Copyright © 2021

All rights reserved

The characters and events portrayed in this book are fictitious. Any similarity to real persons, living or dead, is coincidental and not intended by the author.

No part of this book may be reproduced, or stored in a retrieval system, or transmitted in any form or by any means, electronic, mechanical, photocopying, recording, or otherwise, without express written permission of the publisher.

Cover design by Rosie Neale

CONTENTS

Copyright
Preface
Jubilee Jeopardy 1
Rosie Neale 2
Chapter 1 3
Chapter 2 15
Chapter 3 22
Chapter 4 35
Chapter 5 41
Chapter 6 52
Chapter 7 64
Chapter 8 69
Chapter 9 78
Chapter 10 84
Chapter 11 88
Chapter 12 99
Chapter 13 114
Chapter 14 121
Chapter 15 126
Chapter 16 131
Chapter 17 140

Chapter 18	144
Chapter 19	154
Chapter 20	166
Chapter 21	172
Chapter 22	183
Chapter 23	188
Chapter 24	200
Chapter 25	214
Chapter 26	224
Chapter 27	246
The End	253
About The Author	255
Books By This Author	257

PREFACE

This book was written between the celebrations of the Queen's Platinum Jubilee and her sad passing in September 2022.

JUBILEE JEOPARDY

ROSIE NEALE

CHAPTER 1

Prelude

The warmth of the evening sun on my face felt heavenly after the cold, dark spring we had endured. I walked along slowly, drinking in the soft balmy air and clear blue sky, and in no particular hurry to reach the church hall. Deb's legendary powers of persuasion had once more involved me in something I did not really want to be part of - the committee preparing for the Queen's Platinum Jubilee.

Even more remarkably, she had managed to convince Sophy to come along as well. Sophy was neither a natural 'joiner' nor a monarchist, but she did warm to the community element of the celebrations, bringing people together. She was determined to ensure that any events were genuinely diverse and open to everyone. The tension between her and Mrs Donnington-Browne, who was a staunch royalist and had only deigned to join our group in order to prevent any namby-pamby left-wing nonsense, promised to be entertaining, at least.

As I turned the final corner and rather reluctantly began to make my way through the lengthening shadows up to the door, I heard a familiar voice behind me.

"Sam! Hold on a minute! I've got something to tell you!"

It was Beth, running after me, and breathless with excitement.

Her sweet, round face was flushed and her eyes were bright and shining.

"Hi Beth. What is it? I can tell it's something incredible!"

She laughed happily.

"It's honestly the best news I've had in months. Daria and Vitaly finally have their visas through! I can't believe it. They are actually due to arrive this Saturday!"

"Oh, Beth, I'm so happy for you. You've all had such a long wait. They must be delighted."

"They really are. They've been sleeping on that cold, hard floor for so long, checking email multiple times every day. They're so desperate to get here at last. And I can't wait to welcome them."

Beth had eagerly taken up the government's offer to support people taking in Ukrainian refugees, as soon as it had been announced. She had been very quickly matched with Daria and her young son Vitaly, from the badly bombed city of Kharkiv, but the bureaucracy and delays since then had been incredibly frustrating. She had plenty of room in the large house she had inherited, and had set up bedrooms, a bathroom and even a playroom for them, months earlier. Friends had donated extra bedding and clothes, as well as toys for Vitaly and everything was ready.

It was all in place, and Beth was full of anticipation, but while Daria's visa had come through relatively quickly, they had endured the stress of a seemingly interminable wait for Vitaly's to be approved, and everything was put on indefinite hold. Staying with friends of distant family members in Poland, Daria was feeling increasingly guilty about taking advantage of their meagre hospitality and Vitaly was apparently suffering from high levels of anxiety and stress.

Impulsively, I gave Beth a hug.

"I'm so pleased for you, Beth. It felt as if it would never actually happen, but now it has. Where do they fly to?"

Beth looked at me rather nervously, out of the corner of her eyes.

"They're flying into Heathrow. I've never been there before and I'm petrified of driving so far. I was just wondering - say no, if you can't - if you would come with me. Well, I really mean, drive me to pick them up."

I could not resist her pleading voice.

"Of course I will, Beth. Anything I can do to help. I have to go to this meeting right now, but we'll talk through how to manage things later."

"I'm on the committee too, as it happens, Sam. Maybe we can walk back together afterwards?"

I agreed and we went into the hall, arm in arm, grinning with the overflowing happiness of good news. Inside, we found that everyone else had found their places, and Deb looked ready to begin.

"Beth, Sam, welcome. We were just about to start without you. But you both look as if something exciting has happened. What is it?"

Beth was bursting to tell her news.

"Daria and Vitaly are finally arriving this Saturday! I'm so happy. It's been such a long wait."

There was a spontaneous outburst of applause around the table. Everyone looked genuinely pleased. The whole town had wanted to do something for Ukrainian refugees, and Beth's visitors would be the first of them to arrive in the area. The war had come as such a shock to us all, and there was a genuine sense of empathy with these poor people, who had so suddenly had to leave their lives behind them. Lives which had seemed so similar to our own.

"That's brilliant news, Beth," beamed Deb. "Is there anything at all we can do to help?"

"Well, Sam has agreed to come to the airport with me, so that is one problem sorted, thank goodness. I was a bit anxious about managing that on my own. Is there anything else? Mmmm, well, I have plenty of donated clothes for them, but they are mostly winter things, so if anyone has anything summery to offer, that would be a good idea. Light tops, dresses, or boy's shorts and T-shirts, that sort of thing."

"I'm sure we can put together a nice selection of clothes for them, Beth. What are the sizes we need?"

"Daria is around a size 14, although I think she has lost a bit of weight with all the stress. Vitaly is 3, but he's nearly 4 now. I think he is quite small for his age and again he looks thin at the moment. Hopefully we can feed him up a bit."

"That's certainly something we can do, Beth. What do you think about us perhaps arranging a Ukrainian-themed lunch for them, in the week after they arrive? On the following Wednesday, maybe. Just a little something to help them to feel welcome in the town."

Sophy nodded.

"That's a good idea, Deb. Nothing too elaborate or overwhelming, but a small lunch party might be just what would help to make them feel part of the community. We could do blue and yellow decorations and some typical English foods and a few Ukrainian things too."

"In addition to your generous suggestion, I could offer English, and possibly music lessons to Daria and perhaps also her son. I attempted to open my own spacious home to a Ukrainian family, but then it was decided that we single men weren't allowed to take in refugees, for some inscrutable reason. Such a short-sighted decision. So I would be extremely happy to play my part in welcoming them to our area."

This was from John Deering, a middle-aged music teacher, with round horn-rimmed glasses and a very grandfatherly appearance, thin untidy white hair and rather shabby, old-fashioned, but obviously expensive clothes. There was an edge of sincere disappointment and just a touch of resentment in his deep, cultured voice.

"I think that's a very valuable offer, Mr Deering," approved Deb. "Improving their English will really be useful to both of them. I assume that Daria is able to express herself reasonably well, since she's been able to communicate with you, Beth, but I'm sure she would welcome some more support with it, and Vitaly will probably know very little at all. And he'll be the only Ukrainian at nursery, when he starts. It's very kind of you to be willing to give up your time for them."

Mr Deering nodded with a hint of smugness. I always found his air of intellectual and social superiority rather irritating, but could not put my finger on why he annoyed me. No one else seemed to mind. Even Deb seemed to find him extremely likeable. Perhaps I had an inferiority complex.

The elegant white-haired lady at the end of the table decided to intervene at this point, her cut-glass accent and somewhat regal intonation rather grating.

"I'm sure she would like to earn some money as soon as possible. I could offer her some paid jobs around the house up at the Manor. We always need reliable help and it's hard to find anyone willing to do domestic work at the moment. Young people nowadays tend to look down on it."

I almost gasped at the snobbery of it.

"I'm sorry, Mrs Donnington-Browne," responded Beth, immediately. "But Daria is a fully qualified teacher, and I really don't think she will be looking for that kind of work."

So that was the famous, or infamous, Mrs D-B. She was

everything I had imagined her to be and more.

"Even so, she might be glad of some immediate work, you know, Bethan. It will take some time for her qualifications to be recognised over here, you know, and she may need to retrain. The subjects she is trained to teach might not be appropriate for our education system. I simply want to offer her the chance of some paid employment as soon as she arrives."

Beth looked flustered. She obviously knew Mrs D-B, and was somewhat intimidated by her, but instinctively wanted to protect Daria from this kind of possibly exploitative job offer.

"I think she'll need some time to settle in, anyway," I said, peaceably. "Once she's here, we can ask her what she would like to do."

"That sounds very sensible, Sam," agreed Deb. "Right, let's plan this welcome lunch first, before we move onto the Jubilee celebrations."

Everyone was eager to contribute something to the event. Sophy offered to do some online research and find some recipes and then cook some Ukrainian specialities for the guests. Celia and Deb promised to make typical English cakes and Stephen said that he would find some suitable Ukrainian music and bring his portable speaker from church to play it with. Mrs Donnington-Browne even promised to ask her gardener to provide some colourful flowers, blues and yellows if possible.

Soon we had plenty of volunteers and enough food and entertainment promised to serve a fairly large group. Beth offered to run a craft activity for anyone, adult or child, who wanted to join in.

"If we make some nice colourful bunting, we could use it for the Jubilee celebrations in June."

Everyone liked that idea.

"Are we going to make it public, or ticketed, or invitation only?"

asked Deb.

No one had actually thought about that.

"We don't want it to get out of hand. Too many people crowding in would be intimidating for Daria and Vitaly," said Sophy. "But I don't like the sound of an exclusive 'invitation only' event. What about very inexpensive paid tickets with the option of an additional donation, the money going to the Ukrainian appeal? I can set up an online booking system quite easily."

Everyone approved of that. We could keep numbers under control but also make it a really worthwhile fundraiser.

"We can have the church hall for nothing for that kind of event," said Celia. "And we'll be donating the food and things, so there should be a reasonable profit to send to the appeal."

I offered to put together a flyer, which we could also post on local social media, and Stephen said he would be happy to put it in the church notices and newsletter. Mrs D-B even said she would mention it to her bridge circle. She seemed genuinely enthusiastic and I felt rather ashamed that I had judged her too quickly. It's so easy to be swayed by externals.

Then it was time to move on to considering the Jubilee celebrations, just over a month away. I knew things needed to be organised in advance, but somehow I just did not feel in a celebratory mood as yet. There was so much that was depressing in the news, from the Ukraine war to the looming cost of living crisis, and it was hard to see the relevance of a royal Jubilee just then. But Sophy had a different view.

"I know some of us aren't that committed to celebrating the monarchy (I'm sorry, Mrs Donnington-Browne, I know you are, but not everyone feels the same way), but I think some community events over the Bank Holiday period could be just what we need. Lots of us have had to miss out on celebrations and life events in the last couple of years, and we need an excuse to get together and have some fun."

Heads nodded around the table.

"Yes, I know, a huge number of people are struggling financially, and feeling very worried about how they can possibly manage their bills in the coming months. But we need to do something to take their minds off it, at least for a few days. Something that won't cost them money they can't afford, but will bring us together as a community. That might even help us to be more willing to support each other in the hard times to come this autumn."

She spoke passionately and powerfully and I felt myself respond, suddenly feeling much more engaged with the whole idea. Deb and Beth murmured approval and even Mr Deering rumbled his approbation.

"That all sounds good, Sophy, but we must remember that the cause of our celebration is the remarkably long reign of Her Majesty Queen Elizabeth II, and that needs to remain central to our events."

Mrs D-B sounded authoritative as usual.

"I agree, actually," said Celia, rather surprisingly. I did not have her down as an ardent monarchist.

"I'm not a great fan of the royal family as a whole, but the Queen has been such an example of faith, duty and loyalty over such a very long time. We shouldn't forget that. And the older people in town will really want a traditional element to our celebrations."

Despite differences in emphasis, we were able to come to a unanimous agreement in the end. We decided on a beacon lighting ceremony at Galley's Hill on Thursday evening, a street party in the market square on Friday afternoon, and a charity concert in the church hall on Saturday evening. Stephen would hold a service of Thanksgiving on Sunday, followed by cake and fizz for everyone, to round off the weekend.

Some tasks were allocated immediately. Sophy agreed to contact local businesses to see if they might donate food and drink for the party, and we all agreed to meet again on the following Tuesday, the day before the planned welcome lunch for Daria and Vitaly.

There was a general sense of positive anticipation as we dispersed. I was glad that I had gone in the end. It was good to be involved and to have something to look forward to, amongst all the doom and gloom.

It was almost dark, but still pleasantly warm, as Beth and I walked back to her house.

"I was surprised at Mrs Donnington-Browne calling you Bethan. I know it's your proper name, but everyone else calls you Beth. Did she know you when you were a child?"

Beth made a noise which was half embarrassment and half annoyance.

"She did. And since my parents died, she has insisted on trying to give me 'guidance' and tell me what to do. She's so naturally confident in her own opinions, she doesn't realise how bossy she is being! I find it hard to stand up to her, even when I know I'm right."

"I didn't know you were that close. I've never met her before."

"No, well, I don't see much of her, especially since the pandemic. She used to insist on inviting me to parties, hoping I would meet someone, I think. But I hate that type of thing and always feel uncomfortable and out of place. They're all so much posher and more confident than me, it just makes me feel dowdy, fat and clumsy."

I laughed sympathetically.

"I know just what you mean! I've never had that level of social confidence and sophistication either. But how did your families get to know each other, if your backgrounds are so different?"

Beth sounded slightly anxious now.

"Please don't tell anyone, Sam, but my family - my parents won the lottery when I was young. They came from South Wales - hence my name. But they couldn't cope with staying in the village, not once they had all that money. It was like being in a goldfish bowl. Everyone knew everything about everyone. So they gave away quite a bit to friends and local good causes, and moved up here, not telling anyone where they were going. They didn't have any close family and just wanted a new start, somewhere far away from their old life. They bought this house and a nice car and settled down, putting the rest in savings. But Mrs Donnington-Browne took it upon herself - no, sorry, that isn't fair. She was kind to my mother, who struggled a bit with fitting into the social scene here. She tried to help, but it always seemed to me and my father as if she was being patronising, although Mum was definitely grateful for her suggestions."

"Did your mother really want to fit in, then?"

"Yes, she did. She wanted to be one of them and tried to lose her Welsh accent and to 'stop being common', as she put it. She insisted on sending me to that awful school, where they all hated and bullied me. I was so relieved when she let me come to your school for the Sixth Form. It was so nice to have real friends for the first time."

I had never heard any of this back story. It certainly threw a new light on her long standing self-esteem issues.

"You know we all liked you from the start, Beth. You never have to be anyone but yourself with us."

She turned towards me and smiled gratefully.

"You have no idea what being friends with people like you and Deb did for me, Sam. And when Mum and Dad were killed in that dreadful car accident … I don't know what I would have done without your friendship. And, to be fair, Mrs Donnington-

Browne helped a lot with the admin and dealing with the authorities. No one was going to argue with her! She definitely smoothed the way. I do owe her a lot. I just - just want her to treat me as an adult now."

We had reached Beth's front door. It really was a lovely house. Not pretentious at all, just spacious and well-designed, and surrounded by a truly beautiful garden, which had been her mother's special project.

"I can only pop in for a few minutes, Beth - Mum's babysitting tonight and I don't want to keep her up late. She's been a bit under the weather lately."

"No problem, Sam - I understand. And I'm always happy to babysit for Chloe, you know. Obviously, it wouldn't have worked tonight, but don't be afraid to ask. She knows me really well now, from nursery as well as our outings, and I - well, I love her with all my heart. You know that. You and Chloe saved me last year. Anything I can do in return is a pleasure."

Her voice was warm with emotion.

"I know that, Beth. We're a team. It's so good to have friends I can ask for help without having to feel embarrassed about it. And it goes both ways! I'm hoping Mum and Dad can have Chloe on Saturday when I come with you to Heathrow."

We went into the study, and Beth pulled out the printed paperwork for Daria's flights. Luckily it was not an early morning arrival, so we had time to make our way down there after breakfast. We decided it would be worth paying for the short stay parking, as it was so close to the terminal. Daria and Vitaly would not have much luggage, but we wanted to make the journey as easy as possible.

"Oh, I can't help feeling so excited, Sam," enthused Beth. "I hope they will like the house and that the town won't be too quiet for them. But just now, knowing you will be driving me down to Heathrow, I don't feel nervous at all, just so very happy and relieved. It's lovely to have the chance to help them, to give them a home."

I agreed wholeheartedly. The sense of helplessness was the worst thing about watching so much tragedy and loss on the news. We had been limited to providing donations for the Afghan refugees, as none had been sent to our area. It felt so good to be able to support real people in trouble, and share some of our good fortune with them.

Mum had fallen asleep in her chair when I arrived home. She looked older and indefinably frailer. I was worried about her, but she was insistent that there was nothing really wrong.

She opened her eyes suddenly and smiled, transforming her face.

"You're back, Sam. How did it go?"

Her voice sounded normal, at least. I told her about Beth's news and she immediately offered to take Chloe for the weekend, not just Saturday.

"Then you can help Beth on Sunday with any settling in issues as well. It's bound to be a shock to their system, suddenly landing in England like that. And she's not used to having guests staying. No, honestly, Sam, it will be a pleasure for your father and me. We haven't had Chloe on her own overnight with us since Christmas."

She brushed away my protests. We shared a cup of tea and biscuits together and then she left, looking much more herself. Maybe I was worrying over nothing.

CHAPTER 2

Introduction

The warm summery weather lasted until Saturday, and Beth and I felt rather as if we were going on holiday, as we set off in bright sunshine, with that special mixture of anxiety and excitement churning in our stomachs. The roads were busy and I had not done any long-distance driving for a while, so I concentrated hard at first, while I got back into the flow.

Beth was so relieved not to be driving herself that she was happy to sit quietly until we were nearly there. My car did not have an onboard satnav, so at that point I needed her to use her phone and help with directions and following signs, once we were locked into the particular circle of hell known as the M25. I heaved an enormous sigh of relief when we finally pulled off and managed to park.

"We've made such good time, Sam. We can relax, and sit and have a coffee before we go down to meet them."

Beth insisted on buying me a cream cake too. The tension of the last part of the journey had been draining, so I really needed a calorie boost before setting off to do it all over again.

It had been so long since I had been in an airport. I had forgotten how strange the atmosphere of eager anticipation mixed with apprehension was.

"It's weird, I have butterflies in my stomach," I laughed.

Beth nodded.

"Me, too. I think it's this place. I - I hope we'll manage to find them and that she sees my sign or recognises me."

To calm our nerves, we decided to move quickly to the arrivals point and found a good spot where everyone coming through would be able to see us. Beth had a cardboard sign with their names written in purple felt pen, nice and clear. We settled down to wait, checking the arrivals board for their flight every few minutes.

"Oooh, Beth, look, their flight has landed! They should be in baggage reclaim now."

But, of course, they only had hand luggage, just a small rucksack apiece, so they emerged much more quickly than we expected. And Beth recognised them instantly, as soon as they came into view. She actually bounced up and down like a child, eyes sparkling, calling out their names.

Daria heard her almost at once and hurried over, holding Vitaly by the hand, her face full of delight and relief.

"Beth! It is you. You have come. Thank you, thank you so much."

Daria's accented English was charming and her luminous smile lit up the thin face, with its beautiful bone structure. Beth squatted down to say hello to little Vitaly, who was looking somewhat overwhelmed, as much by the noisy chaotic environment as by our welcome. From her capacious bag, she pulled out a brown soft toy rabbit and gave it to him. He looked up anxiously at his mother, but when she nodded, he took it and hugged it to his chest. He tried to say thank you in English, his small mouth struggling with the difficult 'th'.

I had tears in my eyes. What a moment! I felt privileged to be there.

Beth introduced me to Daria, and I tried the few words of Ukrainian I had managed to learn on an online app. Hello, welcome and my name is Sam. Not a lot, but Daria's face lit up as I mouthed the words as best I could.

"I'm afraid I can't say much more than that, Daria, but I will try to learn more," I said.

"If you would like to learn my language, I would be so happy to teach you."

"I would love to. Thank you."

Beth checked whether they needed anything to eat or drink before we went back to the car. It turned out that they had been on a low-cost flight from Poland, and had not had enough money to buy any refreshments, so they were both very hungry and thirsty. We went to sit in the same café Beth and I had already visited and Vitaly's eyes grew round as he saw the food Beth ordered for him. He tried to be polite, but after the first mouthful he just had to wolf it down.

"We - we did not have much to eat in Poland," explained Daria, who was also eating hungrily. "The people we stayed with were kind but very poor, and we could not take their food from them. And everything was very - very plain. Bread and fat, sometimes cheese or sausage. Almost never vegetable - vegetables? Is that right?"

"Your English is very good, Daria. But we will have to feed you up, now that you are finally here, won't we, Beth?"

Beth nodded. Her eyes were on little Vitaly, gulping down his food, his hands shaking a little. Her lips quivered slightly.

"Yes, Sam. We certainly will."

Back at the car, Daria and her son climbed into the back. I had borrowed a booster seat for Vitaly, so that he would be safe and comfortable on the journey. I explained that I would need to concentrate for the first part of the trip, and we made our painful way out of the airport and into the crawling rows of traffic on the motorway. Once I had a moment to look, I saw that the two passengers had fallen asleep holding each other's hands. Beth looked round and saw them too.

"Poor things, they are exhausted," she murmured.

I nodded silently. Let them have their sleep. They must have been up so early to catch their flight. Soon, Beth dropped off as well. I drove carefully and steadily home and pulled up on the drive at Beth's house. After a few moments, all three of them woke up. Beth gave her head a little shake and smiled tremulously at me.

"Thank you so much for driving, Sam. I didn't get much sleep last night, in the end."

"You're very welcome. Glad to help."

Vitaly seemed to be much livelier after his rest and some food, and bounded after Beth and into her house, excited to see where he would be staying. Daria was more hesitant and looked anxious as she walked up the steps to the front door. I smiled at her.

"It's a lovely house, Daria, and Beth is a wonderful hostess. I'm sure you will be happy here."

"You are right, Sam. It is a very nice house and Beth is so kind. Vitaly will be better here, I think. Poland was not good for him. But I wish my husband could be here with us."

Of course, her husband was still in Kharkiv, fighting with the Ukrainian forces. On the front line and in serious danger every day. It must always be there in the back of her mind.

"I know it's not at all the same, Daria, but not so long ago I lost my husband to Covid. He was a doctor. If you ever want to talk about how you are feeling, I'm here for you."

I faltered a little as I spoke. I did not want to imply that she had lost her husband when he was still alive, just fighting a long way away. But I needed to show her that I might be capable of understanding how she might be feeling.

Daria smiled gratefully at me and reached out to touch my arm briefly.

"Thank you, Sam. I think I understand what you are saying. I would like - I would love to talk to you about Bogdan. And to hear about your husband too."

The kindness in her was amazing, after all she had been through. So sensitive to the needs of others.

"Come on, let's go in. Beth will be wanting to show you your room."

As we walked into the cool, shady hallway, Daria sighed with pleasure.

"This is a beautiful house. Beth did not say. We are fortunate."

Beth was inside, holding Vitaly's hand. As she showed them the downstairs rooms, they both gasped and exclaimed at the space there was. Beth had obviously worked hard to clean everything until it was spotless and very tidy, but it still had a lived-in, homely feel. Daria was delighted with the kitchen and asked if she would be able to do some cooking.

"Of course, Daria. Whenever you want to. We can eat together if you would like to, but, if you would prefer to cook separately for you and Vitaly, I will quite understand."

"Oh, no, Beth, we would love to eat with you. But I would be so happy also to cook for you sometimes, if you permit me."

"I would really love that, Daria. Especially on days when I am working in the nursery. We can shop together so that I can buy what you would like to cook."

I could see that these two were going to get on. There was an instant bond. I did not really need to stay, but it would be rude to leave before they went upstairs. Beth led Vitaly up to the room she had set up for him and his eyes grew large with excitement and amazement when he saw the Thomas the Tank Engine quilt cover, the soft toys and the slightly battered wooden train set on the floor.

"Me? Mama - my?"

He looked questioningly at his mother and Beth. Daria reassured him that it was all for him and he immediately went and sat down with the trains. Beth sat on the bed near him, smiling.

"This is your bedroom, Vitaly. You can sleep here. Your mother will be right next-door."

As Daria translated, Vitaly's face changed and looked pinched and much younger. He ran to his mother and buried his face in her skirt, clutching her legs. She stroked his head, comforted him in her own language, and then explained to me and Beth what the problem was.

"I - I am sorry, Beth. My son has been sleeping with me since the war began and he is frightened to sleep alone. The bad dreams come every night."

Tears started in Beth's sympathetic eyes.

"Oh Daria, of course, I totally understand. Please tell him that this can be his playroom and he can sleep with you for as long as he wants to. Let's go and show him your bedroom, so that he can see where you will both sleep."

Daria took her son's hand, talking quietly and soothingly to him, and we all went to the room Beth had set up for her to sleep in. It was charming, with slightly faded floral wallpaper, a double bed with a quilt to match the curtains and a pretty dressing table, where Beth had put a vase of fresh spring flowers.

"It is beautiful! I will sleep so well here. We both will, yes, Vitaly? It will be so good to have a bed after a long time sleeping on the floor. There was no extra room in Poland, so we were sleeping in the main living area."

"I'm so happy that you like it, Daria. It is yours, so please change whatever you want to. There are some clothes in the wardrobe for you and some in the other room for Vitaly. I hope the sizes are right, but we can get more if not."

Now tears filled Daria's intensely blue eyes and her lip trembled.

"Oh, Beth. You are too kind. I - I don't know what to say, how to say thank you. You are an angel sent from God, I think."

Impulsively, she put a hand on Beth's arm.

Beth flushed and stammered a little as she brushed away the thanks.

"Oh, no, Daria - it's nothing. It's the least I could do. And everyone helped, donated things. We all want to support you and make your life here as comfortable as it can be. You'll see - they're all longing to meet you."

"She's right, Daria," I confirmed. "The whole town is keen to support you both. We're planning a celebration lunch on Wednesday and lots of people are eager to meet you both. Anyway, I think I had better be going and leave you to settle in. Can I come round in the morning, to see how things are, Beth?"

Beth smiled gratefully at me.

"Please do. I would love that."

Waving to little Vitaly, I left them and went downstairs, feeling that the arrival had gone very smoothly. First step of the mission accomplished.

CHAPTER 3

Chorale

I slept heavily that night, after an emotionally draining day, and woke up feeling rather sluggish. I missed Chloe's cheerful morning face and her partly comprehensible chatter, but it was a pleasant change to be able to get up slowly for once. Mum had messaged to say that everything was going well, so I knew I had no need to worry, and I would have her back that evening.

But when I looked at my phone, there was a message from Beth. She sounded rather anxious and was keen for me to go over as early as possible. I made myself move more quickly and walked over briskly. It was fresher that morning and there was a hint of dampness in the air that helped to wake me up.

Beth almost flung the door open to me when I rang the bell, and gave me a quick hug.

"What's wrong, Beth? I thought you sounded a bit upset in your message."

She smiled waveringly.

"It's all fine, really, but maybe it won't be quite as easy as I thought it would be. Vitaly had terrible nightmares and woke up screaming in terror three or four times in the night. Daria said that's normal for him, but I found it so upsetting. I didn't feel I could go in to them, but I felt so helpless, hearing him cry out like that. Poor little boy."

I had my own experience with disturbing dreams, but this seemed like far too many for one night. I shuddered in sympathy.

"I think it's not surprising really, Beth. Kharkiv was bombed heavily and then he had all the trauma of leaving home, without his father, a terrifying journey, and then that protracted delay in Poland, with so much uncertainty. It is bound to take time for him to settle and for things to improve."

Beth nodded.

"I know. It's just hard to hear so much distress in a little child. I want to take the pain away from him, but I can't."

I put my arms around her.

"Don't put it all on yourself. Even his mother can't take it away. You are doing a wonderful thing, helping him and Daria. But they've been through a traumatic time and it won't always be easy, giving them the support they need. Anything I can do to help, let me know. Maybe, if he continues to struggle, we can get some kind of family counselling, but it won't be easy with such a young child, especially as he doesn't speak much English yet."

Beth let out a short sob and then had herself under control.

"That's a great idea, Sam. Thank you. We'll get there."

"Of course. But it can't be rushed."

"There's another thing I wanted to ask you, Sam. Daria really wants to go to church this morning. I guess she's Russian or Ukrainian Orthodox really, but she doesn't seem to mind going to another denomination - she's keen to go to our local church today. Would you come with us? I'm really not that comfortable with church, especially Anglican. I did go to chapel back in Wales, but that's so long ago, and it was so different."

I was not really a regular churchgoer either, but I did not want to let Beth down when she needed me. I had been to the occasional service and had enjoyed the Christmas season, but attending every week, with a lively and sometimes noisy toddler, had never become part of my routine. I tried to watch some of the online services, but other things always seemed to get in the way, now that the pandemic was more or less over.

"Of course I'll come, Beth. It'll be much easier without Chloe. The service doesn't start until half past ten, so we've got plenty of time to get there."

Beth looked very relieved as she led me into the kitchen, where Daria and Vitaly were just finishing their breakfast.

"Good morning, you two. I hope you slept well and are settling into your new home."

Daria looked up, her face illuminated by a radiant smile.

"Good morning, Sam. So nice to see you. Yes, we slept well. A few bad dreams but not as many as usual. And Beth has made us a very nice breakfast."

Eager to show off the new words he had learnt, Vitaly pointed and named the food proudly.

"Toast! J-j-jam! Cereal! Milluk!"

Laughing, I applauded him.

"Have you learnt all that this morning? Wow - you will soon be speaking English fluently."

Beth pointed to a jar of Marmite.

"And what is this?" she prompted him.

"Yuk!" he said, pulling a face.

"Neither of them liked the Marmite, Sam. I think Daria thought it might be chocolate spread of some kind and the shock was horrible when she bit into it. It was so funny to see their faces!"

I could not help laughing.

"I guess it's an acquired taste. I like it, but Thomas hated it. He couldn't stand the smell and I stopped buying it. I haven't tried it on Chloe yet."

"I just thought they ought to have something typically English, but bacon and eggs would be going too far on their first morning. I did give them marmalade as well, and that went down much better."

Daria was smiling and nodding along.

"We are so happy to try all your foods. And I am looking forward to cooking some Ukrainian dishes for Beth."

"Why don't you sit and have a coffee with Daria, while I go and get ready for church, Sam?"

Beth sounded more confident about it, now that she knew I would be there too. I agreed and poured myself a cup.

"There is something I would like to ask you, Sam. You are a mother and will understand, I think. I was not sure how to say it to Beth and it is not easy in another language, although I did look up some words online first."

"Of course, Daria. Anything. Ask away."

Daria put her arm around Vitaly's thin shoulders and gave him a hug.

"It is Vitaly. Before the war, at home, he was sleeping on his own and he was going to the toilet alone when he needed to. Since the bombing, he - he can use the toilet in the day but at night, he - is it right to say that he wets the bed?"

"Of course, I understand. I think it happens very often when children have had a shock or a bad experience and he isn't very old yet."

Daria nodded.

"I know, I am certain that he will get better in time. But in Poland I had some - I think they are called diapers?"

"We call them nappies in the UK. I know what you mean."

"I have nearly finished them and I need to buy some more. But I do not know where to get them from."

"That's not a problem, Daria. We can get them from the supermarket. But for Vitaly, at his age, it might be better to get some kind of pull-ups. That is a nappy which is like a pair of underpants. It will feel more grown up and normal to him, and as he begins to get used to going to the toilet on his own at night, he can pull them up and down himself."

Daria was concentrating hard, trying to understand me, and with the help of gestures she seemed to see what I meant.

"This would be perfect. Can we also get that from the supermarket?"

"I should think so, but we might have a better choice and price online, especially as he is a little older. Let me have a look and order some for you."

I pulled out my phone, did a search and found the perfect thing quickly. I ordered two packs to be delivered to me on the following day.

"I'll bring them round to you tomorrow. I'll get some nappy sacks to put the dirty ones into and a bin with a lid for you to keep in the bathroom."

"You are so kind, Sam. You and Beth are doing so much for us. I will say a special prayer for you both."

Slightly embarrassed, I looked down at Vitaly and smiled.

"Time to clean your teeth, Vitaly, and go to the toilet before church."

Daria took him off to get ready and I was left alone with

my thoughts. There were so many unexpected pitfalls here. We would have to learn quickly and be sensitive to cultural differences. Beth was right. It was satisfying to feel that you were making a difference, but it was not all going to be plain sailing.

The wind had picked up and the clouds looked rather stormy, as we walked down to the church together. Beth had dressed up for the occasion in a floaty summer dress, which she found rather hard to control in the strong gusts. She had even asked me whether she should wear a hat, and I was very glad I had persuaded her that it was not necessary.

She seemed to go to church only for weddings and funerals, which probably explained her nervousness. I was somewhat unsure of myself, too, not knowing what type of service it would be, but at least I knew that Stephen was not one for excessive formality. Surely it would not matter too much if we did the wrong thing at the wrong time.

A large lady with a friendly smile welcomed us in and guided us to our seats. As we were looking through the hymn and service books, I was grateful to see Celia come over.

"You must be Daria and Vitaly. I am so happy to meet you," she said quietly, only just audible above the organ music. "Would Vitaly like to come to the children's group instead of sitting through the sermon?"

I looked doubtfully at Daria.

"There is a special group for children so that they don't get too bored during the talk. Do you think Vitaly would go?"

She whispered quietly to him in their own language. Vitaly was clearly conflicted. He wanted to go but was nervous about going alone.

"Would he come if I went with him?" volunteered Beth. "I know you want to be here for the whole service, Daria, but I don't mind missing the talk. I can bring Vitaly back to you if he is unhappy."

When it was explained to him, Vitaly nodded vigorously, his eyes shining. Celia bustled off, telling Beth that she and Vitaly could go out with the other children just before the sermon.

"Do we not stand for the whole Divine Liturgy?" enquired Daria anxiously.

"We stand for part of the service and sit for other sections, Daria. Don't worry. Stephen, the vicar, will tell us when to stand and when to sit."

She looked a little puzzled, but nodded and began to look through the service book. It looked as if it would be a communion service. Another hurdle. Was it acceptable for Daria to take communion in an Anglican church? I had never taken it myself. On the extremely rare occasions when I had been present at that type of service, I had not even gone forward for a blessing, and I certainly did not feel that I had either the understanding or the faith to take the bread and wine.

I looked at the service booklet myself. On the first inside page, before the service started, it said that members of any Christian denomination could take communion, so that was a relief.

Suddenly the music changed and Stephen, wearing robes and looking very smart, his unruly hair combed back neatly, for once, walked past us up the central aisle to the front. Everyone stood up, and Daria prompted Vitaly to stand too. She crossed herself and bowed her head as Stephen began to speak, welcoming us all. As he looked at the congregation, I saw his eyes rest on us for a moment, before moving on, and he evidently decided to add to his normal preamble.

"I would like to extend a special welcome to Daria and Vitaly from Ukraine, who are with us this morning for the first time. It is lovely to see you here and we would like to welcome you most warmly to our Christian fellowship here."

Vitaly heard his name and looked up at his mother questioningly. Daria flushed slightly, but smiled shyly back at the people turning round and craning their necks to look at us. Suddenly someone - perhaps Stephen, I could not see - started a round of applause and everyone joined in, filling the church with the sound of their appreciation.

As it died away, Stephen began the responses to start the service and then we moved on to a hymn. It was not one I knew, but I did my best to follow the tune and sing along. Daria, too, attempted to keep up and I could hear Beth's sweet clear voice from the other side of Vitaly.

The service swept us along with it, with Stephen telling us when to sit or kneel, and when to stand, what to join in with, what to sing. I could see Daria focusing all her attention on following the service book, and what was said and read. Vitaly was surprisingly settled and patient, given he could not understand more than the odd word of what was going on. He had clearly become very used to waiting patiently, and not having his personal needs or enjoyment considered.

Suddenly, it was time for the talk and the children went out, Beth leading Vitaly by the hand. He looked back at his mother rather anxiously, but she smiled and nodded and he trotted off fairly happily.

Stephen was a good speaker and drew us into his sermon about Jesus turning the world upside down, raising up the poor and humble rather than the rich and powerful. He linked it with the important work of the Food Banks, many of them set up or supported by churches. I was sorry that Beth was not there to hear it, since she regularly volunteered at our local branch. Daria's eyes were fixed on Stephen's face as she concentrated on every word he said. As he finished with a blessing, she crossed herself again.

The children came back in just before communion, bringing

with them pictures they had made. Vitaly proudly showed his mother what he had done and she smiled and hugged him. Beth looked happy and much more relaxed. She whispered to me that he had been fine, no problems at all, and the other children had been curious, but friendly.

"We are still taking Covid precautions over communion," announced Stephen. "Each person will receive a wafer and individual glass of wine at the altar rail. You will consume it there and then leave the empty plate and glass on the table in the side chapel as you walk back to your seat. The stewards will show you what to do and invite you up. I would like to stress that members of any Christian denomination are welcome to take communion with us. Please do bring up any children for a blessing, and I will also be delighted to give a blessing to anyone who does not feel able to take communion at this point."

He seemed to be smiling at Daria as he spoke, but I was also relieved to know what was going to happen. Some parts of going to church were almost like joining a secret society, where everyone else knew exactly what to do and your ignorance made you feel like an outsider. Stephen had made this ritual much clearer and more welcoming, more inclusive.

When it came to our turn to approach the front, Daria actually led the way with Vitaly, as if she knew better than I or Beth did what was coming. She waited for Stephen to speak and responded with 'amen', before taking her plate. She then ate the wafer and drank the wine with eyes closed. Vitaly crossed himself as Stephen blessed him, head bowed. Beth and I had both opted for a blessing. I found it strangely moving.

"May the Lord bless you and keep you, may he make his face shine upon you and be gracious to you, the Lord lift up his countenance upon you and grant you his peace."

I had a lump in my throat as I followed Daria and Vitaly back to our seats. Special words, but also spoken by my very good friend Stephen, with sincerity and feeling.

The last part of the service went past very quickly and soon we were shaking Stephen's hand on our way out.

"Daria, it was lovely to welcome you to our worship. I'm sure you found many parts of it different."

"Yes, Father, very different. It was less - less formal and also less - sad? No, that is not the correct word. I do not know how to say it."

"Less solemn perhaps. I would be happy to talk you through the service and how it works once you have settled in."

"That would be very helpful, Father Stephen," said Daria with enthusiasm. "I would like that."

"Please, feel free to call me just Stephen, Daria. Most people do."

Daria ducked her head in assent, but it seemed to me that she would find that difficult. She had obviously been brought up to show respect to priests and Stephen had inherited that honour.

As ever, I was impressed with Stephen's natural rapport with children. He squatted down to Vitaly's level, pointed to his picture and used gestures as well as words to say that he liked it. The 'thumbs up' seemed to be universal. Vitaly's smile lit up his thin face and he tried out his English, the 'th' already sounding more natural.

"Thank you."

Daria looked proud of him and prompted him to address Stephen directly.

"Thank you, Father Stephen."

Waving happily, Vitaly trotted out into the churchyard.

Stephen held my hand for a moment when it was my turn.

"Lovely to see you here, Sam. Thank you for coming with them. No Chloe today?"

"No, she's staying with my parents, so that I can help Beth out for this couple of days. I - I enjoyed the service."

"I'm glad. Hope to see you again soon."

Back at Beth's house, she started to put lunch together, while I chatted with Daria about the service.

"May I ask, Sam, why you had a blessing and not the holy elements?"

Embarrassed and unsure of myself, I tried to give her an acceptable answer.

"I don't go to church regularly. I go sometimes, but I didn't feel - somehow it would not have felt right to me to take the bread and wine."

Daria looked puzzled.

"Do you not believe in God?"

What a personal question! I did not know how to answer. No one British would have asked me that. But it was a fair enough question in the circumstances. Did I?

I took a moment to think about it. It was not a central part of my life, that was for sure. I would not be able to call myself a Christian. But who did I call on, when Chloe was in danger? Who did I pray to during that dreadful afternoon on the church tower? I had to admit it. When I was *in extremis*, I called out to God and I did believe that there was someone there to hear me.

"Yes!" It came out more positively than I had expected. "Yes, Daria, I do believe in God. But I - I don't really know exactly what I believe. I sometimes went to Sunday School as a child and know some of the famous Bible stories, but I just haven't thought things through. If you don't mind, I will try to come to church with you more regularly, if I can manage it, and find out more about what I do and don't believe."

Daria still looked puzzled, but she reached out her hand to me in welcome.

"Of course, Sam. I will be very happy to have you with me. My faith - what I believe - it is so strong, I feel sad that you do not have this. It has been my strength through the war and leaving my home, my country and even Bogdan. I will pray you find this strength too."

It felt so strange to be having this conversation on a normal Sunday morning in Beth's comfortable sitting room. It was so personal, so deep, in a way I normally, like most people, tended to avoid. I had never even talked about religion to my mother, a regular churchgoer. Thomas had been a man of faith, who prayed regularly, but he had not attended a place of worship except sometimes at the hospital, and we had just not discussed it, apart from agreeing on a church wedding. Yet here I was, talking about the most fundamental issues with a relative stranger.

I was relieved, when Beth popped her head round the door to say that lunch was ready. She called Vitaly, who was upstairs playing with his trains and we sat down to eat quiche and salad together. Daria insisted on saying grace before we started. She spoke in Ukrainian but said she would look up the translation later that day. Vitaly was obviously used to waiting to start and sat quietly until she said he could begin.

"I'm going to do a roast dinner tonight," said Beth. "A proper English Sunday dinner. But chicken rather than beef."

"That sounds yummy," I approved. "I wish I could share it with you. But I will be home with Chloe this evening and I've invited my parents to eat with us, as a small thank you for looking after her this weekend. I'm making lasagne tonight as it's Chloe's favourite."

After lunch, I said my goodbyes, telling Beth that I would be over on the following day with the pull-ups for Vitaly. I hoped, for her sake as well as his, that Vitaly would have a more settled night, but it was unlikely that things would begin to calm down as quickly as that.

CHAPTER 4

Capriccio

It felt so good to have Chloe back. I had not realised that I had missed her that much. Spending time with Vitaly had aroused all my maternal feelings and I gave her lots of hugs. She seemed happy to be back with me, too, although she had clearly enjoyed her time with the grandparents.

She loved her lasagne. It had been one of the first proper meals she had fed herself with and although she was messy, it was worth it to see her relishing her food like that. Mum insisted on staying for bath time, despite her very obvious fatigue. She enjoyed the fun we had with the water and Chloe's gleeful giggles when I put foam on my nose and blew it off.

After a much better sleep, I got Chloe ready straight after breakfast. Beth invited us in when we arrived with the pull-ups. I was not sure how Chloe and Vitaly would react to each other, but they hit it off straight away. Vitaly brought down his trains and they played happily together. Since Chloe was still in the early stages of talking, it did not seem to matter that they could not communicate in more than single words and basic phrases. Chloe had always loved trains and taught Vitaly her favourite sound: 'choo choo'.

Daria was delighted with the supplies I had brought, and put them straight upstairs in the bedroom. Vitaly had slept better, she said, and the bad dreams had been less frightening, although they still woke him up every few hours. He already loved the soft toy Beth had given him at the airport and cuddled it as he went to sleep and whenever he woke up. He had given it the name Krolyk, which was apparently one of the Ukrainian words for rabbit.

Beth had taken the day off from her work at the nursery to help them to settle in, but she had a proposal for me for the following day.

"I am going to work tomorrow and Vitaly is coming with me for a taster session. He should get some free provision, once all the paperwork is done, due to his age, but Caroline at nursery would like him to join before that and she even said that she would cover the cost. It will help him to learn the language much faster and to make new friends here."

"That sounds great, Beth - what a good idea."

Beth nodded, but had more to say.

"He's only coming for an hour or so tomorrow and I know it's one of Chloe's nursery mornings. Would you be able to take Daria to the Citizens Advice Bureau for me? I've made her an appointment for that time. There's so much to organise and we need some help and guidance."

"Of course I will, Beth. The person you really need is Deb, as she's brilliant at all that kind of thing and already volunteers at the CAB, but Daria hasn't met her yet. We'll introduce them on Wednesday at the lunch and I'm sure she'll be a great help."

"I hadn't thought of Deb. I'd forgotten she did that. But anyway, the appointment is made and it will be good to get things started. At least we need to know exactly what to do."

Daria looked up and smiled.

"I am sorry that there is so much to organise. It is very kind of you to use your free time to help us."

"You are very welcome, Daria. I only wish there was more I could do to support you and other refugees. I'm sorry our government has made it so complicated and difficult for you."

"Oh no, I understand. It is important. Official things must be done like this."

The next day, having dropped Chloe off at nursery for her play morning, I went to pick up Daria. Beth had given her a key, and she was very cautious about making sure that everything was shut and locked carefully. I asked her how Vitaly had responded to going to nursery with Beth.

"He was happy, as he really misses his own nursery in Kharkiv, and his friends there. But he was also very anxious about how it would be. I do not think he would have gone without Beth. She sent a message from the school to say that he is fine and enjoying playing with other children."

We walked quickly into town and found the CAB office. I had not intended to go in to the appointment with Daria, but she insisted, and it was good to see exactly what she had to do, in order to register for benefits and prepare to be able to work. The adviser was very helpful and made the process seem more straightforward than I had anticipated. The time flew by and soon it was time to go and pick up Vitaly.

It was immediately obvious, when he came out, that he had enjoyed himself. He was bouncing with excitement and talked very fast in Ukrainian about everything he had done. He insisted on Daria telling him some more English words and longer phrases, so that he could also tell me what he had been up to.

"Oh, Sam, it is so wonderful to see him like this again! It has been so long. He has been so quiet, so scared, not like himself at all. My heart is bursting with happiness and thankfulness."

Her voice was full of emotion.

I gave her hand a quick squeeze.

"I can only imagine. Bless him. I am so pleased for you."

I left them at Beth's house, promising to see them on Wednesday at the special lunch. It had been a very encouraging morning and a good start to their new life in the UK.

The committee meeting on Tuesday evening went, in general, very smoothly, with two exceptions: a simmering row between John Deering and Celia about the concert, and Mrs D-B's insistence on giving patronising and unwanted advice and detailed instructions to Beth.

I knew that Celia could be hot-headed and struggled to control her temper, but it was clear that the older man was equally stubborn and determined to force through his own wishes. He was, however, better at disguising his emotional reactions under a cloak of sweet reasonableness.

"It's a charity concert, and we need as many people as possible to come along and pay for tickets and refreshments. That's why I want the children's choir to sing. I know they're not experienced musicians, but they performed really well at Christmas and all their parents and grandparents will want to come and support them."

Celia was trying very hard to keep a rein on her bubbling temper.

"But for such an important royal celebration, we need the very best music we can muster, Celia. My amateur choir sings to a very high standard, in four-part harmony at the very least, and we have some excellent experienced soloists."

"That's all fine and good, and I'm very happy for them to take part, but we really need a diverse set of performers to appeal to a much wider range of tastes."

Sophy murmured her support for this aim, but did not risk

intervening between the two antagonists.

"There are very few groups in the area which meet the requisite standard. I would not want our Jubilee celebration to be ruined by poor quality offerings. It would be embarrassing and would reflect badly on our committee and its preparations."

"No one expects a polished performance from children, Mr Deering. I think you have completely the wrong idea about what this concert is about. It needs to be fun and inclusive, so that we can make as much money as possible, and involve as much of the community as we are able to."

At this point, seeing Celia flushed with temper and John Deering's mouth set in a stubborn line, Deb took over.

"I'm sure everyone will appreciate the wonderful music your choir will perform, Mr Deering, but Celia is right. We do need to attract a wide audience, who might not all be interested in pure classical music. Let's come back to this discussion in our next meeting."

Neither of them looked entirely satisfied with the outcome, but Celia looked to be the happier of the two. Both accepted Deb's firm ruling with a brief nod of the head, however.

As for Mrs D-B, I could see why Beth found her attitude irritating. She seemed to believe that Beth needed micromanagement and insisted on offering unwanted directions, from suggesting food to serve to her guests, to telling her how often to wash sheets and change towels. Beth took it pretty patiently, but in the end she snapped.

"Look, Mrs Donnington-Browne, I'm grateful for all your help and advice, but I really do know how to run my own household. I've done it for years now. I'm not a child any more. And I will do things my own way, in discussion with Daria."

A look of respect edged into Mrs D-B's determined grey eyes.

"Very well, Bethan. I apologise if I seemed to be interfering. But please do ask if you need any support or advice. I am only too happy to help."

Sophy reported that we had sold all the tickets for the Ukrainian lunch on the following day, and that half of the people who signed up had made additional donations, so there should be a healthy profit to pass on. Everything was arranged and she had already made a start on the Ukrainian speciality food, some of which took a great deal of preparation time and had multiple stages.

"I really hope I don't mess them up! Daria will know if they are not right and some of them are quite a challenge."

CHAPTER 5

Giocoso

I arrived at the church hall nice and early, as I had promised, to help with the lunch preparations. Mum had insisted on coming to the meal, too, so she was bringing Chloe along later. I hoped that she was not overdoing it. She looked very pale and had deep shadows under her eyes that morning, but she insisted that she was fine and that I should not make a fuss.

Sophy, Celia and Deb were there already and had begun setting out tables and chairs. I took over the easy routine tasks and left them to add the creative touches. Blue and yellow colours were everywhere and it soon looked very welcoming and celebratory.

Before long, others were arriving with their food offerings and other contributions to lay out on the tables. Stephen set up his phone with the speaker to play Ukrainian folk and pop music, and the flowers arrived from Mrs D-B's garden, blue and yellow as she had promised, with some white marguerites in addition. Sophy used glasses to arrange them into attractive little posies for each table.

The guests started coming in even before the appointed time, enthusiastic about welcoming our first Ukrainian refugees. To start with, people milled around chatting rather than sitting down at the pretty tables. Deb asked me to keep an eye on her friend Claire's son, Adam, for her.

"He's a bright lad, but he's had some difficulties with school and needed quite a lot of specialist support in his early teens. He still has these unusually strong enthusiasms and obsessions and she's quite anxious about him. He's totally obsessed with the situation in Ukraine and has told her that he intends to go out and fight against the Russians as soon as he finishes school this summer. He just won't listen to reason. He was determined to come today and meet Daria, and Claire's just a bit worried that he will go over the top and embarrass himself, and her. She's working today, so she can't make it herself."

She pointed him out to me and I made my way over, wondering how to strike up a conversation with a teenager I had never met. He was extremely tall and thin, even gangly, with a very long, straight, floppy fringe covering most of his face. He was wearing a black t-shirt with the Ukrainian flag prominently displayed on it and the single dark eye that was visible, slightly enhanced with eye-liner, was bright with excitement and interest.

"Hello, there. You must be Adam. I'm Sam, Sam Elsdon. Deb mentioned that you would be here, and that you were very interested in the situation in Ukraine."

Not exactly the most creative way to start, but I had to begin somewhere.

He looked down at me with an air of puzzlement as to why I might choose to talk to him, and just a touch of contempt for someone he perceived to be too close to his mother's age. But he had evidently been well brought up, and the good manners triumphed, after a moment's struggle.

"Oh, er, hello, Sam. Yes, I am going out later this year to do humanitarian work and I then intend to enlist in the army over there, as soon as I possibly can."

No small talk, then. Straight at it.

"That's very brave and committed of you. It must be quite complex to organise all the permissions and travel. Are you going to go out and work with a British charity over there?"

He looked a little taken aback. He seemed to have expected me to try to dissuade him.

"Well. er, it's not arranged yet. I have to finish my A levels first. But I am definitely going, whatever anyone says."

"I see. Joining up with a recognised charity is probably the best place to start, so that you can be useful as soon as you arrive, and you can be sure that all the regulations have been met. Do you drive? I know they are always keen to have drivers."

He flushed with annoyance.

"No, I haven't been able to learn yet. It's very expensive and I don't have a part-time job."

"Oh, I understand. It might be worth passing your test before you go, though. Have you started learning some Ukrainian? I've been using an online app and have picked up a few words and sentences. It's quite a challenging language, with the different alphabet."

He was looking increasingly baffled and frustrated by my attitude. Instead of telling him not to go, that it was too dangerous, I was raising all kinds of boring practical issues he had not thought of.

"No, and I don't have time, with my A levels to study for. I expect everyone speaks English there anyway."

"Oh, you can do this in just a few minutes a day. And I'm not so sure about the English. Even Daria finds it a challenge, and most of the soldiers you see on the news need translators. It certainly makes sense to start picking up some words and phrases, so that you can fit in more easily and understand orders. And you'll need to be able to understand road signs and things."

"Humph," was the sound he responded with.

"Do you go to a cadets group? They would provide some very basic military training which would certainly serve you well in the field. Even scouts would help with the outdoor way of life and camping side of things."

He stared at me rather helplessly. I felt rather sorry for the boy. He was so keen to be involved, but just had no idea how best to do it.

"I - I never got on with scouts or other group organisations. I'm an individualist. But I'm determined to do this anyway."

"It might be worth getting in touch with the local cadets to see if they can give you any help, though."

Just then my mother arrived with Chloe in her buggy. I almost laughed at the expression of profound relief which came over what I could see of Adam's face as I turned away. He certainly was not adept at hiding his feelings.

I was just making sure that Mum took her seat straight away, as she was looking rather weary and drawn, when Beth, Daria and Vitaly came through the door. The small boy looked slightly intimidated to see so many tall adults standing around, but his face brightened when he spotted Chloe and he waved enthusiastically at us. Daria was a little flushed and seemed slightly overwhelmed, but she brought him straight over to Mum's table.

"Sam! It is so nice to see a face I know. Have they done all this just for us? It is so kind."

"Hello, Daria. Yes, it is to welcome you and Vitaly, and also to raise money for the Ukraine appeal, but no one wants you to feel intimidated. Come and sit with me for a couple of minutes, and then I'll introduce you to some of the people who have organised and arranged it all."

Gratefully she sat down next to my mother and gradually her

face returned to its normal colour. Beth bustled around setting up a low craft table for collage work on some bunting and took Chloe and Vitaly over to start it off. She soon had a couple more volunteers, Sophy and Celia, and the children began to have fun finding things to stick onto the red, white and blue triangles.

Mum talked quietly to Daria about her journey to the UK and how she was settling in with Beth. Daria began to look much more at ease and responded willingly, expressing her enthusiasm about what she had seen of the local area, as well as the welcome she had received from her hostess. I was just going to begin to introduce her to some of the other guests, when John Deering came over and addressed her, rather self-importantly as usual.

"I am quite simply delighted to meet you at last, Daria. My name is John, John Deering. I don't know if anyone has mentioned to you yet that I have offered to teach you English."

Daria stood up and put her hand out rather hesitantly.

"That is very kind of you, Mr Deering. I would like to improve my English so that I can teach in this country. If you can help me, I will be very thankful."

"Grateful," he corrected immediately, taking her hand and shaking it with the ease of long practice. "I am sure that I can enable you to make excellent progress, provided we work diligently together. Here is my card. Please send an email or telephone me to arrange a suitable time for your lessons to begin. I can teach your son too, if you wish, but he will be a beginner, so I think it would be better if we worked separately. He will, in any case, absorb a great deal of language from his environment, with little effort, since he is so very young."

Daria agreed, listening humbly to the older man, impressed by his air of competent confidence.

"As you can tell, Mr Deering, Daria already speaks very proficient English," I intervened.

I was still finding him irritatingly condescending. He looked down his nose at me and responded, with a smile, to Daria rather than me.

"She is right, you speak very well, considering you have only just arrived in England. With some expert help, I am certain that you will soon be an extremely competent anglicist. I will need to assess your comprehension and writing skills in addition, of course. So please do get in touch without delay. The sooner we can begin, the better."

He smiled smugly at her and moved away.

"What a nice old man!" exclaimed Daria. "So like a grandfather and so helpful."

"Mmmm," I replied noncommittally "He is not as old as he looks. But he should be able to teach you well, I think. It won't be colloquial English, but the formality of his style could be quite useful to you in applying for work. He said he might teach you some music too. I think he still takes pupils for piano lessons, although he no longer teaches at the posh private school he used to work in."

Daria looked at me in surprise and delight.

"How wonderful! I have always wanted to learn the piano. You people here are all so very kind. Some of those I met in Poland said that the English were very cold, and unwelcoming or unfriendly, but here you are not like that at all."

I took her over to meet Deb and they were soon talking about all the bureaucratic requirements Daria would need to fulfil. I knew Deb would be well-equipped to help her and her natural air of confident competence was very reassuring. They arranged to meet up on the following day and start the process of completing the necessary forms.

Suddenly Adam approached and interrupted their conversation, speaking very fast and rather loudly, looking only at Daria and completely ignoring the rest of us.

"Hello, Daria, I am Adam, Adam King. I wanted to talk to you about the war in Ukraine. I hear that you are from Kharkiv. I know that the bombing was very heavy there and there was a lot of damage to the infrastructure. Can you tell me about it? What was it like during the bombardment? How did you manage afterwards? Were there many serious injuries? How effective are the defence forces? I am going to Ukraine to help to defend your country soon and I need to learn as much as you can tell me."

Flabbergasted, as much by the speed of his delivery as by his multiple questions, Daria stared at him, open-mouthed.

"I - er - I do not know what to tell you," she began, but Deb immediately took charge and defused the sudden tension.

"I know you are very interested, Adam, and I'm sure that Daria will talk to you in detail about Ukraine another time, but this simply isn't an appropriate occasion. She needs to settle in here and take her mind off the war just now. Come with me and we can start serving some of the hot food."

For a moment, I thought Adam was going to refuse and he certainly grunted in a sulky way, but a minatory look from Deb was enough to make him trail after her.

"I am so sorry, Sam. I did not know how to answer him. I did not understand some of what he said."

"Don't worry at all, Daria. He's just a teenager and very passionate about Ukraine and what is happening there. Come and say hello to Stephen from church instead. You remember him?"

"Of course, Father Stephen. I would be very happy to speak to him again."

Soon everyone was sitting down, chatting happily and enjoying the food. Sophy had really gone to town with her Ukrainian specialities. She had decided that *borscht* would be too messy to transport and eat, but had made several flavours of *varenyky*, which Daria said were very good, and an Olivier salad. Mrs D-B said it was just like a Russian salad, and Deb jumped in to cover up the slightly awkward moment by praising Sophie's Ukrainian cakes, which were really delicious, even though they did not look exactly as they apparently should.

Everyone made at least one triangle of bunting, which was colourful, if not neat. Even Chloe had managed to squiggle something in felt pen and stick on a ready made flag, and Beth had added her name for her. The music made a pleasant background to what was a very happy event. Vitaly grew in confidence and tried out his English on more and more of the guests, thriving on the praise and appreciation he received. Daria looked on proudly.

"Oh Sam, this is a wonderful thing. I love to see Vitaly so happy and to see people enjoying Ukrainian food and music. And the English food is very good, especially the - scones, is that how you say it? Thank you so much for everything."

"The pronunciation of scone is a minefield, I'm afraid. I say it to rhyme with 'one', but a lot of people make it rhyme with 'own'! There is no right way to say it. And it's even controversial whether you put cream or jam on first."

Daria laughed.

"English pronunciation is so difficult, but I did not know that English people also disagree about it. There is so much to learn."

"It's a tough language, I can see that. Especially the spelling. But you already speak so well."

"Oh no, but I will work hard to improve. I am so happy to have lessons from Mr Deering. Thank you so much for organising it all."

"It's Deb and Sophy you should be thanking, Daria. They had the idea for the lunch and did most of the organisation."

"Let us go and thank them then, please. I must tell them how pleased we are."

Deb and Sophy were both clearing up in the kitchen when we found them. They looked delighted with Daria's reaction to everything and received her grateful thanks with typical self-deprecation. But you could see in their faces the satisfaction of a job well done.

As Chloe, Mum and I were finally leaving, with Beth and her guests in tow, Adam approached us again.

"I must just say to you, Daria, before you go, that if you need anything, anything at all, I will be happy to help. I can help with learning English, if you like, until I leave for Ukraine."

"Thank you so much, Adam - is that right? That is your name? It is very kind of you. But Mr Deering has offered English lessons."

Adam looked annoyed and frustrated.

"I'm sure you can help with some English conversation practice later on," I soothed, feeling sorry for the lad. "Your language is certainly more up-to-date than Mr Deering's. And there may be other things you can do to help."

"OK, I suppose that will have to do. Here is my email and phone number, Daria. I really do want to be of use to you."

He handed her a scruffy scrap of paper with his details, and turned away, his irritation visible, even from behind, in his jerky movements and stomping walk.

"Poor Adam!" I said quietly. "He's obsessed with your country, Daria and he means well, but …"

Daria nodded sympathetically.

"When the war started, many young men at home were like this, so eager to fight. But war is not an adventure. It is terrible and many were hurt or killed."

"He seems rather young for his age," commented Mum. "But I don't know enough teenagers to judge properly."

She sounded really tired and a new surge of anxiety shot through me.

"I think we'd better go straight home, Mum, and not walk Beth and Daria back today. Chloe looks worn out and she has nursery again tomorrow morning."

I knew I had to be tactful if I was to persuade her to come away.

"You're right, darling," she sighed wearily. "It's all been very exciting for her. Lovely to meet you, Daria, and you too, Vitaly."

Vitaly actually did look exhausted, his small head drooping as he trudged alongside his mother, but he managed to raise the energy to smile, wave, and practise his English 'goodbye'.

When we got home, I insisted on Mum staying for a cup of tea and tried to make her put her feet up and rest.

"I'm worried about you, Mum. You really aren't yourself."

"You don't need to be concerned about me, Sam. It's probably only that I still haven't recovered from the Covid we had at Easter. I've just never got my energy back. Your father seems to be back to normal, but I just can't seem to shake it off, however hard I try. I keep falling asleep in the evenings and I never used to do that. But the doctor is insisting on doing some other tests to make sure it's nothing more than that."

I smiled down at her affectionately.

"Please let me know what comes out of the tests. And you must rest more. From what I hear, that's the only way to get over it."

"But I get bored and depressed doing nothing at home, and I feel as if I'm preventing your dad from enjoying life."

"Now you know that is just not true, Mum. But I can see that you're feeling down, however much you try to hide it. Would it help if I came over and helped around the house? I could do some of the heavy cleaning. You know I have the time now that Chloe goes to nursery."

Mum's bottom lip quivered and her eyes filled with tears, but she snapped back at once.

"Definitely not. You have enough on your plate with your own house and Chloe to look after. Do stop fussing. I'm absolutely fine, and seeing you and our darling Chloe does me more good than resting, doesn't it, my sweetheart?"

Right on cue, Chloe put her arms around mum's legs and laid her head on her knee, saying something which sounded very much like 'love Gammer'. She couldn't manage 'Grandma' yet, so 'Gammer' was, and might perhaps remain, her version. My heart melted into a rush of tenderness and I knelt down to hug them both.

CHAPTER 6

Andante

The next few days felt distinctly quiet after so much excitement, back to a more normal routine for me and Chloe. According to Beth, Daria had started her regular English lessons with John Deering, Vitaly was attending nursery three mornings a week, and his nightmares had lessened, both in frequency and severity. Deb was helping with the complex bureaucracy of obtaining all the required documentation and permits.

"I was wondering whether she is able to get any regular news of Bogdan? It all looks very chaotic and violent in that part of Ukraine on the news, and she must be feeling so worried."

"She tries not to let me or Vitaly see it, but I know she is anxious about him. On a few occasions, since they left Ukraine, he has been able to ring and speak to her, but only when they are in a truly safe area, which seems to happen very rarely. Mainly she is able to glean scraps of news from the Ukrainian group chat they have set up and there's a messaging group of other wives and relatives as well. Sometimes she hears that someone has seen him, safe and well, and she feels better for a little while."

"It must be awful for her - and for him too, although I don't suppose he has much time or energy to think about it."

"She asked me if she could light a candle in her bedroom when she prays for him. I suggested she have it downstairs, as it would be safer. I'm a bit obsessive about fire risks, as you know. So she's made a kind of little shrine, with a photograph of him and a candle holder in front of it. I think she finds it comforting."

"That's so kind of you, Beth. You are being such a good host."

"Not really, Sam. I do my best, but sometimes I feel so inadequate. I wish I spoke Ukrainian and could speak to Vitaly in his own language."

"How is his English coming on?"

"I'm astonished at how fast he is picking it up. He can put together some of his own sentences already. At nursery, he likes to play with the younger children at the moment and I think that's because of the language barrier, but he is picking things up all the time and even starting to learn his alphabet."

"Wow – that's brilliant. Of course, they use the Cyrillic alphabet over there. It made learning the language on the app much more of a challenge. Even more to get your head around. I must take Daria up on her offer to teach me. I would love to learn Ukrainian really properly. Such a challenge."

"I wish I had your type of brain, Sam. I've always been hopeless at languages, as you know. But I've started to put up signs on things around the house, with their names printed on them in English. I thought it would really help Vitaly to learn to read, as well as pick up the sounds of the words. Useful things like 'toilet' and 'kitchen'."

"What a good idea! Don't be so hard on yourself, Beth. You are such a sensitive, thoughtful person. You are doing everything you can to help."

Beth was not good with compliments and I could almost hear her blushing over the phone.

"Not being a mother myself doesn't help. There are so many

things I just don't know about parenting. But I am trying to learn. I would really like to adopt one day, you know."

I had never known Beth to have any kind of romantic relationship, yet she had told me before how desperate she was to have a family of her own. I hoped it would work out for her. She would be such a wonderful mother.

The next committee meeting on Wednesday evening was less tense, partly because Celia could not make it. John Deering said that the two of them had finally agreed on a list of performers, but were not yet able to come to a consensus on an outline programme or running order.

"She is insisting on that rather plump, spotty teenager, Jessica, closing the concert. I believe that the girl wants to sing *Candle in the Wind*. Not very appropriate to my mind. And will a young girl's voice alone, with only a piano accompaniment, be strong enough to finish the concert on a high? I am personally not in favour of it. She had a few piano lessons with me a while ago, but showed no exceptional aptitude or talent."

"Jessica? Oh, she has the most wonderful voice. That will be a real climax to the programme. She has the ability to communicate very powerfully with an audience. We were all in tears after her performance at Christmas."

I was glad that Deb had spoken up, otherwise I would have had to defend Jessica. I knew what an amazing singer she was. But, as Celia's protégée, probably not likely to be popular with John Deering.

"I love that song," contributed Beth. "I remember it from Princess Diana's funeral."

"I am certainly not of the opinion that a link with that sad day makes it suitable for a Jubilee celebration event! In any case, I will need further discussions with Celia, I suppose. It does make things run more smoothly to have a single person in charge of an event like this, who can make swifter and more effective decisions, but I don't suppose you would sanction that at this point."

A bare-faced power grab. Fortunately Sophy was very much against excluding Celia.

"I understand what you are saying, Mr Deering, and cooperation and delegation are always more difficult than doing it all yourself, especially for someone as experienced as you. But that is what community events are all about. I think we would all be very grateful to you if you would continue to collaborate with Celia."

John looked rather flattered at her mode of expression and bowed his head in acceptance.

"If you consider it to be of value, of course I will continue to share with her the benefit of my expertise in organising musical entertainments."

Everyone smiled in relief, hoping that this was the end of our concert conflict.

When the meeting concluded, Sophy came over to talk to me.

"I'm trying to arrange a picnic in the park for Saturday, Sam. The weather forecast looks pretty good, Annette's actually got a day off and it seems ages since we all got together. Emily's definitely coming, and Deb is going to try to make it, but may be taxiing the kids around. And of course Daria is bringing Vitaly. I'm pretty sure Beth's coming too. Can you make it? I know Annette's dying to see you. Don't worry - I promise it's not a coffee morning!"

The smile on my face wavered a little at her last words. Last summer's events still had the power to hurt me, just when I least expected it. I tried to laugh it off lightly, but Sophy knew immediately what had happened and put her arm around my shoulders.

"I'm so sorry, Sam. I know it was much too soon and not funny at all. I didn't mean to upset you."

I managed a slightly shaky grin.

"I know you didn't, Sophy, and most of the time it is fine. It just pops up suddenly and I relive those awful moments, when I thought I might lose my precious daughter ... But of course, it didn't happen, and we have to go on living. In fact, I'm hoping Jackie might be able to visit me for a couple of days in the summer holiday. It would be lovely to see her again. I have so much to thank her for."

Sophy nodded.

"Poor thing. I feel so sorry for her. But I really didn't intend to stir up all those memories for you."

"It's not your fault. You can never know what will trigger it."

"Anyway, do you think you will be able to come to our picnic? Around half past eleven, near the pond?"

I nodded positively. I owed my friends an awful lot too, and it would be lovely to spend time with them all. Chloe's rigid routines had somehow taken over my life and I had not made the effort to arrange to meet up with them regularly enough.

"Thanks for organising it, Sophy. Do we all bring our own food and drink or are we sharing?"

"Easiest to bring our own, I think, but I'll bring a few extra things to share. So glad you can come, and sorry again for upsetting you."

"You didn't. It was nothing. Just a blip. I'll see you on Saturday. Looking forward to it."

Chloe and I were among the last to arrive at the park. She had managed to spill milk all over herself that morning and the clean-up process made us late, rushed, and unusually tense. But as soon as she saw Elise and the other children playing with toys with Beth and Vitaly on the blanket, she toddled off happily enough, little train in hand, and I breathed out the tension in a big sigh. She might be more independent physically now, but she really did demand a lot of attention. It was a tricky age. Mobile enough to reach much more, but not old enough to have any sense of danger.

I turned back from watching her walking off, to see the others, sitting in a circle around the children. Smiling and waving at my friends on the other side, I sat down next to Annette. She had always been slight, but she looked painfully thin, her smiling face drawn and pale, eyes slightly sunken and surrounded with deep shadows.

"It's so lovely to see you, Annette. It's been far too long."

"I know, it seems ages. I've really missed you."

"I used to see you on Tuesday at nursery pick-up. Has Simon changed his day?"

A deep frown appeared on her face, her lips narrowed and pursed, as if a terrible anxiety had returned all at once.

"We - we've had to take him out of nursery, Sam. With everything so expensive now, it just wasn't possible. He misses the other children, but it can't be helped."

I squeezed her hand.

"I'm so sorry. I know things are really tough just now. You know I will help if I can."

Annette looked down, a tear glittering on her pale eyelash. Her hand was shaking slightly.

"Give me a minute, Sam. I'm OK, really I am. It's just that when people are kind to me, it sets off the emotions. I know you understand. I did want to ask you something, but it can wait until later. Tell me how Chloe is. Is she talking much yet?"

I gave her the time to get herself under control by talking about my daughter and the pleasing progress she was making in communicating what she wanted. I was worried that she was so fragile. Not like the Annette I knew - proud and tough, independent and determined. The sudden rise in the cost of living was so cruel to families living close to the edge, as many with young children were forced to.

Deb arrived just then, somewhat flustered from rushing around delivering her children to their various hobbies. As if on cue, we all moved nearer to each other so that we could talk as a group.

"Sorry I'm late, everyone. The boys needed ferrying to opposite ends of the town and Jack is in a cycle race this morning, so it was down to me. So lovely to see you all! I've missed getting together like this. Shall we try to do it at least every month? If we don't plan it, it just won't happen."

Murmurs of agreement all round. Life just gets in the way, especially when you have young children or a demanding job.

As we began to catch up on what had been happening in each other's lives, I could sense a growing tension next to me. I felt that Annette was needing to speak, to me at least, and maybe to the whole group.

"How about you, Annette? How has life been treating you?"

She took a deep breath, glanced round the whole group and then looked down at the ground, a deep patchy flush on her pale cheeks.

"It's - I have to tell you, it's been really tough. Everything is so expensive now and the electricity price is impossible and only going to get worse. We've - we've had to give up the car. It isn't just petrol, it's repairs, insurance, road tax. It's just not worth it. I have a bike now and John has a moped, as he works further away."

There was a murmur of sympathy, which encouraged her to go on. But it was obvious that every word was hurting her.

"But it means I can't even go for a job caring for people in their homes, which would pay more per hour, because I don't have transport. And with my hours at the care home being mainly four until midnight, it's really hard to get extra work. I can't do babysitting or anything. I tried offering ironing, but no one wants to pay for that any more. So many people are in the same boat as we are."

She was talking faster now, more fluently.

"John and I talked about it. It's hard for me to do, but I have to try to use my contacts to get more work. I don't like doing it. You know that. But - I could do cleaning for someone on a Saturday morning, when John can have Simon. I wondered if it would be useful to you, Sam, as you're on your own, and it's so hard to get anything done with a toddler under your feet."

My brain raced. I wanted to help, but I had never wanted to have a cleaner. Partly because I knew I would be embarrassed about the state of the place. I would be tidying up so much before they came that it would hardly be worth it! But also because I was somehow uncomfortable with the idea of having someone working directly for me, almost like a servant. Not logical, but it was there, as a barrier in my head.

"Well …" I hesitated, trying to hide the reluctance in my voice. I would ask her to help my mother out, but without transport that was out of the question.

Deb and Sophy both jumped in together.

"Mrs D-B!"

"What do you mean?"

Annette was completely confused.

"Mrs Donnington-Browne at the Jubilee committee. She wanted to get Daria to help with various things around the house - or rather the 'manor' as she put it. I'm sure she would be delighted to pay you for some work."

"And I can babysit for Simon," I added.

"No, Sam, I would love to look after Simon for Annette."

It was Daria's clear accented voice which cut through all the offers of help.

"I need to give something back to this town, these wonderful people, who have welcomed me and Vitaly so warmly. And I have much time."

I could already hear the increased confidence in her voice when speaking English. And she had no trouble following our conversation now. She was a very quick learner.

"That would be really kind of you," said Sophy. "It would certainly make things easier for Annette. Any other ideas?"

She sounded unusually emotional. She was close to Annette and obviously knew how much it cost her to ask us for help, even though it was only more work she was looking for, not monetary support.

Emily spoke up, her business-like approach refreshingly matter-of-fact in this emotionally charged situation.

"I wonder if you could offer cat-sitting for people who go away on holiday or for the weekend, Annette. I often get asked if I know anyone who does it. Dog people tend to take their pets on holiday with them, or use kennels if they can't, but cats are different. They often hate the cattery, which is really expensive anyway, and people would rather leave them at home, but need to have someone to go in each day, feed them and check that they are OK. Empty the litter tray if they have one, fresh water, all that sort of thing. How are you with cats?"

Annette's eyes brightened.

"I've always loved them! We had two at home when I was growing up. I'd love to have one now, but with vet's bills and food we just couldn't afford it."

"Perfect!" said Sophy, sounding much happier. "I can make you some business cards. And as you're a carer, you're already DBS checked, which is a big selling point."

"You're right, Sophy. And I can hand out cards to my customers," confirmed Emily.

"And we can put it on the local Facebook group."

The enthusiasm for this idea was evident. Finding something that Annette would like to do, that could even become an extra business for her - it felt like a great solution.

"We're just coming into the peak holiday season, too, so it couldn't be better in terms of timing," said Emily.

As ever, Deb took charge.

"That's a fantastic idea, Emily. We'll all help with publicity, accounts and babysitting as needed - although I know you want to do most of that, Daria. It's great that you should want to contribute like this, so soon after arriving here. In the meantime, we can ask Mrs D-B if she would be interested in you helping round the house. I'll contact her and, if she agrees, we can go on Monday morning, if you're available then, Annette. Daria could try looking after Simon for an hour or so while we go and meet her."

I could see that Annette was overwhelmed and close to tears again. I put my arm around her bony shoulders and gave her a hug. She nodded to Deb and I whispered in her ear.

"It'll be fine. We'll sort it. Thank you for asking for our help. I can imagine how hard it was."

She reached up to her shoulder and gave my hand a convulsive squeeze.

"I've been so worried. About money, losing our home, having enough to eat even, but also about asking you for help. I feel as if a heavy weight has been lifted off my shoulders."

I could not help feeling guilty that I had not been thinking about her financial situation before. I knew she and her husband had relatively low-paid jobs and that they did not have any savings or family support in the area. I should have realised how the enormous price rises would affect them.

Even though I had been largely insulated from the issue by Thomas' death in service payment, I had still been aware of everything costing more and was considering when and how I would need to return to work, to make the money go further. But teaching, while not exactly highly paid, would at least cover childcare costs and bring enough in to make a difference.

We all knew better than to offer Annette money directly. She was too proud for that. But I was already thinking of little practical ways to help, like inviting her and Simon round for lunch, or doing some baking to share.

As I walked back with Beth, Daria and Vitaly, I noticed that Beth was very quiet. She had been fully engaged in playing with the children, keeping them happily occupied, while we chatted, but I knew that she had heard the conversation with Annette, because I had caught her staring in our direction.

"What's wrong, Beth?" I asked quietly.

"I feel so awful! I have so much. I even get money from the government to help with looking after Daria and Vitaly. And poor Annette is in so much difficulty. It's just not fair. I don't deserve it. I wish I could give her money, but I know she wouldn't take it."

Beth's frustration and guilt burst out of her.

"I know how you feel. I think we all reacted like that. But you are doing great things with your good fortune, Beth. You're volunteering at the Food Bank, you do a great job for very little pay at the nursery, and now you are offering a home to Daria and Vitaly. You have nothing to be ashamed of. We'll all do our best to support Annette. But the fact is, there must be lots of families in the same dire situation."

Beth nodded vigorously.

"I know. We are having to help more than double the numbers we had last year at the bank. I'm getting very friendly with several of the women, who have to come in more regularly now, and they are facing the most terrible hardship. I'm afraid some of them may lose their homes. Some are asking for food you don't need to cook because they can't afford to put the cooker on. And donations have actually gone down, because everyone else is feeling the pinch."

"I think I would like to donate regularly, Beth. Can you get me a form or send me a link? I do put things into the box at the supermarket, but I really want to do more. And if we put a link on the Facebook group, I'm sure other people would help."

Beth looked a little more cheerful.

"You're right. We could do some fundraising activities too. Thanks, Sam. You always manage to make me feel better."

With new plans burgeoning in our heads, we walked on more happily, enjoying the spring sunshine.

CHAPTER 7

Fugue

The following day felt blustery and somehow autumnal, as Daria and I walked to church together. Beth had opted to stay at home and look after Chloe and Vitaly, so we were able to talk properly.

"How are the English lessons going, Daria?"

"I think I am making much - sorry, a great deal of progress, Sam," she said enthusiastically. "John - he asked me to call him by his Christian name - teaches me grammar, helps with my accent and vocabulary, and then we talk about the history of England, especially in this place, and what is happening here now. He is so interesting and knows so much.

"Mmmm," I responded. He was obviously enjoying himself, pontificating to his heart's content. "We generally say 'first name' nowadays."

"Thank you, Sam. It is helpful to me to know also how younger people speak. But John is teaching me so many things. He talks to me about everything, politics, current affairs, the royal family, everything. I feel that I am learning much about England as well as improving my English. He tries to guide the way I think by showing me the background."

I rather wondered what kind of politics he would be discussing with Daria, but could not ask her to explain without undermining his position as her tutor.

"And now he is also teaching me how to play the piano. Beth has a piano too, so I can practise. He is a very good teacher and so kind to me, like a grandfather or an uncle. He sits beside me on the piano bench - or is it a stool? And he guides me how to hold my hands. It is difficult, but I enjoy it so much."

A small alarm bell rang in my head. But I was probably misinterpreting her words.

"I'm happy for you, Daria. Glad you are able to have fun while you are learning. And I can tell that your English is improving all the time."

"Thank you, Sam. I am reading books and watching the television as well. John says I must immerse myself as much as I can."

"It's definitely the best way to learn. And it's clearly working!"

Daria slowed down a little and turned to me, concern on her face.

"One thing is a problem to me, Sam. Everywhere I go, on my own or with Vitaly, but never if Beth is with me, I am meeting Adam. It is as if he is watching me or following me. He likes to talk to me and ask me about Ukraine, and that is kind and nice of him, but it is sometimes too much. I do not want to talk about it all the time. I do not want Vitaly always to hear of what our life was there. He has my phone number now and sends me messages and questions many times every day."

"Oh dear. That doesn't sound right."

Potential stalking behaviour. Something to be concerned about, always. He was only a boy, but boys were often slaves to their hormones and not good at balance. And it sounded as if he might already have some other issues, which might make him more prone to obsession.

"Leave it with me, Daria. I will speak to Deb. She knows his mother very well and will hopefully know what to do for the best. It may be better, for now, to ignore most of his messages, and not to stop and talk to him for very long if he comes up to you. Just say you are in a hurry and you'll talk to him another time."

She nodded, looking relieved.

"I will try to do that. I do not want to make him angry, and I know he is being kind and helpful, but I am finding it all strange and difficult."

"I'm not surprised. Don't worry. You did the right thing by telling me."

At that point, we arrived at the church. I was starting to get used to the pattern of the service and what to do, but still felt completely out of my depth about what it all meant. I would have to speak to Stephen about it some time, but on my own. Daria would not understand. She was so devout, and so sure of her own faith.

I rang Deb later, while Chloe was having her rest that afternoon.

"Oh no! Claire was worried that he might be far too interested in Daria, as well as Ukraine, and it sounds as if she is right. Apparently, he's been missing quite a lot of lessons at school in the last couple of weeks, too. She's desperately anxious about him. He's - well, he's young for his age, not streetwise at all, and hasn't had any girlfriends that I know of. Daria's so young and attractive and far too kind to push him away or snub him."

"It sounds as if he has a real crush on her and is taking it to extremes. Do you think Claire will be able to handle it, or do you or I need to have a talk with him?"

"I'll see what she says. To be honest, she is at the end of her tether with him at the moment and doesn't feel that she has any influence over him. She did tell me that he had started learning Ukrainian on an app though. And she found him researching camping equipment! Apparently he said you had suggested it was a good idea to learn the language and get used to sleeping outside."

I laughed.

"I was trying to get him to be more practical about his plans. He seemed to want me to tell him not to go, and was a bit put out when I suggested he work with a charity, learn to drive, join the cadets and start learning Ukrainian!"

"That was really clever of you, Sam," said Deb admiringly. "I wouldn't have thought of that. Much more effective than pleading with him not to do something so risky."

"I suppose, over the years in school, I've picked up a smidgeon of child psychology."

"You might be the best person to speak to him, then. I'll talk to Claire about it first, but you're probably better than the rest of us at engaging with a teenager like him."

"Well, he seems to behave more like a fourteen or fifteen-year-old than an adult, and I'm very used to trying to persuade them to put some work into my subject …"

"Exactly. And you know that young people often listen better to someone other than a parent."

This was true. It was only too obvious at every parents' evening. Parental advice was just not welcome. I really needed to enjoy my time with Chloe while she was young. It would probably not be too long before she was rebelling against everything I suggested. That was a rather sad thought.

I asked Deb how Mrs D-B had reacted to the idea of Annette doing some paid work for her.

"She was absolutely delighted! She said she is always looking for reliable people. And there is a lot to do in such a large old house.

I'm taking Annette to meet her tomorrow, but I think she will definitely offer her some work, on a flexible basis to fit around her shifts at the care home. She was very pleased that she is already DBS checked, too."

"I'm glad. Anything we can do to help Annette without offending her. I felt so bad that I had not thought about how difficult this rampant inflation would be for her."

"Me too. It's scary how many people will be suffering."

I told her about our idea of putting a link to donate to the Food Bank on our local Facebook group and she said she would very much support that. I knew that her fertile mind would soon be coming up with other ways to help the community, too. You could always count on Deb, not just to have ideas, but also to put them into practice, promptly and with sometimes intimidating efficiency.

CHAPTER 8

Presto

The start of the Jubilee celebrations seemed to be rushing towards us, borne on the unseasonably strong winds. One of our main worries was the prospect of heavy rain. May had begun well, but deteriorated into extremely changeable weather, with bright sunny periods interspersed with violent stormy showers, and we were all concerned about the street party, in particular.

In the end, we decided that we would just have to try to find as many gazebos and awnings as possible and Sophy suggested, in addition, stretching a large sail over one part of the square. It would not be possible to move such a large group into the church hall if the rain came, and there would be many vulnerable older people there, as well as families with small children.

We had decided to make it a ticketed event, so that we knew who to cater for, but we did not charge for the tickets. There was an option on the website to donate towards the cost of the food, but we did not want to exclude anyone, just because they could not afford to pay for a ticket. We even distributed some paper application forms, mainly to the elderly, so that those without computer skills could still come. Beth had taken some to the Food Bank to make sure that families who were really struggling would be invited.

"A lot of the local businesses are donating items, especially Mr Patel's bakery, which is being incredibly generous. Including his famous doughnuts! And we've had over a hundred people sign up already! Quite a few are giving money towards the party, so we can afford to buy in what we don't have and pay for ingredients for the home-made cakes and other dishes."

Sophy sounded really satisfied with the way things were going. She and Deb made a great team and, with contributions from everyone, we felt that we were on track for really successful celebrations and community events.

John Deering and Celia were making progress in organising the charity concert on Saturday and had decided to share the proceeds between the Ukraine fund and the local Food Bank, after Beth explained how desperate some local families were. There was still some friction between them, but John was putting on an air of extreme patience, and eventually accepting some of Celia's excellent suggestions.

I had suddenly become aware that I had not seen my detective friend, Daniyaal, for far too long. He had been forced to cancel one of our ad hoc monthly meetings due to a work issue, and I had to pull out of the next one because Chloe was unwell. So it had been several months since we had spent time together and I decided to invite him along to the beacon lighting ceremony. Sophy had booked a good band and it was shaping up to become a less formal, more fun event than I had envisaged.

He was keen to meet up and talk, but would only be able to come for an hour or so.

"They've asked us all to be available from around ten in the evening, just in case there is any trouble in town, when people have possibly been drinking all day. But I will definitely come for a while. It seems ages since I last saw you."

"It really does. I would like to introduce you to Daria, too - my new friend from Ukraine. She's such a lovely person. Shall we meet there? I'll have to help with setting things up at the start, so it makes more sense if you come along at about half past eight."

"Sounds great. I'm looking forward to it already. See you soon."

But first, I had a rather difficult task to attempt. Claire had seized on the idea of me talking to Adam about Daria with the desperation of a drowning swimmer, according to Deb.

"Anything you can do to help him to understand what is and is not appropriate in the adult world. She really needs help. His father lives away on the south coast and doesn't see him much at all, as he has his own new family to worry about. And Adam seems to feel the need to be a man's man, in spite of how he chooses to look. It feels as if he is forcing himself to go against his natural instincts. As if he has to prove himself somehow."

"Oh dear, that's such a shame. It never works to make yourself go against your real personality. But young people have so many pressures on them nowadays. It's a hard world to grow up in. I don't envy them at all. And the pandemic just made things even more difficult for them."

Deb heaved a worried sigh.

"I know, I'm already getting anxious for my two. At least they both love sport for now, and that gets them out and mixing with other people. Do you need me to come with you to speak to Adam?"

Unusually for Deb, this was clearly not an offer she wanted me to accept, I could see that in her eyes.

"Don't worry, I'll be OK. Did Claire say when or where I could meet him?"

"She is hoping that you can meet him 'by chance' when she sends him to the supermarket tomorrow. About eleven o'clock, I think, but I'll check with her and message you."

"So he's not expecting me to want to talk to him? I'm not sure if that's a bad or a good thing. I suppose it's possibly better that he doesn't know I've been in contact with you, or that his mother has prompted me to speak to him."

The closer our projected meeting came, the more my stomach churned with apprehension. Why on earth had I agreed to do such a difficult and probably ineffectual thing? Interfering in other people's family lives was sometimes disastrous and almost never had the desired effect.

At least I would be able take Chloe with me, which somehow gave me more confidence, confirming that I was a parent and was actually grown-up enough to be capable of offering unwanted behavioural advice to an eighteen-year-old. But how could I possibly even start a conversation like that with him?

In the end, with the aid of several messages from Deb, we both turned up at the supermarket simultaneously and indeed almost bumped into one another. I took a deep breath and dived in.

"Oh, hello, Adam. Do you remember me? Sam Elsdon from the Ukraine lunch. Can I please have a quick word with you?"

There was recognition in his eyes, or rather his eye, as the left one was completely covered with his long straight fringe of dark brown hair. But as I asked to speak to him, there was obvious wariness and reluctance in what little I could see of his face.

"Why? Have you been speaking to my mother?"

His abruptness was not encouraging, but at least I could honestly reply in the negative, and that seemed to persuade him to comply. There was an empty bench next to the car park and I led him over to it and turned the buggy round to face me. Chloe stared intently at Adam. He seemed to find that unpleasant and avoided catching her eye.

Reluctantly, he sat down next to me. Hostility oozed from every pore.

"What is it you want with me?"

Not quite rude, but verging on it. But I could understand his reaction. What was a middle-aged woman (as he would see me), with a toddler in tow, doing talking to him?

"This is quite difficult for me, Adam. But I have to tell you that I am speaking to you on Daria's behalf."

"Daria! What is the problem? Is she OK?"

He responded with instinctive anxiety, concern for her. That was positive, at least.

I managed to keep my voice neutral and calm.

"She's had a quiet word with me. She's been finding receiving so many messages from you a bit over the top, Adam. And although she is glad and grateful that you are so interested in her country, she doesn't really want to talk about it every time she goes out. As you will imagine, it brings back all kinds of difficult memories for her."

"But - " was all that came out at first, in a strangled voice.

"I know it's very important to you, because you plan to go out there soon. I understand that. But you have to remember that Daria came here to get away from the war, to be safe with her son, and she's naturally also very anxious about her husband Bogdan, who is fighting with Ukrainian forces near Kharkiv. So she doesn't want to be reminded about it all the time."

Abruptly, Adam surged to his feet and began walking to and fro in an agitated manner.

"You don't understand! Yes, I need to know more about Ukraine. That's obvious. I must prepare myself for what I will find there. But Daria - well, she's wonderful, amazing. So beautiful and sensitive. Not like anyone I've ever met before. I - I really love her. I want to help her in any way that I can."

Oh dear. More than a crush. To him, a genuine first love. I felt deeply sorry for him.

"Adam, I hear what you are saying. I can tell that you have genuine feelings for Daria. But you have to remember that she is married, and that she loves her husband very deeply. It wouldn't be right to interfere in that. He's the father of her child and they have their own life together, which can hopefully begin again one day soon."

He sat down again, hands shaking a little as he dashed the fringe out of his eyes. He looked even younger, vulnerable and wounded. I wanted to give him a hug and tell him that it would be all right, that he would recover, but I knew that would not be well received.

"I - I understand. I will try to keep out of her way," he managed to get out in a very quiet, slightly tremulous voice.

I could see his lower lip quivering and knew that he would not want to lose control of his emotions in front of me. Best to bring it to a swift conclusion if at all possible.

"Thank you, Adam. That's very mature of you. I know that when you care for someone, you want the very best for them. And for Daria, that is settling in here and eventually being reunited with her husband. But I do fully respect your feelings and recognise how hard this will be for you."

No verbal response, but a convulsive deep breath. Time to leave him to allow his feelings to come out in private.

"Thanks again. I'll see you soon. And I wish you all the best with your exams."

He snorted contemptuously.

"What do exams matter now? That's the last thing on my mind."

"I know, Adam. But they will be important to you later," I soothed. "Anyway, goodbye for now."

I turned away, moved the buggy so that Chloe could not carry on staring fixedly at him, and made my way over to the shop. I hoped that I had not made things worse. My heart was touched by his pain, remembering how hard setbacks could feel at that age.

There was sympathy in my voice when I told Deb what had happened. She was inclined to laugh at first, but sobered up when I explained how he had reacted.

"I thought he would really lose his temper and have some kind of meltdown, to be honest with you, Sam. I'm amazed you managed to keep him so calm."

"I think it's probably because I took his feelings seriously instead of ignoring them. Don't you remember how acutely painful things were when we were teenagers? How it felt like the end of the world if someone you fancied laughed at you or ignored you?"

"Mmmm, you're so right. And we had each other. Adam's a bit of a loner, I gather. Poor lad. Hope he gets over it soon."

I heartily agreed. I was rather anxious that he might be pushed into some kind of self harm or other damaging behaviour.

"Can you ask Claire to keep a fairly close eye on him for the next few weeks, Deb? It'll be best if she doesn't mention it at all to him, but if she could just be more tolerant and positive with him than usual, it might help him to recover more quickly. Especially as his exams are starting so soon."

Deb agreed and said that Claire would be so relieved that he would not be pestering Daria any more that she would be only too pleased to be extra nice to him.

Later that day, I met Daria near the park. Vitaly was not with her but she was smiling and seemed excited.

"Sam! How happy I am to see you. I have such good news."

"That's good. Tell me."

"Oh Sam, Vitaly is getting so much better. He goes to the toilet on his own at night again now. He does not need the pull-ups every day any more, but we keep them to make him feel safe. The nightmares are much less. And last night, I woke up in the morning and he was not there. I was worried, but he was sleeping in his own bed. He said he looked in there on the way back from the toilet and thought he would try sleeping by himself."

"Wow! That's astonishing progress in such a short time, Daria. He is really settling in well here. You've done a great job of making him feel secure."

Her face was illuminated by such deep happiness, it brought a lump to my throat.

"He is so very happy here. He asked to stay with Beth this afternoon rather than coming for a walk with me. He feels safe and comfortable with her. I think he will sleep in his own room from now. He says I make noises when I sleep!"

I laughed.

"You mean you snore!"

"Yes, that is it. He made a joke of it. He is growing up so much. So much more independent. The nursery has helped with that."

"You must be so very proud of him and so relieved that he is beginning to recover."

"Yes, Sam. I was so worried that he might never get better. He suffered so much in Kharkiv with the bombing and on that difficult journey out of the country. It was all so hard, so - trauma? Is that the word?"

"Traumatic."

"And he was so young, but old enough to know that bad things were happening and that Bogdan and I were frightened too. Life here is so different. I think that is why he is getting better so soon."

I nodded.

"That's probably true, Daria, but the trauma has not gone away, you know. He will probably have times when he seems to go backwards, to go back to wetting the bed or coming to sleep with you where he feels safe."

She agreed gravely.

"Yes, but it is so good to see him doing things I thought he might never do, or not for a long time. He is a strong one."

"He really is. He's a special little boy. But he is strong because he knows that he is loved, and that makes him feel safer."

Daria flung her arms around me.

"You are so kind, Sam. You understand us. And you make me understand things."

I explained that I had talked to Adam on her behalf.

"I don't think he will follow or approach you any more, Daria. At least I hope not. And there should not be multiple messages every day. He - he really does care for you and now understands that what he did was not the right thing."

"Thank you, Sam. It was kind of you to solve this problem for me."

"I can't help feeling sorry for him. He is so very vulnerable."

"He is very young."

She was relieved, but her mind was fully centred on Vitaly that day. She had no energy or emotion left for pity or to reflect on what it might mean to Adam.

CHAPTER 9

Con brio

All of a sudden, as it seemed, we had arrived at the week of the Jubilee. The weather continued to be erratic and often very wet and everyone I met discussed it endlessly, in the vain hope that talking about it might somehow drive the rain away.

Mrs D-B was particularly fractious at our last full meeting before the beacon lighting.

"I simply do not understand why the weather has to ruin our special events. It is actually June now! It's supposed to be blazing or flaming, isn't it? Her Majesty deserves a wonderful celebration, not a damp squib."

"I don't think the weather was good at the last Jubilee either, was it?" Deb said. "I seem to remember a very cold and wet boat pageant on the Thames."

"All the more reason for it to be good this time. I am sad to say that it will, in all probability, be the Queen's last such event. It should live in the memory as a golden period, not a miserable bedraggled flop."

Murmurs of agreement ran round the table. It was so frustrating.

"I promise you that we will have a great weekend, whatever the weather, Mrs D-B," Sophy soothed.

She and the rest of us actually addressed her like that now. She could be difficult and tactless, but she was definitely not as bad as I had been led to expect. Annette said she was quite easy to work for, as long as you followed instructions very carefully and did not act on your own initiative. She had very high standards, but was not overly unreasonable in her requirements and focused more on the work being done well than the minutiae of timekeeping.

"Oh, I know we will, Sophy. But it is particularly the events in London I am concerned about. Will Her Majesty even be able to attend them if the weather is inclement?"

"I'm pretty sure she has some health issues anyway at the moment, Mrs D-B. They say she has mobility problems, so she's already had to miss some important occasions. But I'm positive she'll enjoy her celebrations and parties all the same. We definitely intend to!"

Deb led us through the calendar of events, checking that all the organisation was on track.

"Sophy, you've confirmed with the band for the beacon lighting, haven't you? I know we booked a while ago, but a reminder never goes amiss. And the pub has permission to put on a cash bar for us, just for the period of the event, but there will be no other refreshments. That should cut down on the mess we need to clear up afterwards. The beacon is ready and we will light it at around ten past nine, just after the Queen has lit her own. No tickets, open to everyone, as there is plenty of space on Galley's Hill. I'm hoping this is the event that will especially appeal to the younger people."

Here John Deering interrupted, rather sententiously and without much relevance to the discussion, as far as I could see.

"An interesting piece of historical information in relation to our event. We call it Galley's Hill, but that is a corruption of the original name, Gallows Hill, the place where miscreants were hanged and left dangling there as a warning to others."

"Oh! That's not a nice thought at all. But it's the best place we could find, so please don't go around telling people that story, Mr Deering. It could feel like a bad omen or even rather disrespectful to the Queen."

"As you please, although I think it is quite appropriate. Hanging was once a popular public event, you know, even for children. I suppose our 'modern sensibilities' don't like the idea now, but it is part of our British history. It marked a kind of democratic participation in the act of justice, as well as providing real entertainment for ordinary folk. Executions are still popular events in the United States, you know. So it is not so very far removed from our Jubilee entertainment, after all."

There was a pronounced but subtle sneer in his voice as he spoke of contemporary views of what is acceptable. The others seemed rather puzzled by his attitude, but were impressed with his knowledge.

"It is a great pity that our history, local and national, has been sanitised in this way."

"I am a great one for history, as you well know, John, but this is not an appealing story to repeat at this juncture, when we are preparing for our historic royal event. Any link between our beacon for the Queen and the punishment of criminals is simply not in good taste."

Mrs D-B, who obviously had permission to address him by his first name, was firm and magisterial. He shrugged and acquiesced meekly enough, but I could see that he profoundly disagreed. I wondered what kind of local history he was sharing with Daria in their lessons.

Discussing the arrangements for the street party on Friday took some time, but it seemed to be well on the way to being fully prepared. Sophy had done a marvellous job with the ticketing system, setting a deadline which meant we had clear numbers for catering. I had volunteered myself and my mother to make some cakes and Beth was determined to try making the special Jubilee pudding, despite Celia's disapproval of the winning recipe.

"It's really a trifle, not a pudding, and it will mean we need bowls and spoons. We were trying to keep it to plates only."

But Beth insisted and said she would provide sufficient small bowls and spoons for at least one or two tables to be able to enjoy the pudding. Daria was planning to help with preparing it, in addition to providing some Ukrainian snacks and sweet treats, and making her first ever scones.

Arrangements for setting up, clearing away and taking down were rather complex, and Deb had put together a full timetable and even collected the names of appropriate volunteers. Fortunately everyone in town seemed to want to be involved somehow, so it had not been not too difficult to round up assistants.

"How is the concert coming along, Celia?" asked Deb.

A look of annoyance flitted across Celia's rather transparent face. She had never been good at concealing her emotions. As she was about to begin her reply, John Deering once again jumped in first, to ensure that his own point of view was heard.

"Well, Deborah, it has been something of a logistical challenge and we have taken a great deal of time discussing a suitable programme. In keeping with the Queen's own musical tastes, I was hoping that we would use exclusively classical pieces, but Celia has insisted that we have a wider range of styles and genres, to reflect current fashions, in addition to the great canon of western classical music."

Celia was a little flushed, but in control of herself, as she responded.

"The Party at the Palace is going to include a huge variety of music and that must have been approved by the Royal family. To my mind, it makes sense for us to appeal to a wide audience too. We want lots of people to come along and enjoy it, not just old people like you and I who actually like classical music."

"I know, we have been through this discussion on numerous occasions, Celia," sighed John, in a long-suffering voice. "I have agreed, submitted to your will on this occasion. I just wish to make it plain to the committee that the programme was not all of my choosing. And it is 'like you and me', dear, not 'like you and I.' You would never say 'like I', would you?"

I found his smug, patronising comments almost intolerable and I could see that Celia was battling with herself, but she had made great strides in mastering her hot temper, and, after all, she had won the argument.

"Anyway, we have a diverse set of performers, providing a really good range of different music, from the school jazz band to John's classical choir. The children's group is singing too, and, of course, the wonderful Jessica. We even have a small band doing a Queen tribute, which seems quite appropriate."

"It sounds excellent," said Sophy. "Just the kind of real community event we were looking for. The more performers we have, the larger the audience is likely to be. Great work, you two."

"Dress rehearsal will be early on Saturday afternoon and the performance begins at seven. A local printer has agreed to do the programmes in return for having his name on them as a sponsor, so everything is in hand, I think. Sparkling wine or elderflower cordial will be on sale during the interval." John took over again, and Celia let him pontificate for a few more minutes.

"I don't suppose there is anything major to organise for your service of thanksgiving, Stephen?"

"No, Deb, it has already been planned and I have printed the orders of service. Celia and the Women's Institute are arranging special Jubilee flowers and will have cakes and tea ready for afterwards."

"You have been busy, Celia. That is a lot to take on. Thank you so much. I don't know what we would have done without you."

Deb spoke with real sincerity and there was a small round of applause. Celia smiled and looked down, blushing slightly but clearly pleased that her hard work behind the scenes was genuinely being appreciated.

CHAPTER 10

Agitato

The sense of anticipation grew as the week went on and the forecast began to look more favourable, at least for the crucial event on Friday. It was a busy few days, as I tried to fit some baking around looking after Chloe. Nursery was closed for the half-term week and she seemed to miss the routine and the other children, so I arranged a couple of play dates as well.

On Tuesday, I received a worried phone call from Beth.

"I'm so sorry to bother you, Sam. I know how busy you are this week. But Daria's had some very bad news. It seems that Bogdan has gone missing and no one knows where he is, whether he has been captured or might be lying injured somewhere. She wants to go to the church to pray. Do you think that will be possible?"

"Oh no, poor Daria. How awful for her. I'll speak to Stephen and see what can be arranged. If he says yes, would you like me to take her?"

"Would you? I would be so grateful. I can look after Chloe for you. I don't think she's planning to take Vitaly. In fact, I don't think she's even told him at the moment. She doesn't want to worry him, and there's really no point if Bogdan turns up fine in a day or so."

"That seems sensible for now. There's nothing he can do about it and it would certainly upset him. Thanks, Beth - if you can have Chloe that makes it much easier. I'll ring Stephen now."

Stephen immediately agreed to open the church for us. I mentioned that Daria liked to use a candle when she prayed and he promised to find something suitable for her. I let Beth know, got Chloe ready and hurried off to meet Daria.

I had never seen her wearing a headscarf before. It was bright and colourful, but far from new, probably one of the very few possessions she had managed to bring from Kharkiv. Her eyes were shadowed and her head was bowed as she came downstairs.

"Mama?" asked Vitaly, confused and uncertain.

She reassured him in her own language and obviously told him to help Beth to take care of Chloe, because he immediately fetched some suitable toys to play with. He waved goodbye happily enough, but still looked a little puzzled.

I did not speak to her until we were outside.

"I am so sorry that you are suffering this terrible anxiety, Daria. I very much hope that Bogdan will soon be found, safe and well."

She fumbled for my hand and held it for a moment, saying nothing. We walked silently to the church, where Stephen was waiting for us. The old stone looked warmly golden and inviting in the afternoon sun and the heavy door stood open, promising coolness and shade inside.

Inviting us in, Stephen led the way to the side chapel, where he had set up a candle to be lit. Daria took out a battered, but obviously precious, photograph of her husband. In the picture, he was a handsome and carefree-looking young man. She kissed it and laid it in front of the candle. Once it was lit, she knelt at the altar rail, hands pressed together, eyes intently closed. I sat quietly behind her with Stephen and tried to focus my mind, looking at the tiny candle flame. It did not help me at all, and I shut my eyes.

Suddenly I felt Stephen's hand on mine and he whispered that he would pray with me. Quietly he prayed for Bogdan's safety and Daria's peace and comfort. I tried to pray myself, but could not find any words, other than: 'please, God'.

We remained there for more than an hour. Daria prayed mainly in silence, but at times in her own language and I tried to share in her prayers as best I could. At last she stood again, crossed herself and bowed her head.

"Can the candle and picture stay here in the church, Father?" she pleaded.

"Of course, Daria. I will need to move them to ensure that there is no danger of fire, you understand, and I will need to put the candle out when I lock up tonight. But, if you like, I will light a candle at my home for Bogdan, too."

I looked at him in surprise. I knew that he did not normally like using candles for prayer. But he was giving Daria the best comfort he could offer, putting aside his own feelings and perhaps beliefs in order to support her. I felt a wave of warm affection for this unassuming, sensitive man.

"I thank you, Father. Would you give me a blessing?"

"Of course, Daria."

As he gave her the blessing, he even made the sign of the cross over her, not at all his usual practice, but a further sign of his love and care.

As we walked back again, I had a sense that Daria was more at peace after her time in church. She thanked me for coming and staying with her. I said, somewhat hesitantly, that I would continue to pray for Bogdan, and that I knew Stephen would too.

"He is a wonderful priest, Sam. Not the same as our priests, but more caring than many of them. He is truly a man of God."

"He is certainly a very special friend to me. He has been there for me through some very bad times, and I can never thank him enough. He won't even accept my gratitude."

Vitaly ran to her when we went in, clearly still somewhat disturbed and anxious. But she hugged him and smiled.

"I have been to the church, my little one. It is well. We should go to the shop and buy some things so that I can make cakes and scones for our party on Friday."

"You really don't have to, under the circumstances," I said.

But she wanted to contribute, and if it kept her busily occupied, that was surely a positive in such an uncertain situation. Beth said she would go with them to help carry things and we all walked off together. I felt easier in my mind, but could only imagine the tormenting thoughts that would fill Daria's mind, especially when she tried to sleep. Even bad news would surely be better than this dreadful uncertainty.

CHAPTER 11

Con fuoco

Beth articulated the contrary view, when I rang to see if there was any news on the following day.

"No news is good news, I suppose."

"I guess you're right, but the anxiety must be terrible."

"She seems to be relatively at peace, since her visit to the church with you, Sam. She is baking furiously and showing me and Vitaly the techniques as she goes. Some of the recipes are really complex, but she is obviously an extremely accomplished baker. She's going to help me with the Jubilee pudding tomorrow, so she wants to get as much of her own cooking done today as she can. The scones are already in the freezer and they taste amazing! I think she used a Mary Berry recipe she found on the internet. We've been watching some old editions of *Bake off* together and she has developed a real admiration for her."

"I'm so glad that she has something to take her mind off it all."

"Keeping busy definitely seems to help, but she is praying regularly too. Her faith is a real comfort to her. I'm amazed at how strong she is."

As a refugee, it was pretty clear that you had to be very strong or you would not survive. Getting to know Daria had helped me to understand and respect all those who were forced to flee their homeland, leaving behind everything they knew and loved, and stepping into an unknown world, fraught with danger. Nobody would do it unless they genuinely had no alternative.

I finished my own baking on the afternoon of the beacon lighting. All of us from the committee had agreed to go along and help with the event, but as it was quite late in the evening, my mother came over to babysit for Chloe, who was already in bed by the time she arrived. I wanted Mum to have a really quiet and relaxing evening, watching the television, since she was coming to the street party on the following day, and that would be quite taxing.

She still looked tired and pale, but the twinkle was back in her eye.

"Do stop fussing about me, Sam. I'll be fine. So far, all that the tests have shown is that I haven't really recovered fully from Covid yet. I would have come earlier to help you put Chloe to bed if I had known that was what you were intending to do."

"She was really tired this evening and ready to go down early. Please have a nice rest, Mum. Go to sleep if I'm late. You can stay here tonight if you would like to. I should have thought of that."

"No, it's fine, your father won't be home until late from his choir practice, so it doesn't matter if I'm late too. We're both looking forward to the street party tomorrow. It should be a really nice event. A proper traditional community celebration of the Queen's long reign. Hope the weather doesn't spoil it."

"I know. Fingers crossed."

Fortunately, the weather that evening was pleasantly warm and dry. I did not think that many people would have bothered to come and stand out in the rain, although the band had a gazebo over the temporary stage to cover them, just in case.

As I arrived at Galley's Hill, I was amazed at how many people were already there, well in advance of the published start time. The community had really come out in support. There were a lot of young people, probably there to support the popular local band, and the bar was obviously going to do a roaring trade. I hoped that people wouldn't become too rowdy, although we were pretty far away from most of the houses in the area. In fact, ironically, it was Mrs D-B's extensive manor house which was the closest.

The experienced band played from eight o'clock, a mixed set of their own pieces and some popular covers. I noticed that they seemed to get louder with every song, and more and more people joined in vigorously with well-known choruses. I was not surprised to see that Mrs D-B looked increasingly disapproving.

"They're doing a good job of getting the audience involved, aren't they?" I said, trying to give an explanation she might find acceptable.

"As you will imagine, it is not at all my type of music, Sam," she said, having to raise her voice in order to be heard. "I can see that it is very popular, but I do not understand why they have to continually turn up the volume. It was more than loud enough at the start."

I nodded.

"I agree, actually, but I think this is how they do things nowadays. I wish I had brought some earplugs! But the crowd is really having fun and that's what we want, isn't it? And there will be a nice big audience for the lighting ceremony."

Mrs D-B did not look entirely convinced, but she did go over to the beacon area on the crown of the hill, to make sure everything was ready for what she, at least, saw as the main event.

Daniyaal arrived promptly just before half past eight and made his way through the gathering crowds to where I was standing. We did not usually hug when we met, a hangover from a misunderstanding over going out for a meal together, but that evening everything felt less formal and I returned his unexpected hug of greeting with enthusiasm. His arm stayed round me for just a moment longer and he gave my shoulder a quick squeeze.

"Lovely to see you, Sam. It has been too long. There is so much to catch up on."

I smiled up at him.

"It really is good to meet again after all this time. I've missed our chats - and the cakes! But talking is not going to be easy with this music. I think it's only going to get louder."

It was indeed hard to make yourself heard and I had to repeat myself right into his ear before he understood. By common consent, we moved back, further away from the small stage.

"We'll have to meet for a proper talk soon, Daniyaal. I wanted to hear how your visit to Wales at Easter went, but there's no point even trying to tell me now."

He nodded, his dark eyes sparkling in the light from the stage area.

Daria was with Deb, having left Vitaly at home with Beth, who was not keen to attend the lighting. She still struggled with large crowds, especially when they were not organised, and this particular event was deliberately far from structured. So she had delegated it to Daria to support the team and was happy to stay at home with little Vitaly.

Daria looked much younger, dressed more casually than usual, in close-fitting jeans and a bright t-shirt, her blonde hair hanging loose and even wearing make-up for once. Her intensely blue eyes were bright with pleasure and I could see that she was thoroughly enjoying the music and the atmosphere.

"This is fun, Sam," she said, as they approached us. "I have not been at a concert like this for a long time."

"Me neither. I'm glad you are enjoying yourself. I wanted to introduce you to my friend, Daniyaal. He's a detective. We met last year, when there was a nasty murder case here involving some of my friends."

Daniyaal did not look entirely happy with the wording of my introduction, but Daria was intrigued.

"You have never spoken to me about that, Sam. How fascinating! I would like to hear more about it."

She put her hand out to shake Daniyaal's in greeting. It was not something most British people would do nowadays in such a situation, but the formality was somehow rather attractive.

Struggling somewhat with the volume of the music, they had a short conversation about her impressions of the area, both, as was normal for them, using very correct language. The Welsh lilt to Daniyaal's voice blended nicely with Daria's accented pronunciation and they seemed to be able to understand each other quite well, despite the background noise.

Then Daria turned back to me.

"But I do not think that John is having a pleasant time at all. He spoke to me, and he is very unhappy with the loud music and all the drinking. He is over there by the beacon, but I think he would like to go home!"

As I looked over, I could see John and Mrs D-B sharing their negative opinions, yelling into each other's faces and ostentatiously putting their hands over their ears.

"Oh, well, each to his own," said Deb peaceably. "They can go home straight after the ceremony if they want to. I don't mind staying until the end to make sure everything is OK."

"I can stay until ten o'clock or a bit later, but have to get back for Mum then. But the band finishes then anyway, doesn't it? And the bar officially stops at half-past nine, I think."

"Beth has said that I may stay to help at the end, Deb. She will put Vitaly to bed, and I have a key, so it is not a problem."

"Thanks, Daria, that's a big help. We'll need to try to move people on when it's over, and I'm hoping to get a group picking up litter before we leave here."

Conversation became increasingly difficult as the volume reached new heights and the crowd joined in enthusiastically with *Sweet Caroline*, such a popular anthem that summer. Even Daria picked up most of the words to the chorus, as we sang along too.

Suddenly the music stopped and attention switched to the lighting of the beacon. Everyone joined in the countdown to nine o'clock, when the Queen would be lighting her own flame in Windsor, and, a short time later, ours was ignited with a great flourish by the mayor and his wife, who had emerged, surprisingly casually dressed, from the middle of the crowd enjoying the music. The flames hissed and flared brightly against the darkening sky.

There were no proper speeches, but the band struck up with 'God save the Queen', which was sung with gusto, although it was clear that not everyone actually knew all the words. Then the music started up again, many in the crowd dancing, now that it was really getting dark.

"I'm going to tell Mrs D-B and John Deering that they can go now. This is not their kind of thing at all. I think there are plenty of us here to help with clearing up. Celia's here too, over the other side, and has already been picking up rubbish from behind the bar area."

Deb strode off to release the older people from their torment. Even in the dim light, from a distance, you could see the relief in their movements, as they turned to make their escape as quickly as possible.

Suddenly, Stephen darted up to speak to us, from behind the stage. He looked very unlike his normal self. He was still wearing his dog collar, but, with a black t-shirt and jeans instead of a suit, he seemed much younger and his eyes were glowing with excitement.

"Hello there. Isn't this great? I haven't seen a proper band for years, not since the last Christian festival I went to. I've been helping with the sound system for them, since I've done outdoor work before and they've mainly played indoor gigs. It's been such a change and so much fun!"

I had never seen him like this before, he was like a completely different person. No sign, either, of the social anxiety or hesitancy that still sometimes inhibited him. I grinned at him.

"I can see you've been enjoying yourself."

Daria looked slightly disapproving. This was not normal priestly dress or behaviour as far as she was concerned. But she still greeted him respectfully, asked for a blessing and crossed herself as she received it.

"Thank you, Father Stephen. It is good to meet you."

"Likewise, Daria. I have been thinking of and praying for you and Bogdan. Hello, Sergeant Evans. I didn't know you were coming. Nice to see you again."

"Hello, Vicar. Sam invited me to come with her. I've really enjoyed it and the music is very good. But I have to go back on duty now, so I will have to take my leave."

As he said goodbye to everyone, and then to me, he gave me another hug and I was sure his lips brushed my cheek. Not expected at all. I was glad it was dark and no one could see me blush. We were not normally tactile, 'kiss and hug' friends, and I felt a little confused by it.

Stephen watched him go and then turned back to me, his face now in shadow.

"That was kind of you, Sam. It looks as if he had a good time. Oh, well, I must go back to the stage. I promised I would help with taking down the equipment. See you tomorrow, I hope."

No hug from him today. I wondered why. My eyes followed him as he ran back to the stage area. I had seen a totally new side to him and it was intriguing.

There were some protests when the bar closed so early, and the owners began to pack things away, but Deb and Sophy were immediately there, calming things down, explaining that we only had permission until then, but that the pubs would still be open when they went back to town. There were some grumbles and moans, as you might expect, but it was accepted with relative good humour.

The band finished their set with a rousing version of Queen's *Don't stop me now*, to riotous applause. No one actually wanted to stop, but as we moved through the crowd, encouraging people to leave, most of them wandered off in loudly chattering groups.

Suddenly I noticed that Daria was surrounded by a group of young lads, who had obviously imbibed more than their fair share of beer that evening. I was pushing my way towards her, excusing myself as I went, when I saw Adam arrive at the spot, full of righteous anger.

"Leave her alone!" I heard him shout, his voice high-pitched and a little shaky.

"Says who?" One of the larger young men confronted him. "We're not doing any harm. Just talking to the lady."

"It is true, Adam, they were just asking me where I am from. They knew from my accent that I am not English. But they were not saying anything bad."

"Just - just don't try anything. I will look after you Daria."

Adam, poor thing, wanted to be the protector, but he just did not have the physique or mentality to pull it off. He projected weakness rather than the tough style he was aiming for. The group just laughed at him and moved in closer, while Daria looked frustrated and embarrassed.

Enough was enough.

"OK, boys, time to move on now, please," I intervened. Not quite 'teacher voice', but enough authority in it to have the desired effect. They moved off, at a deliberately slow pace.

"Nice to meet you, Daria," said the biggest of them as he left. "Hope we see you again soon."

"You see, Adam? They were being nice to me. I know they had drunk too much, but I know how to - how to manage them. I do not need or want your protection."

Daria sounded annoyed.

"I - I'm very sorry, I didn't mean to offend you," mumbled Adam. "I was only trying to help."

He turned away and stalked off, his face so red that it was even visible in the faint light from the stage.

"Poor Adam!" I sighed. "He wants so much to be a hero. And especially your hero."

"Do you think I should have thanked him, Sam? I do not want to upset him."

"No, not at all, he needs to learn. But I can't help feeling sorry for him."

"I, too," said Daria, quietly. "It is hard being young and alone."

The hilltop now had the seedy and uncared-for look of the morning after. Those of us who were left bustled around with torches, litter pickers and recycling sacks, while others extinguished the beacon and worked with Stephen to help the band to clear away their instruments from the temporary stage. Taking that down would wait until the morning, but the portable generator had to be moved and anything valuable taken away. I had to leave before it was finished, but at least felt that I had done my part to ensure the success of the event.

When I reached home, I found my mother fast asleep in her chair and snoring gently. The sleep had smoothed her face, taking away the tense lines around her eyes and forehead, which I had hardly been aware of until they were gone. I stroked her hair back from her face tenderly, feeling a rush of affection for this brave, caring, and stoic woman.

I made her a cup of tea before gently waking her. As soon as she awoke, the creases appeared again and I was shaken by anxiety. It quavered in my voice.

"Mum, thank you so much for babysitting. I'm sorry it's so late. You really need your rest."

She smiled lovingly at me.

"I told you not to worry about me, didn't I, Sam? I'm fine. I do need to rest, the doctor told me that, but also that I should keep my mind busy and try some regular gentle exercise. He's not sure if it is Long Covid or a post-viral fatigue syndrome, but the treatment and prognosis are similar. I just have to be more patient with myself, and you know I find that hard. But keeping an eye on Chloe for you is never a chore. It's what I want to save my energy for."

I grasped her hands in mine.

"I can't avoid being anxious, Mum. How can I help you? There must be something I can do."

"Well, he suggested swimming would be a good idea. What about you and Chloe coming swimming with me once a week? I think there's a suitable session at my local pool."

I leapt at the chance.

"That's a fantastic idea, Mum. It will be very good for me and Chloe as well, and it's always easier to make yourself do that kind of exercise when you've agreed to meet someone. Let's start next week, if we can."

My heart was lighter when she left. At least it was not something worse, although I knew it could take a very long time for her to fully recover.

CHAPTER 12

Vivace

The morning was warm, but heavy with humidity and occasional drizzle, and heavy rain or even possibly storms were threatening. The street party was due to start at two o'clock, so everyone held their breath, hoping for a dry period, if only for a few hours. After all our hard work, it would be so disappointing if it was ruined by a deluge.

I was needed in the market square early to help with setting up, so my parents came over to look after Chloe and bring her down later for the party. I was feeling rather tired and jaded after all the excitement of the previous evening, but the adrenaline soon kicked in, and I was full of anticipation as I drove down to the centre of town, the car loaded with cakes and table cloths.

Stephen and Celia were already there, along with Sophy and Deb, putting up trestle tables and chairs and setting up the gazebos. Mrs D-B was supervising volunteers, including her own gardener, hanging the huge sail from the lamp posts near the town hall and other helpers were adding even more bright flags and bunting to the already colourful market square.

Thanks to Deb's amazing powers of organisation, everyone knew what they had to do and things gradually fell into place. Beth and Daria were due to arrive later with their food, since we did not want anything which needed refrigeration set out too early. Several of us had taken food preparation training, and we wanted to ensure that everything was done safely. We were determined that there would not be any chance of food poisoning.

I was surprised to see Adam's distinctive figure helping a group at the other side of the square to set up folding benches. I waved a greeting, but he either did not see or chose to ignore me. Not surprising, really, after the embarrassment of the previous evening.

I was pleased to finally meet his mother, Claire, who came over and introduced herself to me, saying that Deb had pointed me out to her.

"I hope you don't mind me calling you Sam. I just wanted to thank you for your kindness to Adam and the way you spoke to him. It has definitely helped. He had a bad evening yesterday - I don't know exactly what happened, he won't talk about it. But, in general, he has been better. Depressed and sad at times, and often grumpy, as usual, but less prone to sudden rages and even occasionally willing to help around the house. I wasn't sure he would come this afternoon, but he agreed, even though he looked awful this morning."

Tactfully, I decided not to fill her in on what had happened last night and focused instead on his helpfulness.

"It's kind of him to be willing to join in with the preparations. He hasn't had it entirely easy just recently and I feel quite sorry for him, but he seems to be coping in quite a mature way, actually."

Claire looked so intensely grateful, that I was glad I had at least given him some faint praise. Tears filled her eyes. I realised that she was not much older than I was, and must have been an extremely young mother. Not an easy task, bringing up a boy on your own at any age, let alone when you were still a child yourself. Even more difficult when that boy had some special needs.

"Thank you so much for saying that, Sam," she said rather emotionally. "Normally people only see Adam's appearance and behaviour, and I know they think I'm doing a terrible job as a parent. But he is such a caring boy underneath. Mostly he cares too much. But he just doesn't know how to show it in a socially acceptable way. And it's so hard to guide him, when he doesn't want to listen to me."

I smiled at her.

"If you've raised a caring son, you've done a great job, Claire. Parenting is very hard, as I'm just starting to learn."

Just then, Beth arrived, on her own, looking quite unlike her normal self, eyes red from crying and her face crumpled, biting her lips in order to try to keep control of her emotions. I excused myself hurriedly and rushed over to her.

"What's wrong, Beth? Tell me."

She drew in a long shaky breath and seemed to steady herself.

"I don't want to ruin the party, and Daria insists that she doesn't either, but I have to let you know. She's - she's had the most terrible news. Bogdan has been found dead. I - I think there's even - even a photograph of his body. It's definite."

The life drained out of me in a rush. What a dreadful thing. I felt quite sick and the heavy lump in the pit of my stomach, which I had felt when I heard the news of my own husband's death, was back with a vengeance.

"Oh Beth, how simply tragic. I don't know what to say. What can we do to make things better for her?"

Beth shook her head slowly.

"There really isn't anything, is there? I think - I think it might help if you talked to her. You know something of what she is going through. And I'm sure she will want to go to church and spend time there, as well as speaking with Stephen, but in the end nothing can or will make this any better."

"Is she still coming down here later?"

"She says she is. She's determined to bring Vitaly in an hour or so. I drove over with all the food, but she's going to walk. They should be here soon."

"Has she told Vitaly yet?"

"I don't think so. I think it's too much for her, hearing the news herself, and then having to explain to such a young one what has happened to his daddy. I know I wouldn't be able to do it straight away."

Beth sounded stressed. I was not surprised.

I knew I could not have coped with coming to an event like this just after hearing of Thomas' death, but in any case Covid had made it very easy for me to shut myself away with my pain and numbness. I could imagine that the shock and grief had probably not hit home with Daria yet.

Guests soon began arriving and the square quickly became busy with excited families in bright summer clothes, and older people with coats and umbrellas. They had experienced many such days and did not trust the British weather. No one checked tickets or reserved seats. The system was only there so that we could have numbers for catering. We would not want to exclude anyone, even if they had not signed up.

My parents made their way over to us with Chloe and I settled them quickly into empty places at a long table in the middle of the square. The rising hum of anticipation was infectious, but I could not respond to it, not now that I had heard Daria's sad news. I went around distributing food and drinks, answering questions and participating in small talk in something of a daze, replying mechanically to people, but not really mentally present in the moment.

As soon as I spotted Daria with Vitaly on the edge of the square, I made a beeline for her and saw Beth doing the same. I gave her a consoling hug, looked searchingly into her face, and then suggested that Beth take Vitaly over to sit with my parents. He was looking excited, but also a little scared by the number of people, the loud hum of conversation and the unfamiliar setting. I knew he would be more comfortable with Chloe and Beth.

"Daria, I am so very, very sorry about your news. What an absolutely terrible blow."

I could not say any more. Tears were filling my eyes and my throat was thick with emotion.

"Thank you, Sam."

I was amazed that she was able to respond so calmly and quietly.

"I think I knew some days ago that this would happen, when I heard that he was missing. But I could not let him go so easily. But all of us in Ukraine have lost someone. I knew it could come to me too. Part of me expected it."

Looking at her white face, frozen and pinched, with blank shadowed eyes, I was overwhelmed with pity.

"Do you have to be here? We have plenty of helpers, and Beth and my family can look after Vitaly for you."

At that, she hesitated and looked questioningly at me.

"Do you think this is possible? I want to help, but I do not feel that I can be useful, just now. I need to walk and think. In my country, the three days after - after someone has died are very important to us. There are traditional things we would do, rituals. But Bogdan will only have a simple military funeral, over near Kharkiv. I cannot be there so quickly. And so I do not know what I should do here."

I put my arm around her shoulders and drew her to the shady side of the square.

"No one would want or expect you to help here after what has happened. Your baking is here. Vitaly will be fine with Beth, you know that. You go and walk. Would you like me to come with you? Just for company. We don't have to speak."

She shook her head decisively.

"Thank you, Sam, but no. I need to be alone. To think about everything. To make some difficult decisions for myself and for Vitaly. I will walk down past John's house and out into the country. I know that way. It will be better for me."

"I understand. Walking really does help, I don't know how or why, but it definitely does. You have my number as well as Beth's if you need us, Daria. Anything at all that we can do."

I gently kissed her cheek and she turned to go. As I watched, she walked off steadily, a gallant little figure, dealing with her dreadful loss in her own way. I understood that she needed the solitude. But I felt incredibly helpless in this sad situation.

I tried to throw myself into the celebrations, but was obviously not making a very good job of it.

"What's wrong, Sam? You look awful."

Deb was very perceptive. I did not dare to look at her as I told her Daria's news. I knew that I would not be able to master my emotions if I did. As I expected, she was shocked and distressed.

"I'll explain to the others, so that no one else asks you and no one speaks to her about it when she comes back, unless she mentions it. What a terrible thing to happen! Awful to be so very far away at the time. Go and sit with your family, Sam. You're not up to doing this right now."

I allowed myself to be persuaded and sat with Beth, my parents and the children, trying to force down a few morsels. Vitaly was eating as heartily as ever and seemed unaware of the drama. That was a relief, at least. Beth was very quiet, but managed to remain calm and steady for his sake. I whispered to Mum what had happened and she squeezed my hand in sympathy, but did not speak about it. She knew me too well.

A few minutes later, I noticed Adam coming back into the square from the street Daria had walked down. He looked very upset, holding his thin wrist against his mouth as if to restrain his emotions. Even his walk looked jerky and agitated. I hoped that he had not followed her or spoken to her. Especially not today.

Suddenly I felt a gentle hand on my back. Looking over my shoulder, I saw that it was Stephen.

"Can I have a quick word, Sam, please? It won't take a minute."

I stood up and went with him to a quiet spot, where no one would overhear us.

"Deb told me the news, Sam. I'm so sorry. How can I help? Do you think Daria would like to talk to me or pray in church?"

"I'm absolutely sure that she will, Stephen. She really likes and trusts you. And I know she will need the spiritual comfort you can offer her. But just now, she's gone for a walk on her own, to think things through and clear her head. When she comes back, we can see what she would like. I'm pretty sure she would like to come to the church again, but I don't want to pre-empt her choices."

"No, indeed. It's important that she can do whatever feels best to her in the moment, that she is in charge of the process. But I will be there, whenever she needs me."

I touched his cheek affectionately.

"I know you will, Stephen. Thank you so much. For everything."

He flushed.

"No need to thank me," he said, slightly brusquely. "You know it is my job."

"I do, but I also know that you go well beyond the call of duty, Stephen. You're a very special friend."

As I made my way back to the family, I caught sight of Annette, little Simon and a burly, good-natured looking man, whom I guessed to be John. She whispered to him and he rose to his feet. He was much taller than I had expected.

"Nice to finally meet you, Sam. I just - just wanted to thank you for everything you have done for Annette. Your support and friendship have meant a lot to her."

He spoke quite shyly but with determination.

"You must be John. It's lovely to put a face to your name. But you don't have to thank me. I know that Annette would do the same for me - in fact, she did, last year, when I was in trouble. We support each other. That's what friends are for."

His face was suddenly lit up with a broad smile.

"It's great that she has good friends here. We neither of us have family anywhere near and having you all around makes all the difference. But any time you need a man around the house or an extra pair of hands, just ask. I'm pretty good at practical things and DIY."

"That's so kind. I might well need to take you up on that. How are things, Annette?"

She smiled happily.

"We're getting there, thank you, Sam. As you know, I've already done some paid work for Mrs D-B, and Emily and Sophy are helping me to get the cat-sitting business off the ground. John will be able to help with it too, when he's not working. They have decided that I should call myself 'the Cat Lady'! Sophy's made me some lovely business cards. We feel as if we're at least moving in the right direction, and still managing, just about, to pay our way."

"I'm so glad," I said. It was lovely to see her looking and sounding more like herself.

"But I'm terribly sorry about Daria's awful news," she went on, soberly. "I just can't imagine how it feels to lose a loved one like that, so suddenly and when you're so far away."

Her hand crept out to touch John and he held it gently in his.

"I know. It's dreadful. I wish there was something we could do, but there isn't. Not right now, anyway."

After a few more words, I moved on and quite literally bumped into Celia, who was looking extremely annoyed and not paying attention to her surroundings. Her face softened as she realised it was me.

"I feel so sad about Daria, Sam. The whole community will support her, you know that, but - well, it's going to be very hard for her."

I nodded dumbly. I could not find any more words.

"I don't suppose you've run into John Deering, have you? He's here somewhere, I know that, but I can't find him right now. I need to speak to him about the concert tomorrow. One of the children who was going to play the violin has fallen and injured his hand, so he can't play."

"Sorry, I haven't seen him at all, Celia. But it's so busy, that isn't a surprise. I'll tell him you need to speak to him if I do catch up with him."

"Thanks, Sam. I also wanted to tell him that Jessica's singing teacher has agreed to accompany her. She rehearsed her song with John playing with her yesterday and it didn't go well at all, but I know she'll be much more comfortable with her own teacher. She has bad memories of her piano lessons with John and I think that affected her confidence."

She paused and took a breath, looking down at the ground.

"I suppose none of this really matters, though, not in the grand scheme of things, not compared to Daria's loss. I'll just have to sort it out myself."

"I have every faith in you, Celia. You're a great organiser."

She coloured slightly, uncomfortable with praise, as ever.

Sitting by Chloe and trying my hardest to engage in conversation with the others and to appear to be enjoying myself, I counted down the minutes for the next couple of hours. It seemed interminable. Finally, there were some enthusiastic thank you speeches, we all stood for the National Anthem and then it was time to clear up. Sophy told me to go home instead, but I felt better being busy and was happy to be moving again. Mum and Dad took Chloe home and I was free to get on, mindlessly clearing tables and dealing with rubbish.

As I was collecting paper cups and plates, I saw John Deering with a litter-picker.

"Have you seen Celia? She was looking for you earlier. Something to do with an injury to one of your musicians."

He snorted rather contemptuously.

"Yes, I spoke with her. She is making a great deal of fuss about something extremely trivial, as usual."

I was taken aback. That was really quite rude. More obviously so than he normally allowed himself to be. He must have seen the shock in my face, because he explained.

"I'm sorry, but it really isn't very important. I met Daria on my way here and heard her tragic news. I tried to persuade her to come to my house and talk about it quietly over a cup of tea, but she was determined to go on walking. Very sad."

I had misjudged him. Celia's worries genuinely were trivial compared to the tragedy of Bogdan's death.

"Thank you for being there for her anyway, Mr Deering." I had never felt able to call him John. Not to his face. "She really wanted time to think and come to terms with her loss on her own, but it was kind of you to offer."

"I've become close to her during our lessons, Samantha. She's a very special person."

"She is indeed."

I had never heard him speak like that before, especially not to me. Perhaps I had the wrong idea about him, and he really was the nice person everyone else seemed to see. Maybe I just always felt inadequate in the face of his assertiveness and relative sophistication. I smiled tentatively at him and went back to my work.

My parents had taken Chloe home, but Beth still had Vitaly with her. He was holding her hand tightly and looked very tired. She was evidently feeling rather overwhelmed.

"Have you heard from Daria, Sam? I thought she would be back by now."

"No, I haven't heard anything. I think you should take Vitaly home, he looks shattered. I'll send her a message to say where you are, so that she can come straight home to you."

Beth looked relieved.

"I think you're right, Sam. I'm worn out too. She'll come home when she's ready, I'm sure."

I nodded thoughtfully.

"I think she's probably lost track of the time, Beth - she'll be so wrapped up in her own thoughts. And she may have walked further than she intended to. Try not to worry. I'm sure she'll be in touch soon."

Finally finished, I walked home wearily. I sent Daria a message as promised, letting her know that Beth had taken Vitaly home. No extra tick to show that she had read it. If she was low on battery she might have switched it off, I supposed, but I was surprised and concerned, all the same.

Mum and Dad left soon after I got home, but they had already got Chloe ready for bed for me. They made such a difference to my life. I did not know how I would have managed as a single parent without their support. Poor Daria would be in that position now. I must ensure that she knew she would get the help she needed, from me and my friends, but also from our whole community.

I tried watching some television, but my mind kept wandering. I was too worried about Daria. Suddenly the phone rang. I was very glad to see that it was Beth. She sounded relieved and anxious in equal measure.

"I've had a message from Daria. I'll forward it to you. She says she is OK, but needs more time and asks me to take care of Vitaly for now. I don't at all mind looking after him, I told her that straight away, but there isn't even a tick to show she's read my reply."

I passed on my theory about her being low on battery, hoping it would ease her mind.

"I'm trying to be calm, trying not to worry, Sam, but I can't help feeling, deep in my stomach, that something is dreadfully wrong. I should be glad that she has contacted me, but I still feel so anxious about her."

"I know what you mean, Beth. It isn't like her not to at least speak to you, and it definitely isn't like her not to come back to Vitaly by now. I guess we have to trust her message for now. Try to get some rest. But ring me straight away if you hear any more or if she comes home."

Clear instructions on what to do settled Beth down a little.

"You're right, Sam. I'll try to get some sleep. I'm worried Vitaly might wake and go looking for her, so I'm going to rest on the sofa in his room and keep my phone on vibrate so that it doesn't disturb him if - when I hear from her. Thanks so much for your support, Sam. It really helps not to feel completely alone with this. I'll be in touch as soon as I hear anything at all."

Like Beth, I was deeply concerned. Daria was not behaving normally at all. But grief can do that. I did not behave at all normally when Thomas died. So I hoped she was fine, but sensed that something was wrong. Would she really walk all night? Looking at the message Beth had forwarded, she did not even send her love to Vitaly. It seemed so unlike her, as if she was so taken up with her own grief that she had no room for him. That was not the Daria I knew. She did not have a selfish bone in her body.

I went to bed and dozed, but could not sleep properly, restlessly tossing and turning. In the end I put the light back on and tried to read a book instead, but did not have the concentration for that either. Scrolling aimlessly through social media was the best I could manage.

Suddenly, there was the ding of a message arriving and almost at once the phone rang. It was Beth. She must be home.

"Beth, thank goodness. Is she back?"

Beth's voice was not normal at all, she was holding back tears. Or trying to.

"No, Sam, she's not back. I've had another message though. I've forwarded it to you."

"OK, hold on, I'll read it. It'll be quicker than you telling me what she says."

The message was bizarre and unexpected.

Beth, I'm sorry to do this to you. I have to go to Ukraine, to find Bogdan's body or his grave. I can't explain more but it is important. A Ukrainian friend is helping me. Please look after Vitaly for me. I know you will be good to him. I'll be back when I can.

"I see what you mean, Beth. It's really strange. Not like her at all. Why would she need to leave like that? Why wouldn't she come home and take Vitaly with her or at least tell him what is happening? I didn't think she was in touch with any Ukrainian friends, either."

"I'm so glad it isn't just me, Sam. It makes no sense to me. If she had come home, I would have paid for a flight for her and she would have been there much sooner. I just don't understand it at all."

"You're right. It's really illogical and very unlike Daria. She was still worrying about missing the street party earlier, and now she's going straight back to Ukraine without seeing her son first? I just don't believe it."

"No, and I messaged back but got no response, so I tried ringing her. It went straight to voicemail."

Something else about the message was bothering me. I read it through again.

"She also never uses contractions like 'I'm' or 'can't'. It simply doesn't sound like her at all. I hope someone isn't forcing her to send these messages."

"Sam! You don't really think that, do you? Surely not."

I took a deep breath and tried to think clearly despite the exhaustion.

"I don't know, Beth, but I don't like it at all. If it wasn't for the children, I would say we would go out now and see if we can see anything at all down that road she was going to walk along, but I suppose that would be overreacting a bit."

"And if she's with someone else, she won't be out there anyway."

"I know. I'll tell you what. Tomorrow morning, if we haven't heard anything more from her, I'll ring Daniyaal and see what he suggests."

I trusted my policeman friend to give me sound advice. I felt better once I had decided that there was a need to involve him.

Beth agreed and we both tried to get some sleep, without much success, on my part at least.

CHAPTER 13

Intermezzo

After another fruitless early conversation with Beth, who was pretty frantic by now, I decided to ring Daniyaal at eight o'clock that morning. Chloe was up and eating her breakfast and I just could not wait any longer.

"Sam? Is something wrong?"

I did contact Daniyaal on a fairly regular basis, but normally by message so that I did not disturb his work. He would then ring me back when he could. So he sounded surprised to hear directly from me, so early in the morning.

"I'm so sorry to disturb you at work, Daniyaal. I really need some advice from you. And - and I feel that this could well be a police matter, in any case."

I explained, as coherently as I could, what had happened. I had rehearsed it during the sleepless night, which made it a little easier, but it was still hard to express my inchoate fears for Daria.

"I'm not really clear why you think it might be a police matter, Sam. You've had two messages from her, so you know that she is safe. It is worrying that she has left her son with Beth and that she is not in regular contact, but you, of all people, should know how devastating this kind of loss can be. She's very young, and might simply be completely overwhelmed by it."

He sounded so reasonable. But somehow I could not feel that she was safe.

"I'm worried that someone might be forcing her to send the messages, Daniyaal. It just didn't sound like her."

"You can forward them to me if you like, Sam. But remember that while she might not use contractions herself normally, the phone's predictive text would probably suggest them. It doesn't have to be suspicious, you know."

"I suppose you're right, I hadn't thought of that."

His sensible and unemotional response made me feel that I was overreacting.

"I'm afraid I don't even think it makes sense to report her as a missing person yet, you know. You have had messages from her saying what she is doing and, as far as we know, she went willingly, with a friend, by what she says. She's not a child and not excessively vulnerable, despite her youth and her grief. She speaks excellent English and is competent and capable, from what you have told me. And she hasn't even been away for twenty-four hours yet. She wouldn't thank you for getting the police out after her, if she's just doing exactly what she said: going with a friend to Ukraine to find her husband's grave or body."

"I'm so sorry for bothering you. I realise now that I have been stupid about this. I guess Beth and I will just have to wait and see what happens, and hope and pray that she comes back soon, or at least contacts us properly to tell us where she is and what she is doing."

"It isn't a bother, Sam. I do understand how scary something like this can be, and for Beth it is a huge responsibility to take on the care of such a young child so unexpectedly. I can contact social services for you if you like."

"Oh no, please don't do that. Between us, we will look after Vitaly. He's had so much upheaval in his life, I couldn't bear it if they took him away and put him with a stranger."

"I understand. Give it a couple of days, Sam, and then feel free to contact me again if you haven't heard anything more. At that point, we can put her on the list of missing persons if necessary. I would come over and talk to you about it, but we are all doing a lot of additional shifts currently, making sure everything goes smoothly for all the rest of the Jubilee events throughout the area."

"That's OK, Daniyaal, I get it. There isn't anything you could do anyway. Sorry for being so pathetically anxious. I don't know why it got to me so much."

"Nothing pathetic about it. You just care about her, that's all. But I don't think you need to worry too much yet."

And he was gone. I sat back in my chair, barely aware that Chloe was trying to attract my attention and wanted to get down from the table. He was probably right, and part of me knew it, but my heart, and my knowledge of Daria, would not let me accept it.

Rather than ringing Beth to pass on what he had said, I decided to get Chloe ready and go over to the house. She and Vitaly could play together and I could talk to Beth better face to face.

Beth threw the door open, even as I began to walk up the path. She had obviously been looking out for me.

"What did he say? What are we going to do?"

While Chloe and Vitaly settled down to play together, I told Beth what Daniyaal had said and how he had reacted, leaving out my own reservations. She seemed reassured on one level, but was still full of anxiety.

"I suppose he is right, but what am I to tell Vitaly? I don't even speak his language. How can I look after him properly?"

I had assumed, somehow. that this aspect of the situation would be fine, since Beth loved Vitaly and he was very much attached to her and clearly felt safe in her house. But, although his transactional English and ability to communicate his needs were improving daily, he did not have the comprehension skills yet to deal with complex issues.

I put my hand on Beth's knee, which was trembling.

"I'm sorry, Beth, I just hadn't thought of that. We'll have to try to find a Ukrainian interpreter to help us. If you can keep things going as they are for a day or so, I should be able to find someone for Monday, I hope. Has he asked any questions yet?"

"Nothing major. He said: 'Mama back soon?' and I said I hoped so. He said something about *tserkva*, which I heard Daria using a lot when we were talking about church, so I think perhaps he thinks that she is there."

"I wonder if she might have gone to find a Ukrainian church? I don't know where the nearest one is, but I know there are some in London. That might be a good place to find an interpreter to help us."

"That's a great idea, Sam. Perhaps Stephen can help us."

"You're right, Beth. He might well know more than we can find out online."

"Why don't you leave Chloe with me and go and talk to him now? She will keep Vitaly distracted and I can take them out for a walk if they get bored, or we can play in the garden."

Beth was starting to recover, now that we had some kind of plan, and I thought it might be good for her to have the children to keep her occupied.

"OK. I'll just ring and see if I can go round now."

Stephen was available, so I walked over to the rectory, my mind whirling with questions and practicalities. Celia opened the door.

"Come on in, Sam. We're so concerned about Daria, poor thing. Stephen is in his office."

She really had mellowed. There was a time, not so long ago, when she would have been warning me not to waste his precious time.

Stephen stood up as I went in, a look of painful anxiety on his face.

"Any news? I could not believe it when you said she had not come home last night. What can have happened?"

We sat down together and I told him everything that I knew, including Daniyaal's reaction. Celia brought in a tray of tea and biscuits and listened in unashamedly, but I did not mind. The more people who told me not to worry, the better, as far as I was concerned.

But neither of them responded like that. Stephen's face grew increasingly worried as I told my story and the frown on Celia's face deepened.

"But - aren't the police going to do anything at all? Surely she should be listed as a missing person at least."

Celia sounded frustrated.

"They think - or rather Daniyaal says - that the messages show she is safe and well, and we just have to wait for her to come home or tell us what she's doing."

Celia shook her head in wonderment.

"But we all know her, you and Beth know her really well. There is absolutely no way she would go away like that, without even seeing Vitaly. They stuck together like glue, all the way from Kharkiv, in all that chaos and danger. She would never abandon him at this point."

"Not even if she knew he was safe with Beth?" I was trying to persuade myself.

"No, definitely not. You know that, Sam. You really do. He's already had such a traumatic time. She would want to make sure he understood where she was going and why. She didn't even send her love to him, did she?"

I shook my head slowly.

"That was one of the things that worried me about her message."

"This simply doesn't sound like the Daria I have come to know," asserted Stephen. "She has a very deep faith, and that would actually help with her grief over Bogdan. And her love for Vitaly is selfless, passionate and unshakeable. She simply would not leave him behind like that."

They were confirming all my own doubts.

"So you agree that something must have happened to her?"

After a hesitation, both nodded their heads solemnly.

"What on earth can we do about it?"

"That's more difficult. I think, if we have no more news by six o'clock this evening, you should ring Sergeant Evans again and make it clear how concerned you are. But even before that, we can do a bit of a search in the area. See if there are any indications of what has happened."

I brightened.

"You're right, Stephen. I know the others would help too. They all liked Daria - like Daria very much."

The past tense had just slipped out. Did I subconsciously think she was dead? I pushed away the dreadful thought and focused on action.

I explained about our need for an interpreter and why we thought a Ukrainian church might be able to help. Stephen was happy to be able to be of use. He knew of a Ukrainian congregation, which met once a fortnight in an Anglican church on the other side of the diocese, and offered to try to make contact for me.

"Thank you both, you've been such a help. I'm glad it isn't just me - that you also feel something bad must have happened."

Their faces said it all. Anxious frowns, tight lips. But at least we now had some idea what to do.

CHAPTER 14

Tutti

Back at Beth's, I told her what Stephen and Celia had said and was surprised to see a look of intense relief on her face.

"Oh Sam, I thought it was just me. You seemed to accept Daniyaal's reasoning and I couldn't argue with it, but it just didn't feel right to me. I'm terribly afraid that something has happened to her. We've become so close, I just know she wouldn't leave Vitaly with me like this."

She was almost sobbing.

"I know, Beth. I feel the same. I'm afraid that I just know, deep down inside, that something bad has happened."

She nodded, fear and dread in her wide grey eyes.

"What can we do?"

"I'm going to contact everyone on our group chat at once and see who can help with looking for Daria."

Soon there were plenty of volunteers. Annette was not working that day and offered to bring Simon and help Beth to look after all the little ones, while the rest of us searched. Emily would use her van to go a bit further on each road out of town and see what she could spot. She even suggested using dogs to try to track

Daria, if we made no further progress that afternoon.

The rest of us would walk in pairs and talk to anyone we saw on the way. We shared a good photo of Daria, so that we could show people exactly what she looked like. Deb, with typical forethought, brought a large-scale map when she came over, so that we could divide the area up into sections and search properly.

"We might not find Daria, but we might find something she dropped or even her phone. What was she wearing, Sam?"

Beth and I described her clothes, bag and shoes, phone and watch. It suddenly felt horribly real. We were searching for clues to the whereabouts of a person we were convinced must have been the victim of an attack of some kind. Something the police should be doing. On impulse, I messaged Daniyaal to say what we were doing. He rang back straight away and sounded very irritated.

"What on earth are you all trying to do, Sam? There's no real indication that something has happened to Daria. You're not just wasting everyone's time, you're creating an unnecessary panic and exacerbating people's natural anxiety about her."

"I'm sorry, Daniyaal. You know I respect your opinion. But we know Daria and you don't. Beth knows her really well. They've lived together for some time now. And we are all absolutely certain that she would not do something like this of her own free will. She would not leave Vitaly. With Bogdan dead, he was – he is the most precious thing in the world to her."

"Certain?"

"Yes, absolutely positive. She's been through the trauma of leaving Ukraine and surviving in Poland for months and she's stayed close to Vitaly throughout. She just would NOT leave her only son without a word to him. It's not credible."

I put every ounce of conviction I had into my voice.

Daniyaal sighed.

"Oh well, I suppose I can put her on the missing persons list. I do normally trust your judgement, Sam. Your interpretation of events seems really rather unlikely to me, based on my past experience of young people going missing, but if I add her to the register, it does mean that her details will be shared with other police forces in the next couple of days, including the Border Force, so we may hear where she is and how she is travelling, whether she might be under some kind of duress. Let me know if you find anything on your search. I may be able to spare a couple of uniformed officers next week if she still hasn't been heard from."

I felt a rush of relief. My friend had listened in the end, even if he did still think that I was mistaken. I gave him Daria's full name and a detailed description of what she was wearing.

"Thank you so much, Daniyaal. Of course I'll let you know if we hear from her or find out anything useful."

Feeling that I had done my best to get the police involved, I went off to search with the others. As planned, we went in pairs, so that we could cover both sides of the various roads we were exploring.

I was paired with Sophy. We trudged down the street which led past John Deering's house, since we knew he had seen her there. On impulse, I went up his long curved drive and rang the doorbell, just so that we could ask him a few more questions and confirm what he had seen, but there was no answer. Of course, he would be at the dress rehearsal for the concert. Celia was there too, but had promised to ask everyone present if they had seen anything of Daria.

Right at the edge of town, the road divided in two, and we took the left-hand fork, leaving the other to Deb and Stephen. We still had pavement for a short way, as far as the bus stop for the small industrial estate, which was in the farmyard to the right of our road. We searched carefully around the bus stop, wondering if she had stopped there or been picked up by a passing motorist. But, although the grass in the area had been well-trampled, there was no sign of anything belonging to Daria.

"Should we go into the business park, do you think? Someone might have seen something."

"It's unlikely, Sam," said Sophy. "With all these Bank Holidays, there won't have been anyone in there for days. We could ask at the farm, though."

We tried, but had no luck. The owner answered the door readily, and called out her whole family, but no one had seen anything at all, and their multiple security cameras were all pointed away from the bus stop and had not picked up anything useful, it seemed. They promised to keep an eye out for her, but we were deeply disappointed to have found no leads or sightings at all.

Back at Beth's house, heads had dropped, and the mood was gloomy. Nothing useful had been found and no one we spoke to had seen anything. Subdued, and sharing a general feeling of depression, we agreed to try something else, perhaps even using dogs, on the following day, after the church service.

Celia had some good news, however. During the rehearsal, she had managed to contact the Ukrainian priest Stephen knew of, and he had agreed to come and meet us at the church on Monday morning, in order to translate for Beth. He was also going to bring a woman from the congregation, who would be able to offer linguistic support going forward.

She had also quizzed John Deering about his meeting with Daria.

"He was very upset to hear that she had not returned," she reported. "He blames himself for not going with her or making sure that she went into his house."

"It's not his fault," I responded rather impatiently. "If anyone is to blame it's me. I sent her off for a walk in the first place. I could have, should maybe have gone with her, but she wanted to be alone and I respected that."

"I know, Sam - it's not your fault either. It was broad daylight, not the middle of the night. She should have been quite safe. Let's focus on trying to find her, not on who is to blame. Are you coming to the concert tonight? It is sounding really quite good."

It was the last thing I felt like doing, but I had bought a ticket and, on reflection, I thought I could perhaps make an appeal in the interval for anyone who might have seen Daria to come forward.

"I'll come, I suppose. It's hard to think of things like that with Daria missing."

"No more messages, I presume?"

"Nothing at all. Not even the extra tick on the messages I have sent her. And her phone goes straight to voicemail."

"Oh dear, it's very worrying. I'll come and search after church tomorrow."

"Thanks, Celia. You've already helped a lot."

CHAPTER 15

Cantabile

Although Chloe loved music, especially when it was loud and had a strong beat, I knew she would not be able to sit still for a whole concert, so she was due to spend the night with Mum and Dad. It would be less tiring for them to have her with them at their house and they were looking forward to having more time alone with her.

I talked to them about what we had done, as I was dropping her off. I valued their opinion, so I was relieved that they thought we had done the right thing in pushing Daniyaal to report her missing, and in searching ourselves for Daria.

"It's a very difficult and worrying situation, but do try to get some rest tonight, darling," said Mum. "You'll be no use to anyone if you collapse from exhaustion."

In fact, I dozed off a couple of times at the concert. Luckily I was sitting near the back, so I hoped that no one had noticed, and that I had not actually snored. The choir pieces were excellent, beautiful music, and well performed, but they did drag on rather, and the soothing classical sounds carried me gently off to sleep. The jazz band, however, just before the interval, was loud and lively enough to wake me up fully.

I wandered around the room during the break, talking to as

many people as possible, asking if they might have seen Daria on Friday afternoon or evening, and showing them the photo on my phone. No one had seen her, but since nearly everyone had been at the street party at the time, that was not entirely a surprise.

I had asked John Deering if I could make an announcement before the start of the second half, but he insisted on doing it himself.

"You look exhausted, Samantha, and you are therefore not likely to be very coherent, are you? I will make an announcement about poor Daria and ask anyone with information to speak to you, Celia or myself."

So, just as the interval was finishing, he stood up self-importantly on the stage and clapped his hands for silence. The buzz of chatter ceased immediately. I had to admit that he had a strong personal stage presence.

"Ladies and gentlemen, may I please have your full attention. As some of you will know, Daria, our town's first Ukrainian refugee, is missing and we are extremely concerned for her welfare. Her absence is entirely out of character and she has not contacted her hostess or her young son. Would you all please examine your memories of Friday afternoon and evening and inform Celia, here on the left of the stage, Samantha, sitting at the back, or me, if you have any information you can offer? She has now been registered as a missing person, so any sighting, however brief, could be of value to the police. Thank you all."

I had to admit that he had phrased it well, better than I would have done after so little sleep. He had sounded unemotional and formal as usual, but that might actually be more effective in this context. I would need to thank him at the end of the concert.

The second half, after John's announcement, was more lively and engaging, including a sweet performance from the children's group, an extremely loud, but not very accurate,

Queen cover from an up-and-coming local band, and finishing with an absolutely exquisite performance from Jessica. I knew she had a stunning voice and the ability to touch the emotions very deeply, but even so, I was amazed at how well she sang *Candle in the Wind*, with the adapted lyrics from Princess Diana's funeral.

The tears rolled down my face unheeded. The wistful mood of the song tapped into my feelings about Daria and they welled up uncontrollably. As she finished, I heard sniffs and noses being blown all around the room, so I knew that I was not the only one to be touched by her. She had an exceptional capacity to move her audience, and clearly the singing lessons were paying off with much improved technique and breath control.

I congratulated her, as soon as I could make my way through the audience to where she was standing.

"Jessica, very moving singing, wonderful. Even better than I have heard you sing before. The musical connection between you and the piano accompaniment was so seamless. I was bowled over."

She looked embarrassed but also very pleased.

"The singing lessons that Mr and Mrs Hambledon are paying for have made a huge difference. My new teacher is amazing, I love our sessions so much. Would you please thank them for me?"

"Of course. I'm sorry that they are babysitting for me and can't be here themselves, but I will tell them all about it."

"My teacher arranged for someone to record the performance, so that we can analyse it together, so I might be able to send it to them."

"They would love that, I'm sure."

I found Celia to congratulate her and, of course, the boss, John Deering, on the success of the evening, saving my most positive comments for Jessica's singing at the end.

"It is not my favourite genre and I still feel that it was an inappropriate choice of repertoire, but I must admit that she performed above my expectations. She was singing quite poorly, out of time and out of tune, when I rehearsed it with her."

Celia audibly took a calming breath and ignored John's slighting comments.

"She was superb, wasn't she? So talented. And her teacher really seems to be bringing the best out in her. I'm so glad your parents made it possible for her to continue her lessons, Sam. It would have been a travesty if a voice like that was wasted."

John appeared to be about to make another derogatory comment, but I interrupted him, asking if anyone had passed on any information about Daria to them. They both shook their heads. No progress at all.

I made my way home, slightly more aware than usual that I was walking alone, as Daria must have done on the previous afternoon and evening, and feeling just a touch more vulnerable than I expected. The town had always felt safe to me in the past, but my confidence was definitely shaken by what had happened. I held my phone in my hand. It made me feel a little more secure.

The dark streets were empty and dreary and soon it began to rain quite heavily. I was soaked through by the time I arrived home. Even after a warm shower, I felt shivery and weak, and only then remembered that I had not eaten since lunchtime. As Mum had said, it would not help Daria for me to collapse, so I made myself some eggs and a cup of tea and soon felt more human.

I went to bed late, in spite of my exhaustion, in the hope that it would help me to sleep, but my mind was full of jangling vivid images from the day and I could not shake a pervasive feeling of dread.

Suddenly, I remembered that I had promised to pray for Bogdan (and had tried, without much success) and that I could and should pray for Daria. For the first time ever, the words came naturally into my head, echoing some of what Stephen had prayed for her husband, as I begged for help for her, strength for Beth, and comfort and peace for Vitaly and the rest of us. As I pictured their faces and held them in my mind, I drifted off into an uneasy sleep.

CHAPTER 16

Requiem

I found the church service highly uncomfortable on the following morning. I had not realised just how many of the words of hymns, prayers and even responses would be able to stir my emotions. In my fragile state, I struggled to join in, my voice often suspended with tears.

I was sitting alone at the back, as Beth did not feel it would be right to bring Vitaly, since he apparently thought his mother might be at church. We had not even attempted to explain to him what had happened. It would be difficult enough in his own language and impossible in English.

In addition to prepared words of thanksgiving for the long and faithful service of Queen Elizabeth, Stephen included heartfelt prayers for Daria's safety and I could hear the empathetic response of the congregation in their vigorous reply of 'Hear our prayer'.

I did not feel up to sharing cake and wine with the others at the end of the service and tried to slip out unseen. But Stephen caught up with me and spoke gently to me.

"Sam! Please don't rush off. Has there been any progress at all?"

I shook my head despairingly.

"Nothing at all. I'm sure something dreadful has happened. We're going out looking again this afternoon, a bit further afield, but I don't think it will help. We were going to try using dogs, but after all the rain last night, I don't see how that can work."

Stephen grasped my hand in his larger ones.

"Don't give up yet, Sam. You just never know."

I agreed wearily and made my way over to Beth's house, walking rather stiffly, as if my tired body was reluctant to move. I had promised to have lunch with her, but I did not feel hungry at all.

Vitaly was looking less contented, more on edge than on the previous day. As I entered, he looked around for Chloe.

"She's not here today, she's with her grandparents. You know, her *babushka*, oh no, that's Russian isn't it? *Babusya*?"

His face cleared.

"*Baba*. Is mama there too?"

I hugged him to me so that he would not see the tears in my eyes. It was all I could do.

"No, darling. Not at the moment."

He looked up at me, a shadowed look in his eyes and nodded. It was a strangely adult reaction. He held my hand as we walked into the dining room for lunch, pork pie and salad, apparently one of his new favourites. He was quieter than usual, but ate well, smiling at Beth when she spoke to him, yet clearly in a more sombre mood.

"How did you manage last night, Beth? I hope you didn't try to sleep on the sofa again."

"Well, I did, but I made it up as a proper bed and I did get a little sleep. Vitaly joined me in the middle of the night and then I slept better."

She looked down at him anxiously, and touched his head lightly.

"Poor little man."

How would we manage if Daria never came back? I could not imagine. Beth had powerful maternal instincts, that much was evident, but this was a great deal to expect of someone who had never been a mother, and had no partner to help and support her. One more thing to worry about. One more thing to put to one side for now.

One by one, other friends turned up at the house, ready to go out again on our probably vain search. Emily had decided not to bring the dogs in light of the previous night's downpour. Deb spread the map out again on the kitchen table and drew in some more areas where we could look. This time, no one was feeling very hopeful, but there was a dogged determination throughout the group not to give up on our friend.

Just as we were about to leave, my phone rang, startling us all. Everyone's eyes turned hopefully towards me in case it was Daria. I shook my head. Daniyaal.

"Hello, Daniyaal."

I knew as soon as I heard his voice, very professional but much lower in tone than usual, that it was bad news. I sat down abruptly.

"Sam, I am so very sorry. I'm afraid a body has been found. I believe that it is Daria. Obviously I only saw her briefly, in the dark, on one occasion. I'm afraid that I need someone to come and identify her more formally."

I gulped hard, feeling very sick all of a sudden.

"I'll do it. Can you collect me from Beth's house?"

I managed to get the words out.

"Of course. Fifteen minutes."

He rang off. I looked down, trying to get myself under control, but of course the others had guessed. Deb came over and hugged me hard.

"You don't have to say anything. Bad news."

"They - they've found a body. Probably Daria. I have to go and identify it - her."

Although they had realised it was not going to be good news, this was a frightening jolt, and there were gasps from the others. Beth was wide-eyed with shock, sitting with her arms around Vitaly, who was standing in front of her chair, looking at me in a puzzled but anxious way. She had gone completely white, and looked as if she might faint.

Deb took control as usual. Her own voice shaking, she told everyone to sit down and asked Beth if she had any brandy.

Beth shook her head dumbly, but Deb went into the kitchen anyway. She made tea and put sugar in it for all of us, adding a dash of vodka into each cup. Beth had bought it before Daria's arrival to make her feel at home, not knowing that she did not actually like the stuff.

The raw spirit cooled the tea quickly and I was able to gulp it down before Daniyaal arrived. It did bring the blood back into my body and give me the strength to stand and go to the door to meet him. Deb came with me and gave my shoulders a squeeze.

"You're so brave, my darling. You can do this. I'll be here when you get back. I'm going to call your parents and let them know what has happened."

I nodded gratefully, unable to speak for the moment.

Daniyaal looked quite different. His face was patchily pale, frozen, and stiff, and he would not meet my eyes. He took my arm and led me gently to his car. Before we set off, he spoke quietly, but with intense sincerity, looking straight ahead, not at me.

"I am incredibly sorry, Sam, that I did not take your concerns about your friend more seriously. I know you don't make a fuss about nothing, but I just couldn't believe you would be involved in another such incident so soon after the last case. We're under a lot of pressure just now and I did not want to create another problem to deal with. I thought you were exaggerating your confidence in understanding Daria's behaviour, after knowing her for just a few short weeks. But that's no excuse. Please forgive me."

Tentatively, I reached out my hand and touched his tense brown arm.

"Of course I forgive you, Daniyaal. You were doing your job and you know more about these matters than I do. But we know Daria - knew Daria. And we knew something was badly wrong."

He turned his head towards me and I could see the gleam of tears in his dark eyes.

"Thank you Sam. Your friendship means a lot to me. I know I let you down, and I will do my best, with my team, to find out exactly what has happened."

His voice had a slight shake in it. Then he seemed to be able to switch back, almost instantly, to his professional persona.

"I think it will be best if I don't tell you anything in advance about where we found the body. I need your mind to be clear of expectations, so that you will notice anything you think is out of place. Normally we would do the identification more formally, often after the post-mortem, but in this case, with our suspicions of foul play, it is essential that we identify the body as soon as possible. So it is still as it was found. I'm telling you that, so that you can prepare yourself for the environment you will find. It will not be easy for you. The scene has not been sanitised. It will be an upsetting sight."

I shivered convulsively. What had I let myself in for? My stomach was churning unpleasantly and my breath was coming fast. I tried some breathing exercises and closed my eyes to focus.

The journey was not long. As the car pulled up, I dared to open my eyes. We were actually on the same road Sophy and I had searched, but several miles further on. I had driven past the spot many times on the way to visit my parents. The road was cordoned off with cones, several parked police cars blocked the view, and there was a small tent over part of the verge and the ditch, next to the overgrown hedgerow.

For a moment I could neither move nor breathe. Although I had been involved in two difficult cases involving deaths, I had only briefly seen one dead body and the experience was not one I was keen to repeat.

"Take a moment, Sam," said Daniyaal calmly. "This is not easy for anyone. There is no rush."

But now that I was here, I needed to get it over with. I looked at him and nodded. He came round to help me to put the blue plastic covers on my shoes before getting out of the car and led me slowly towards the tent. Several people approached to speak to him, but he waved them away.

"Not right now. This is important."

He held back the door of the tent to allow me to enter and came in beside me. Inside, there was a strange bulky figure, covered from head to foot in blue overalls and masked as well. I could not even tell their gender.

"I'm sorry, doctor, I know we should be in full protective equipment, but we have at least covered our shoes."

The figure looked up at us and grunted.

"The scene is not exactly pristine anyway, Dani. It'll do for now."

She - I knew now that it was a woman - moved aside to let me see what was in the ditch, half folded onto itself. A silly voice in my head told me that it might not be her. But I knew it was wrong. It had to be her.

The pale blonde hair was matted with a large patch of something very dark and sticky and also full of dirt and wet leaves. The head was leaning forwards onto the chest, half-turned away from me, but I could see her long dark eyelashes, the beautiful cheekbones, the pale full lips. A dark bluish mark was evident on the side of her long graceful neck. Her light blue blouse was crumpled, filthy and wet, but I recognised at once the flower embroidery on the collar.

I took this all in like a flash photograph, in an instant. I knew it would stay with me.

Nausea surged uncontrollably from nowhere and I felt myself sway as the darkness swirled up from my feet. Daniyaal's arm was round me immediately and he pulled me away, out of that dreadful place.

"It's all right, Sam, I've got you. Sit on the verge here and put your head down."

I retched painfully several times before I could slowly lift my head.

"Sorry," I mumbled.

"Don't be. It's perfectly normal. I am so sorry to do this to you, especially with someone you really cared for. I take it that I was correct, the body is Daria?"

I nodded, then remembered from somewhere that I had to say it aloud.

"Yes. It's Daria."

The sickness came back for a moment. How could that terrible object in the ditch be my lovely friend? I shut my eyes, but the image was still there, burnt onto my retina.

I felt no grief, no sadness. The revulsion was still strong but it was turning into a deep anger, even fury. How could someone have done this? With new determination, I turned to Daniyaal, the nausea under control now, the anger bubbling in my voice.

"Tell me what you know. Who found her?"

His concerned face swung sharply back as if I had slapped him.

"Are you sure you want to do this now, Sam? You've identified the body and that's enough. More than enough."

I could feel a cold hard rage giving me the strength to speak out clearly now.

"No, Daniyaal, it's not enough for me. This - whatever it is - is a disgusting act of violence and betrayal. I want the person caught. I'll tell you everything I know, but I need to know what you have already worked out, to fit in the pieces. There's been enough time wasted already."

The hurt came back into his eyes at that and I softened my voice.

"I'm sorry, I wasn't having a go at you. It's just the truth. Please tell me where you are and let me help."

"OK, Sam. If you think you are up to it. You go and sit in my car. I must speak to the team, see what more we know. Then I'll come and talk to you."

He stood up, dusted off his trousers and reached down a hand to help me to my feet. Once I was up, I realised how weak I felt and I staggered a little, but then found my balance and moved slowly to the car, sitting down heavily and leaving the door open, needing the air. I tried leaning my head back and closing my eyes, but the stark image of Daria and my own angry response to it refused to allow me to relax.

Opening my eyes again, I tried to study the area dispassionately. It was certainly remote. No houses to be seen. No bus stops or other signs of habitation. The hedges were unkempt, hiding the fields behind them. I had driven past this spot so many times, but there was nothing, nothing at all, to distinguish it from the mile before or the mile after. Not even a bend in the road.

Why would someone have killed Daria here? I knew it could not have been an accident. The messages told us that. The killer had wanted to pacify Beth, to make it seem as if Daria had left of her own free will.

But why here? I could see uniformed officers combing the nearby verges, hedges and fields for clues, indications of what might have happened. After the heavy rain of last night, it was not likely to be an easy or pleasant task.

I suddenly realised that I ought to let the others know. I could not bear to speak to them just now, but put a simple message on our group chat.

It is Daria. She is dead.

It sounded brutal. But what else could I say? As I read the words, tears pricked my eyes and the profound sadness of the situation hit me, as if writing it down made it real. My lips quivered and a painful ache grew in my chest. Wrapping my arms tightly around my body, I tried to control the shivers.

CHAPTER 17

Furioso

By the time Daniyaal finally returned to the car, I had myself more under control, deliberately putting the sadness to one side and giving rein to the anger instead. He looked searchingly at me and seemed to see what he needed to in my face.

"Right then, Sam. I'll put you in the picture, as far as we have it so far, and then drive you back to Beth's. I know that I can trust you to keep investigational details private, as you have done before, but you and your friends are going to be important, even possibly crucial witnesses, at least to the background of this case, so I think it is right, at this point, to tell you what we know."

I nodded, tensely, waiting.

"OK. The body was discovered this morning by an elderly lady walking her dog in the area. She often parks up a mile further on, by the entrance to the old quarry, apparently, and then walks down the road in this direction as far as she can manage. She said she used to pick blackberries here as a child and has fond memories of the area, although it seems a pretty ordinary, nondescript sort of place to me."

I grunted assent. Not a place I would have chosen for a walk, especially with a dog, since there was often fairly fast traffic coming in both directions. But in the past it would have been a quiet country road.

"Her dog was off the lead and would not come back when called, so she followed it to the ditch and - and had a terrible shock. She managed to pull the dog away from the - the body and put it back on the lead but then had to sit down for a few minutes."

I nodded. I could totally understand that reaction. Poor thing.

"She does not carry a phone on her, so she had to go back to the car to call us. She keeps an old mobile for emergencies in the glove box, luckily. But she was very shaken by what she had seen, so I think it took her quite a while to get herself up and back to the car, and then she had to remind herself how to use the phone, so there was a long delay between the discovery and us arriving here. She could not even tell us clearly where she was. She likes to talk, but is not very focused in her thoughts, especially in descriptions and details."

I could hear the frustration in his voice. And, if a dog had found and interfered with the body, I could understand why the doctor had said that the scene was not pristine. What with the rain, wild creatures, and then a dog, it certainly had not been left untouched. Ugh. I knew that she was dead and would not feel it, but it somehow seemed disrespectful to the woman she had been.

I had to ask, although I knew he probably would not yet know.

"How - how did she die? Do you have any idea?"

"Well, until the post-mortem we really cannot be sure, as you know, but there are signs of a major wound on the back of her head and there's obvious bruising on her neck. But she could, of course, have also been drugged or even poisoned. What I can say for certain, and this must remain between the two of us for now, is that she did not die here. Lividity, which is visible even as she is situated in the ditch, makes that very clear. She was killed elsewhere and left here."

That made sense. I could not see a reason why anyone would have chosen to kill her at this spot. Not left here, though, but dumped here, as if she did not matter, like rubbish. Thrown in a ditch to rot. It could have been a long time before she was discovered. The anger in me boiled higher.

"How long ago, can you tell yet?"

"Again, we cannot yet be sure, but the likelihood is that it was Friday rather than later. It looks as if she has been here for a while. Certainly before the rain last night and most likely quite some considerable time before that. Hopefully we will get a more accurate time of death after the autopsy."

In a strange way, that was reassuring. I had been imagining poor Daria possibly held captive somewhere, forced to send those messages, but at the mercy of a cruel killer or even a gang.

"I'm glad, in a way, that she wasn't still alive somewhere when we were looking for her yesterday. That would have been an awful burden to carry."

Daniyaal looked at me, understanding in his eyes.

"For me, too, Sam. I would hate to think that if I had only listened to you, she might still be alive. I would find it hard to live with that. Let's hope that the autopsy shows she died quickly and without suffering."

"Did you find her phone?"

"Not yet, but we haven't moved her yet and it may be under her body. It was important to get her identified as soon as possible, so that we can work properly on the case from the outset, knowing who the victim is, and confident, given the messages, that this is murder, not some kind of accident. I'm very grateful to you for being willing to do it. I know what an ordeal it has been."

"What happens now?"

"I'm going to drive you back to Beth's house. I have plenty of officers here dealing with the scene and can call on more if needed. If you and Beth are up to it, I think I need to begin taking down some more detailed information from you, so that we know where to start our investigations."

"I'm up to it. I have to be. I want to help as much as I can. We have to find the murderer as soon as possible. This is a vile killing, disgusting, cruel. Of course I am up to helping."

Daniyaal looked at me gratefully but with concern in his eyes.

"I am aware that coming here and seeing her like that has added a layer of trauma for you, especially as you had become so close. I am extremely sorry about that. One thing I can say with reasonable certainty is that, so far, there is no sign of her having been sexually assaulted. She seems to be fully clothed, with no visible signs of interference in that area. But obviously we'll know more when we move her."

I felt as if the air had been knocked out of me. I had, for some reason, not thought of rape or sexual assault as a motive, but it was a logical one. Daria was so attractive, she could well have become a target, walking alone, even in daylight. It had happened to women before. So it was a genuine relief to think that she had not been molested in that way, that her last minutes had not been contaminated by that kind of horrific experience.

"Thank you, Daniyaal. That is some kind of comfort, I suppose."

CHAPTER 18

Basso continuo

Most of my friends had left when we arrived back at Beth's house, but Deb was still there waiting for me, as promised. Without speaking, she gave me a long hug and then took us both through into the kitchen. Putting the kettle on for tea, she brought a ready-plated lunch for me out of the fridge and set it on the table in front of me.

"I know you don't think you're hungry, Sam, but your body needs fuel. I can see that. Try to eat something at least. What about you, Daniyaal - sorry, Sergeant Evans? Would you like something? Some toast perhaps?"

Daniyaal smiled.

"Unless I am interviewing you formally, Daniyaal is fine, Deb. You are right - Sam needs to eat and recover after the shock she has had. And I would really appreciate some toast. I need to be ready for a very long day and night of work."

So we sat together at the table. Deb made the toast and we all had tea. She had put sugar in mine, although I never normally took it, as an extra boost of energy.

I knew Deb would want - no, need - to know what had happened, but for a few minutes I focused on trying to eat. Once I managed to get past the first few mouthfuls, I realised that I was actually quite hungry, despite the lurking nausea, which returned whenever Daria's image flashed into my head. So I ate slowly and carefully, deliberately, taking my time over it, chewing each mouthful thoroughly and swallowing it down, even though at first it seemed impossible.

"Where are Beth and Vitaly?"

Deb's face clouded over further and her voice held a tremendous amount of sympathy.

"She's taken him for a short walk to the park, to feed the ducks. He loves that, apparently. We decided that we couldn't try to explain about Daria straight away. He knows something bad has happened. That was obvious from our reactions and we could see the impact of it in his face. But we thought - we decided we would have to wait until the Ukrainian interpreters are here tomorrow to explain to him where - where his mother is."

Her voice cracked at the end, and a few tears fell, but she sniffed defiantly and went on.

"I'm going to stay here tonight, in order to help Beth. We can't leave her on her own with this huge burden of responsibility. She says there is plenty of room for you to stay too, if you don't want to be on your own. I've spoken to your parents and they are keeping Chloe for at least another night. They sent you their love and told you not to worry about rushing home."

Now I felt tears pricking my eyes too. My dear friend and my parents were so thoughtful and caring. I was so lucky to have such support.

"Thank you so much, Deb. You always know how to make things a little better. I think I should stay here too. Company will help."

"Can you - can you bear to tell me what has happened?"

I nodded, but looked down at the crumbs on the table while I spoke.

"Daria - her body was found this morning by a dog-walker, in a - in a ditch. It has to be murder. Her head - it seems clear. But we don't know exactly when or where or how or why."

I swallowed hard and tried to focus on not throwing up the food I had just eaten.

Deb touched my hand gently.

"That's enough, Sam. I understand."

Daniyaal intervened.

"You will understand, then, Deb, that I will need to speak to all of you as soon as possible, so that I can get some kind of timeline of what happened on Friday. If you can give me the contact details of the others, that would make things much simpler."

"Of course. Do you want to start with me?"

"If you feel able to answer a few questions, that would be great. I'll record it as before, if you are still happy with that."

She nodded.

He took her gently through the events of Friday afternoon. How she had spotted that I was looking unwell and heard about Bogdan's death. How she saw me talking to Daria as soon as she arrived at the party with her son, and then watched her walking off alone. There was not much more that she could add.

Daniyaal was about to start questioning me, when Beth and Vitaly returned. She looked exhausted, and he was quieter than usual, his eyes big and dark in his thin little face. Deb immediately reacted by suggesting that she take him to buy an ice cream from the corner shop. She demonstrated eating one, and he laughed briefly and agreed. I was really pleased that he had the confidence to go with someone he did not yet know well.

Beth slumped into a chair and I offered to make her a fresh cup of tea.

"That would be lovely, Sam. I'm in such a weird state. I don't know how I am supposed to feel, in myself. I just know that I can't give in to my sadness when I'm responsible for a defenceless child. It is so surreal spending time with Vitaly, when I know he has lost both his parents, and I – I can't talk to him about it or even try to comfort him. I don't know if I'm doing the right thing or not. Poor little mite."

She was speaking erratically and her breathing was all over the place. I caught her eye and she tried to calm herself, taking slow steady breaths, exhaling for longer than she inhaled.

"This is indeed a very difficult situation for you. I know we've met a few times before, but I just need to know now if you are happy for me to call you Beth?"

Daniyaal's calm but sympathetic voice seemed to help her. She nodded.

"I need to speak to you and Sam, as you will imagine. I can't begin the investigation properly until I've done that. But I think it would be best if I spoke to you both together, now, if that would be acceptable to you. It will save time and be easier for the two of you. I'll record it, if you are willing, so that we can untangle things later."

Beth and I looked at each other for a moment and then agreed. Better to get it over with now.

This time, Daniyaal started with how Beth had been matched with Daria and anything she knew about her background in Ukraine, family, friends, where she lived.

Beth did her best to respond, but the information was necessarily rather sketchy. She knew very little about any family other than Bogdan, and Daria had no friends that she had been in contact with in England, as far as she knew. Some of her online contacts were from the Kharkiv area, which made it easier to discover news of her husband. We had never heard

Daria mention anyone she was really close to in the British Ukrainian community and we knew she had no relatives here or left behind. Beth thought she might have a distant cousin now in Germany, but knew that they were not close.

He probed further as to how Daria was able to communicate with other refugees here and people back in her country. Beth explained about the Ukrainian group chat Daria was part of, which passed on news as they heard it, but she definitely did not know any of the names of the members. She had, understandably, never been shown any of the messages, since they were all in Ukrainian and, more than that, in the Cyrillic alphabet, so she would not even have been able to identify familiar place names.

He had some searching questions about how and from whom Daria had heard of Bogdan's death. Was it from UK-based Ukrainian contacts or friends or direct from her own country? Beth was not sure, but knew that there was actually a photograph, either of his body, or of the burial taking place. It had taken any uncertainty out of the bad news. She had not wanted to ask to see it, that would have been intrusive, and deeply inappropriate in that terrible moment.

Then we moved on to examine the street party itself. Our account was not exactly coherent, but we were able to fill in each other's omissions to a certain extent. It was only as we talked through the full timeline that I remembered seeing Adam coming back up the street Daria had left by, looking upset.

"He might have seen her, might be able to tell you if she was with anyone," I said.

I had to explain exactly what had happened at the beacon-lighting ceremony and, in response to more questions, about Adam's obsessive crush on Daria.

"I didn't know about that, Sam. Daria didn't say anything to me when she came back. She just said how much she had enjoyed the event, that it had made her feel young again."

"I know the incident upset Adam a great deal, but I don't think it was all that important to Daria, really. She was obviously used to handling the kind of admiration and interest she got from those lads, although she had found Adam's previous intense behaviour much harder to cope with. That's why I had to speak to Adam about following her around and pestering her. She didn't quite know how to deal with him."

Daniyaal frowned.

"Being put in his place like that, by someone he really admired, would have had a major impact on a teenager, you know. I am very surprised that he chose to come to the street party, where he knew he was likely to see her again. After that kind of humiliation, you would normally want to hide away, in my experience."

"He may well have wanted to apologise to her and get it done as soon as possible. I was rather worried that he might have followed her to try to speak to her, when I saw him coming back. I thought that might be why he looked a bit strange. Well, you may think he always looks odd, but I mean unusual for Adam. He did have a massive crush on Daria, but, from what his mother told me that day, he seemed to be getting over it, once I had that talk with him."

"How did you try to persuade him to leave her alone? That's a tough thing for you to be asked to do."

"It wasn't easy, but he actually took it very well. I reminded him that she was married and it wasn't appropriate for him to have such a close relationship with her. It seemed to me that his feelings were really deep, but also very genuine, and that he was willing to back off, in her best interests, even though it would be very painful for him."

Daniyaal looked incredulous.

"That's a very unusual reaction from someone of his age. Or anyone with a sexual obsession like that. I've had to deal with stalking cases and they are very difficult to resolve. I've never seen that kind of response."

"I understand that, but he genuinely did seem to be maturing, to be able to want the best for Daria. He wasn't really a stalker, you know. Just an immature boy with a passion for someone ultimately unattainable."

"I will definitely need to speak to him as soon as possible, Sam. It could be very important. Both anything that was said between them, and what he might have seen, at the time or afterwards."

"I know. Deb is close to his mother, so she should be able to arrange it for you."

I told him about John Deering having seen Daria on his way to the party and that he had offered to take her to his house for a cup of tea, but she had insisted on walking on.

"He's the last person I know to have spoken to her. I guess you will need to see him as well."

"Of course. If you can put me in touch with him, I'll do that as soon as I can."

"Well, if Beth doesn't mind, he could come here now, if he's not busy. I do have his contact details, because of being part of the committee."

"Yes, please, Sam," replied Daniyaal, when Beth had indicated her agreement. "The more I can get done now, the better."

I rang John quickly and he immediately agreed to our request. I was relieved not to have to inform him of Daria's death. The news had spread rapidly, especially among the committee members. He sounded rather shaken, and certainly less confident than usual, unsurprisingly. He seemed to have really cared about Daria. It was the best thing I knew of him.

"Is the inspector not going to be involved in the case this time, Daniyaal?" I asked, while we waited for him to arrive.

"She's been called to a triple murder not far away, gang related, and that's really her speciality. But she will be overseeing things from there and I will have another DS to help me. I think it's likely that she will take on the responsibility of looking into the possibility of a gang connection for us."

"Is that at all likely? Daria didn't have anything to do with that sort of thing."

"I know, but there are gangs involved in people-smuggling and the sex trade in the big cities near here, and you never know who might have been part of her chat group. She was a very attractive woman. And we do know that some refugees have been targeted, as so many of them are unaccompanied women with children."

"What a horrible thought! I didn't realise."

Beth looked stricken and I felt so bad that I had let Daria wander off alone. I could have, should have gone with her. I had not realised that she would be so vulnerable.

"It's probably nothing like that, Sam, given the messages and where her body was disposed of, but we will have to cover every angle, with a murder like this."

Daniyaal was reflecting on what he had been told so far.

"The other possibility, I think, could also stem from the beacon ceremony. The group of young men who surrounded Daria. I know that you said they seemed good-natured enough, but they could have met her again on that Friday afternoon. They are not likely to have attended the street party. She would not have been in a good mood to deal with them then."

"That's certainly true, and I didn't see them at the party, but - "

"They could have reacted badly, killed her without really

meaning to, and then dumped the body."

I sat back, trying to think it through.

"They didn't seem like that kind of group, but I suppose you could be right. You never know how people will behave, especially under peer pressure. But would they have bothered with the phone messages?"

"Well, sending them would provide more chance to cover their tracks, as would be the case with anyone who was involved with this murder. All the necessary information would have been in her phone for them. It's something I will have to try to follow up, anyway. Do you have any names? Or descriptions?"

"I didn't recognise any of them and certainly don't know their names. But I would know them again if I saw them, I'm pretty sure of that."

"I'll ask my officers to question other people at the event and see if we can find their identities. It's a bit of a long shot, I know, but at least it is a lead I can pursue."

Deb came back with Vitaly, chocolate still around his mouth from the ice cream he had clearly enjoyed. Beth whisked him off to wash and then have a quiet play in his room and Daniyaal asked Deb to contact Claire, and arrange for him to speak to Adam as soon as possible.

She looked a little anxious as she rang her friend and her voice was unusually hesitant. But it was clear, from her reaction, that Claire was actually eager to help, and offered to bring him round within the hour.

"It seems she told Adam the bad news this afternoon and he immediately asked her to arrange for him to speak to the police, surprisingly enough. So I suppose, this way, it works out well for her too."

Daniyaal looked astonished, and I felt a distinct shock which seemed to strike me in the chest. I had definitely not expected that. And I felt anxious about it, for some reason that I avoided exploring.

CHAPTER 19

Counterpoint

The doorbell rang. Deb went to answer it and brought in John Deering. He looked a little uncertain when he saw me and Daniyaal sitting together.

"Let's go into Beth's living room," I suggested. "It will be more comfortable."

The others agreed, but Deb said that she would stay and tidy up in the kitchen and start preparations for dinner. I did not know whether John would be happy about me being there with Daniyaal, but I was not going to give him the chance to object if I could help it. I felt the need to know as much as I could about Daria's last hours.

"This is Detective Sergeant Evans, Mr Deering. He handled the previous murder investigations here. You can trust him completely, and be really open with him about anything you have seen or heard."

John gave me a strangely quizzical look.

"I hope that I would always be open and trusting with the police, Samantha. That is, of course, the normal way for a law-abiding British citizen to behave."

Back to his rather condescending manner, which so irritated me.

But he relented.

"But thank you for introducing me. I am sure that Sergeant Evans is extremely competent. Is it definitely murder, then, Sergeant?"

"I'm afraid so, Mr Deering. Everything we know thus far appears to rule out accident and it certainly cannot possibly be suicide. We do not have the post-mortem report yet, of course, but there are very clear indications of foul play here. Hence my desire to speak with you as soon as possible, since you appear to have been the last person to see her alive, other than her killer."

John sat up rather straighter, folded his hands in his lap and took on an extra air of self-importance.

"My evidence could be crucial, then. I will endeavour to be as accurate and clear as possible then."

He agreed to Daniyaal recording him.

"Since you do not have another officer with you to take notes, that would seem to be the most sensible option available to us."

He sounded somewhat disapproving. He always seemed to expect things to be done in the traditional manner.

"My colleagues are all busy scouring the scene at the moment. We will take more formal statements later, at the station, if necessary, but for now I just need to hear everything you can tell me, as a key witness."

"Of course."

He inclined his head, with almost regal condescension. He must have been spending too much time with Mrs D-B.

"So, Mr Deering, can you please take me through exactly what happened when you met Daria on Friday afternoon?"

"Certainly. I left my house a little later than I had hoped, due to a malfunction with my cafetière, which spilled coffee and grounds all over the kitchen table. Since I was still suffering from a severe headache, engendered by the excessive volume of the entertainment on the previous night, it took me longer than usual to make the normal preparations for attending an event. I would estimate that it was around half past two when I finally set off, but it may have been a little later than that."

He spoke with pompous precision, as if he was reading out a prepared lecture.

"I had just emerged from my property via the garden gate, when I was almost knocked over by a passer-by, whom I then quickly identified as Daria. She was walking extremely fast and was nearly blinded by the tears streaming down her face. In her distraught state, she initially failed to recognise that I was the person she had so nearly overturned. It was evident that she was deeply moved by some overwhelming emotion."

I was surprised at the mention of tears. She had seemed very calm, almost too calm, when she left me.

"I asked her what was causing her to be so upset, since no one had yet thought to inform me of her husband's sad demise."

He looked rather accusingly at me. I did not respond to this obvious provocation.

"Her first response was: 'Adam'. She was unable, at first, to explain clearly how he had offended, but it seems that he had accosted her a few minutes previously and insisted on trying to excuse himself to her, for what appears to have been his boorish and uncalled-for behaviour at the beacon ceremony, persisting in such a way that she became very distressed. She felt herself obliged to explain her sudden bereavement to him and the simple act of putting it into words released an overwhelming flood of grief within her. She and Adam appear to have parted on very uncomfortable terms, both extremely upset and emotionally disturbed."

Oh dear. That seemed to explain Adam's appearance on his return to the party. How very sad that he should have chosen that moment for his apology.

"Seeing how very lachrymose she was, I pressed her to come back to my house and calm herself, offering her some light refreshments, but she was obdurate and determined to continue on her way. She maintained that you, Sam, had told her that walking helped when one was in distress, and she therefore insisted on leaving me."

Another accusatory stare. I ignored it once more.

"Now that I have been made aware of Daria's tragic fate, I feel somewhat responsible for allowing her to depart in that manner. I should have pushed her to remain. She was a delightful and committed pupil, both in her English studies and, more recently, in piano lessons, and I am devastated by the news of her passing. I am sorry that I cannot be of further assistance to you, Sergeant. I only wish I could contribute further useful information to your inquiry."

Having delivered himself of that seemingly well-rehearsed speech, he sat back, his chosen facial expression of grief jarring with his evident satisfaction at making an articulate and effective statement.

"Thank you very much, Mr Deering. That was extremely helpful. I would like to pose just a few additional questions, if that is acceptable to you."

Daniyaal was quite able to hold his own in the formality stakes.

John acquiesced readily.

"Firstly, can you confirm which direction Daria took when she left you?"

"Certainly. She continued down the street towards the edge of town. I am not aware which fork she took at that point, since I turned to make my way to the celebration in the square."

"Did you notice any other pedestrians walking in her direction, or any particular vehicles driving past you?"

John paused for a moment and closed his eyes.

"No pedestrians, at least none I remarked. There were several vehicles which passed me, including a black van and, I think, a red sports car, but I was thinking of Daria's sad situation rather than my surroundings, so I cannot be certain."

"Do you remember when you arrived at the party?"

"I'm afraid not, Sergeant. Feeling somewhat distressed by my encounter with Daria, I walked slowly and, when I arrived, I managed to find myself discreet tasks behind the scenes, so that I would not need to speak to anyone. The whole event was extremely busy, not to say chaotic, with people coming and going at will."

"Thinking a little further back, you said that you became intimate with Daria during your lessons with her. Did she ever mention Ukrainian friends or contacts to you?"

John looked severely at Daniyaal.

"I would hardly have said 'intimate', Sergeant. That would be an inaccurate use of language. However, I think I can claim to have become well acquainted with her, since we discussed a wide range of issues together, in order to further develop her ability to express herself in the English language. I believe that she did mention a friend who formed part of an internet group of which she was part. A young man who had known her husband, to the best of my recollection. Unfortunately I know nothing more about him, not even his name. But you may be able to discover that on her mobile telephone."

That was the first I had ever heard of such a friend and I was a little surprised that Daria would have mentioned him to John rather than to Beth or me. Was he someone she was embarrassed about or felt uncomfortable with? It could be a lead for Daniyaal, anyway.

"That is very useful indeed, Mr Deering. One more thing. You were present at the beacon event, I believe. A group of young lads had a confrontation with Adam and Daria at the conclusion of the evening. Did you see them?"

"I'm afraid Mrs Donnington-Browne and I left early, so I cannot help you there, Sergeant Evans. And I would not recognise any of the younger crowd who attended that ceremony anyway. We move in very different circles."

"Thank you, anyway, for your valuable assistance thus far. I think that is all I have for you currently. Here is my card. Please do not hesitate to contact me if you remember anything else, however small."

"I certainly will," responded John.

He rose to his feet, shook Daniyaal's hand, nodded slightly dismissively to me, and left.

"Was that really helpful, Daniyaal?"

"Well, leaving aside his rather pretentious way of speaking, it was quite revealing in places. I certainly now have several leads I can follow up."

Deb knocked quietly and poked her head around the door, looking somewhat concerned.

"Have you finished with John? Has he gone? Claire and Adam have just arrived. He won't let us sit in on his interview with you, I don't know why. But he doesn't seem to mind you being here, Sam."

Her tone of voice betrayed even more anxiety than her face.

"Deb, it'll be fine. We have some idea what it might be about, after talking to John Deering. Try not to worry."

"Oh, I'm not worried at all." she said airily, patently lying. "Claire is a bit anxious, that's all. She can be overprotective sometimes. He's very immature and quite sensitive. He does have some kind of diagnosis, I believe. I know he's now officially an adult but - he still seems like a boy in so many ways. You - you will be gentle with him, won't you, Daniyaal?"

Daniyaal nodded.

"From what you have said, I am aware that he may have particular vulnerabilities. I will not push him too hard. And remember, this is only an informal interview. Sam can be the responsible adult for him this time, but if it should come to more formal questioning down at the station, I will ensure that he has the right kind of representation."

She looked immensely relieved.

"You're so right. He is vulnerable in so many ways. Thank you. Claire and I will wait together in the kitchen. I'll send him in to you."

Before he arrived, Daniyaal explained to me why he would prefer it if I stayed, that it would be better both for him and for Adam if there was an adult witness to their discussion. I nodded my understanding. A safeguarding issue on both sides.

Unlike John Deering, Adam looked anything but controlled, and sounded anything but articulate. His floppy fringe was unusually greasy and uncombed, and he repeatedly pushed it away with his right hand. His protuberant Adam's apple bobbed up and down quite distractingly, and he kept flicking at an elastic band on his left wrist.

Daniyaal deployed his usual calm approach and that seemed to reassure Adam. His voice became a little less uncertain and he was able to relax back slightly into his chair. He agreed to being recorded, impatiently, obviously eager to get on with it.

"Now, I have been told that you asked to speak to me, Adam. What is it that you want to say?"

There was a long pause, while Adam all too obviously struggled to marshal his thoughts and find the right words.

"It's about Daria. I saw - I spoke to her on Friday afternoon. And

I saw her with someone else afterwards. I thought - I thought I should tell you. I - I cared for her very much. I want the - the murderer to be caught and punished."

He stopped and finally took a breath, his hands trembling.

"That is very public-spirited of you, Adam. I wish everyone was as ready to come forward and talk to us in these difficult circumstances."

The words should have been patronising or even sarcastic, but Daniyaal actually sounded sincere, and Adam responded like a drooping flower to water.

"Yes! I must do what is right. For Daria. It's hard to talk about. I - I have been stupid, I know that now. I don't know why I behaved that way. It seems strange to me, when I think about it now. But it was as if I couldn't help myself. She was - was so very beautiful, not just on the outside, you know? She had a beautiful soul and it shone from her eyes."

I was taken aback. It might have seemed to be only an adolescent crush, but this boy had just expressed something very profound and very true about Daria.

Daniyaal brought him back to the facts, but I could see that he, too, had been impressed with Adam's suddenly articulate expression of a special kind of love.

"In what way did you behave stupidly, then, Adam? Can you please explain to me what you mean?"

Back to earth, faced with his own shortcomings, Adam lost confidence again.

"I - have they told you - do you know what happened at the beacon lighting? OK, then you know that I overreacted and that I embarrassed Daria very much. I didn't mean to. I just - just wanted to protect her, to keep bad things away from her. But, as usual, I messed up. I'm no good at saying the right thing. I always do something stupid."

He felt very sorry for himself and with typical teenage self-obsession, it was all about him.

"But I felt so bad about it. I agreed to help at the street-party because - I really just wanted to apologise. I had to, to get it off my chest. But I wanted to say sorry properly, in a mature way. To explain that I really cared about her."

"I can understand that," replied Daniyaal, quietly.

"So, when I saw her leaving the square, after talking to you, Sam, I - well, I followed her. Well, actually, I took a shortcut and managed to catch her up. Just by the children's playground, you know."

He spoke more fluently now, immersed in what was clearly a painful, but already often recalled, memory.

"I spoke to her. She looked so strangely at me, as if she was hardly aware that I was there. I didn't know her husband was dead. I would never - never have bothered her if I had known. I tried to explain, to apologise, but the words all came out wrong. She didn't really seem to listen. I touched her hand, to try to make her understand, to get through to her how sorry I was to have offended her."

His voice thickened with emotion, occasionally squeaking into falsetto.

"She pushed my hand away. I didn't know what was wrong. She had never looked at me like that before. I thought I must have upset her very badly. I begged her to accept my apology."

Deeply sorry for him, I had to look away for a moment from the naked hurt in his face.

"Suddenly, she started to yell at me. She told me Bogdan was dead, that she did not care what I had done. She began to cry, to sob. I didn't know what to do. I said - I said she needn't worry, I would look after her. I know it was a stupid thing to say. When I look back, I can't understand what made me say it. But it came out all on its own."

He took a deep breath and looked stricken.

"I can still hear her voice. 'You?' she said. 'You are just a boy. What can you do?' I felt as if she had slapped me in the face. But she was right. I was stupid. I should never have said it. I should have understood. What it is to lose someone. Just a boy. I don't think I'll ever forget it and now - now it is the last thing I will ever hear from her, the last image I have of her, tears all down her face, terrible pain in her eyes. And all I could do was make it worse."

He burst into tears and buried his face in his shaking hands.

I could not leave him like that. I went over to him and put my hand gently on his back, passing him a clean tissue.

"Don't be so hard on yourself, Adam. I know it wasn't the right time or the right thing to do, but you actually had good intentions. You meant well. Daria will have understood. And, in the end, it may have helped her, talking to you. When I last saw her, she was very calm, much too calm. The grief was all bottled up inside her. You may have enabled her to release it. That's not a bad thing."

"But now she's dead, and I can't put it right."

"I know, but that isn't your fault. You didn't kill her, did you? So you will have to let it go, hard as that is to do."

Daniyaal intervened, his voice professional, unemotional.

"Thank you, Adam, for telling me that. I understand that it was difficult for you. It fits with some other witness statements we have and it is very helpful to know just what was said. You mentioned that you also saw her with someone."

Suddenly Adam sat up straight and spoke clearly.

"Yes! It was him, that John Deering. He's always talking down to me, sneering at me, making me feel small. I really hate him. My mother says he's a nice, kind old man. He's not nice to me! But anyway, I was watching Daria, almost running down the road, so desperate to get away from me, and he came out and almost knocked her over. Then he grabbed her hands and stopped her, talked to her. He even put his arm around her. She didn't push him away. She let him put his arm around her. I couldn't watch any more, I turned round and came back to the party. But he was with her. He was definitely with her, and that's the last I saw of her."

Poor Adam. He thought he had seen the murderer. He was brave enough to report it, too. He was not to know that we had already heard about the meeting.

Daniyaal kindly explained that we already knew about John's encounter with Daria. Adam looked flabbergasted, then revolted.

"Did you see anyone else in the vicinity, Adam?" asked Daniyaal. "Anyone on foot or in a vehicle?"

But Adam had been blinded by his own emotions and had noticed nothing at all.

"I am sorry to take you back to the incident at the beacon lighting, but I have a further question about what happened then. I need to know if you recognised any of the young men who surrounded Daria that evening. Do you know any of their names?"

Adam's face hardened at the recollection. He audibly ground his teeth.

"I will never forget what they look like now, but I don't know any of them, although the big one might have been at my school about four or five years ago, I think. And I'm pretty sure I heard one of them calling another Micky, but I could be wrong about that."

"Please try to think back more carefully when you have time, later on, Adam, and get in touch with me immediately if you remember anything else. Take my card, so that you can get straight through to me."

Adam looked vaguely confused, but took the card mutely.

"That's all for now, then. Thank you for taking the initiative in coming to speak to me. I will probably need to speak to you again."

He seemed completely exhausted by the interview, so I went and fetched his mother, who looked anxiously at him for a moment, but then whisked him away to take him home.

"Poor lad," I said, sympathetically. "That last meeting must have really preyed on his mind. I'm glad he was able to get it off his chest."

"Mmmm," murmured Daniyaal, noncommittally. "He did have a motive for being angry with Daria, though, Sam, and could possibly have gone back later and confronted her as she walked back. Does he drive?"

"No, that's one thing I do know. I suggested that he learn to drive before going out to Ukraine to fight. So I don't see how he could possibly have dumped her body out in the countryside. He would have needed help and I can't imagine anyone doing that for him."

Daniyaal received a important message on his mobile and had to leave, but thanked me and Deb for helping him to see so many witnesses so quickly. It was true - we had already learnt a lot about what happened that afternoon.

CHAPTER 20

Missa solemnis

That evening the four of us shared a roast chicken dinner and we adults made an effort to be bright and sociable, for Vitaly's sake. Beth looked awful. The shadows under her eyes and tension in her cheeks made her look quite unlike her normal self. But her eyes were warm with love and care when she looked at the little boy, and she did everything she could to make him feel comfortable and at ease.

Once he was safely in bed, we were able to let the masks drop.

"What a dreadful day!" sighed Beth.

Deb and I agreed wholeheartedly. It felt like an eternity since the morning church service. I knew that Beth was worried about the future as well as our present difficulties. What would happen to Vitaly? Could he stay with her? How might that work? But none of us had the energy to discuss it that evening. We tried television, but everything grated, nothing appealed. In the end Beth put some music on. She explained that her father had loved hifi and she had therefore inherited a really good system and plenty of records and CDs to play.

She chose something at random and it turned out to be Dusty Springfield. That soulful voice, full of hidden emotions, had a powerful cathartic influence and soon tears were pouring silently down my cheeks. I looked over and saw that Deb and Beth were both in the same state. Somehow it felt right to give these tears to Daria, to mourn her in this way. I tried to switch off the awful image from this morning and remember her as she had been, so happy that her son was settling in well and recovering from the trauma of the war.

We were all exhausted and went to bed early, but none of us slept properly. I was constantly jerked out of a doze by a powerful physical hit of shock as the picture of Daria's body forced itself back into my conscious mind. And it was obvious, in the morning, that the other two had fared little better.

"Did you sleep well, Vitaly?" I asked, speaking slowly and clearly. I knew that he had practised that question and answer.

"Yes, thank you, Sam," he said, rather proudly. But he looked pale and Beth said he had slept with her for most of the night and been disturbed by more regular nightmares. He knew something was wrong, knew his mother should be there, but did not ask for her. As if he were already sure she was gone, and he did not want to be told the truth about it.

We had arranged to meet the Ukrainian party at the church at eleven o'clock and walked silently down together. I was looking forward to being able to communicate with Vitaly, but also dreading it, and I could sense the same dichotomy in Beth, who moved increasingly slowly and heavily as we approached the church. It had never been a place where she felt comfortable.

Stephen and Celia met us at the door, both also looking tired and anxious.

"Come and meet Father Mikhail. He seems very kind, and he and the lady he brought with him are both deeply concerned about Vitaly, after what has happened."

Inside the church, standing in the side chapel, where Daria had lit her candle for Bogdan, stood a large weighty figure dressed in a dark cassock and wearing a strangely shaped black hat. His face was grave, but his eyes brightened when he saw Vitaly. Next to him, was a small, rather round middle-aged lady, modestly dressed, and wearing a traditional colourful headscarf. As soon as she saw the little boy, she held out her arms and said something which sounded like '*malenky*'.

It obviously meant something to Vitaly, because he ran to her, talking very fast in his own language. I heard Beth breathe a sigh of relief. The lady looked up and smiled at us.

"This little one says that you have all been very kind to him and his mother. He feels safe with you, especially with the one called Beth. He wishes he could tell you how much."

Beth trembled and bit her lip as she stood next to me. I squeezed her shoulder affectionately. We had known that Vitaly was happy with her, had been from the start, but it was so good to have that confirmed from his own mouth.

In the end, we all went into the rectory to talk. The church seemed too solemn, too holy. The atmosphere was very different with the orthodox priest standing there. He exuded an aura of otherness, and the impact was powerful. Very different from Stephen's informal approach.

We explained in more detail to him and the lady, whose name was Nadiya, what had happened, both Bogdan's death in action in Ukraine, and the terrible events leading up to the tragic murder of Daria. We told the story together, filling in for each other when emotion got the better of us.

Nadiya agreed to explain to Vitaly what had happened, but suggested that he sit with Beth while she spoke to him, so that he felt secure. Beth put her arms around him and held him close, as he took in the dreadful news, one thing after the other, shrinking further into himself with each sentence. He said something to Nadiya, in a heartbreakingly tiny and broken voice, then turned and buried his head in Beth's shoulder, shaking with sobs. She was in tears too, hugging him tightly, trying to reassure him physically, although she could not comfort him with words.

"He said that he suspected something bad had happened to his mother, and knew she had been upset about his father, but he hoped she might only be ill and that she would come back to him, if he prayed enough."

This was too much for the rest of us, and much use was made of handkerchiefs and tissues. Even the serious priest looked moved.

"He will be frightened about the future too," he said gently. "Do you know if he has surviving family members?"

Other than the distant cousin Beth knew of, there was no one.

"If I can, if it is allowed, I would like Vitaly to stay with me," said Beth in a quavering voice. "I know he will soon pick up English and it seems cruel to move him to be with strangers."

I could not help but gasp. That was quite a thing to offer. Did she really know what she would be getting herself into, the commitment it would be?

Stephen exchanged glances with Father Mikhail and then intervened.

"I think we will need to speak to social services and the police, but I'm absolutely sure that they will be willing to leave him with you for now, Beth. Longer term, it will depend on many things out of our control. But I'll speak to social services on your behalf, if you like. I have a few contacts in the department."

"I'll talk to Daniyaal about it and make sure that the police are happy with that," I offered. "And we'll all give you help and support, Beth. You know that."

Nadiya agreed to tell Vitaly that he would stay with Beth for now, without making any long-term promises we might not be able to keep. She also offered to provide phone translation support for Beth, in case she got into difficulties. Vitaly's reaction was instant - he flung his arms round Beth's neck and snuggled into her arms, like a much younger child, needing the comfort of her physical touch.

Father Mikhail then suggested that we go back into the church and light some candles and pray together. He repeated it in Ukrainian and Vitaly looked up, gulped and nodded agreement.

The short ceremony was moving, even though we did not understand the words, intoned in a musically deep voice. Vitaly stood by the altar, head bowed and crossed himself just like Daria used to. The priest pulled special candles from his capacious pocket and lit them one by one. Bogdan's picture was already there and we promised to bring a photograph of Daria later that day. Beth and Nadiya stood on either side of Vitaly, supporting him. The little boy looked so tiny, but was making such an effort to be grown-up. It was heartrending.

Before he left, the priest gave Vitaly a special blessing and spoke comfortingly to him in Ukrainian. Nadiya explained that he was talking about Daria's strong faith and how she was now with God, so Vitaly, while he would naturally miss her, should try not to be sad, but rather live his life well to honour her and Bogdan's memory.

He kindly promised Stephen that he would come and assist in conducting the funeral, when that was permitted. He explained that she would need to be buried rather than cremated, as that was not acceptable in her type of church.

As they left, Vitaly waved enthusiastically and then took Beth's hand, ready to walk home. Despite his terrible loss, he was able to live in the moment and be glad of small things. It was harder for the rest of us to put out of our minds the situation and its consequences, short- and long-term.

"I'll get in touch with my contact in social services immediately, Beth, and I rather think that, under the circumstances, someone is likely to pop out and see you this afternoon to see how things are going."

Beth nodded, but looked unsurprisingly apprehensive. Even the words 'social services' were intimidating when you had never had any contact with them.

"Don't worry, Beth," I reassured her. "I'll go and collect Chloe and have lunch with my parents, but I'll come back later to keep you company when they visit."

Deb had a volunteering shift that afternoon, but promised to help out with any bureaucratic demands. Giving Beth and Vitaly a big hug, she set off, leaving us to walk home quietly together.

"This is very brave of you, Beth. I have so much respect for you, offering to take on such a responsibility just now."

"Oh no, Sam. It isn't brave at all. I'm honestly terrified, if I try to think of how it will work out, but I'm only looking at one day at a time just now. I know that it would be dreadful to lose Vitaly, I just couldn't do it. I - I love him, Sam, more every day."

Vitaly heard his name and looked up, smiling into Beth's eyes.

"I love you, Beth," he said, still struggling with the 'th' sound, but speaking clearly and positively, knowing what he meant.

I could not speak. It was too much. I knew Daria had taught him the phrase, and had heard him say it to 'mama' more than once, but to hear him, so soon and so deliberately, say it to Beth, was wonderful.

"I love you, too, little one," she responded. She bent down and hugged him tightly.

"We'll manage together, won't we?"

He obviously did not understand what she meant, but nodded vigorously. I surprised myself by sending up a little prayer of thanks for a bright moment of love in a very dark time.

CHAPTER 21

Crescendo

Before going to collect Chloe, I rang Daniyaal to update him on the situation with Beth and Vitaly, but also to find out how the investigation was progressing. He was happy to hear that Stephen was contacting social services for us and seemed comfortable with the idea of her continuing to care for Vitaly, provided they approved of the set-up.

"Poor little boy. Terrible to lose both parents so suddenly. Being with someone he knows will be the best thing for him right now, but Beth could do with some additional support, I expect."

"We'll all rally round, but yes, I think you are right. How are things going for you?"

He sighed heavily.

"This is another very difficult case, Sam. There are a few small leads, of course. I have people checking all the local traffic and monitoring cameras for a black van or red sports car, or any other vehicle which might have been in the neighbourhood, but it is a long slow job. My colleagues are going door to door along the road, in case anyone noticed something, however small."

"I can see it would all take a lot of time."

"Yes, it feels as if we are working flat out, but getting nowhere.

We have not yet made any progress in tracking down the group of young men we would like to speak to, but that investigation is ongoing, of course. We hope to get some photographs from the school, which you and Adam could perhaps look at, but it's not a quick or easy process. We will eventually have some forensic evidence once it has all been analysed, of course, perhaps some DNA even, but we will need a suspect to match it to."

"It's so frustrating. Have you found her phone yet?"

Another sigh.

"We have. It was under the body. But the battery and SIM had been removed and the phone smashed, so it is doubtful whether we will ever be able to extract anything useful from it. The tech department is trying but it looks pretty hopeless right now. And her group chats were all end-to-end encrypted, so we cannot access them on the internet. We do not even have the first names of her contacts to start with."

I was really disappointed about that. The phone had seemed likely to offer vital clues.

"You sound very tired, Daniyaal. Have you had any break at all?"

"Not as yet, Sam. We know how important the first few hours are after finding a body. But, in this case, everything seems to lead to a dead end. It could be a very long haul."

He sounded almost defeated, very unlike himself.

"I know you will find out what happened, Daniyaal, and I know you won't give up. Please look after yourself. If it is going to take time, you really need to pace yourself."

"You are right, Sam. In fact, I am just going to have some lunch and make sure my team does too. We will not work effectively if we are exhausted. Thank you. Please do ring me if you, or any of your friends, think of anything which might help."

"Of course. See you soon."

I felt desperate to help in some way. Perhaps going through the street party again would help. One of us might remember something useful. Something which had seemed unimportant, but could potentially unlock the case. So much had happened since then, that Friday afternoon seemed to belong to the distant past.

I messaged all my groups, asking them to think back to the street party and the beacon lighting, and really try to analyse who they had seen, what they had been doing and when. It was not much, but it was better than nothing. It might eliminate someone with an alibi at least. And I knew that the police would be trying to interview as many of them as possible over the next few days. If they went over it mentally now, they would be better able to answer any questions.

Making a start myself straight away, I asked Mum and Dad what they had noticed at the party, while we were having a quick lunch together.

"Well, obviously we were mainly focused on Chloe and what she was up to, as well as Beth and sweet little Vitaly, but I suppose we did notice other people as well, mainly your friends, of course, as we recognise them."

Mum sounded less tired and both of them had clearly enjoyed having Chloe for long enough to set up their own routines with her. I loved to see the way my parents related to her, and how she listened intently to them, in almost the same way she did with me. It had been a great weight off my mind over the last couple of days to know that she was safe and happy.

"Did you see anyone leaving the party early, or coming and going unexpectedly?"

"I think a number of people did take their children home to use the toilet and then come back, as there were no facilities in the square. And, of course, there were people milling around and mingling by all the tables, not many just stayed in one seat for the whole time, so it is difficult to determine who was where."

Dad was right, unless you were carefully observing one person, it was almost impossible to pick out who might have left early. There were no allocated seats and the ticket system was really just to ensure that we catered for sufficient numbers. We had no idea who had actually attended. I was starting to feel as pessimistic as Daniyaal had sounded.

"I did see that tall lad with the long hair over his face leaving and I noticed him coming back a bit later. I only remember because he looked so very upset when he returned. I watched him slide behind one of the gazebos and find a corner to hide in, poor boy. He looked as if he wanted to have a good cry."

"Did he stay there for long, Mum? It could be important."

"I think so. I'm pretty sure he was still there when you all started clearing up."

"That's really helpful. We know he spoke to Daria, but didn't know if he had gone back later to see her again."

"Well, I couldn't swear to him being there all the time. I wasn't paying a lot of attention, but I did feel a bit concerned about him and kept glancing back in his direction, so I think he probably stayed there the whole time."

It might not let Adam off the hook, but certainly made it less likely that he would have been able to slip away for a second time unnoticed.

"I think the vicar popped off to see someone just after he came over and spoke to us, Sam, but he wasn't gone long, maybe half an hour or so."

Dad spoke quite tentatively.

"That's not nearly long enough for him to be involved in this, and, anyway, I'm absolutely certain he didn't have anything to do with it," I answered, rather too vehemently. I could not cope with Stephen being a suspect again. It had been far too distressing the last time.

"I do remember seeing a delivery van halfway down the side street, Sam. Some time after Adam returned. The driver was obviously frustrated at not getting a reply when he knocked on the door, and because it was a terraced house right on the street, he couldn't get round the back to leave his parcel. He looked up and down the road as if he was trying to think what to do next, but in the end he took the package back to the van with him and drove off."

I had not realised how observant Mum was.

"Was it a black van, Mum?"

"I don't think so, Sam. But it was a dark colour and didn't have any business markings on it. That's how lots of them are nowadays."

"I don't suppose you could describe the man."

"Not really. He was quite tall and on the broad side. He had mirrored sunglasses on, they looked so strange. I don't think he had a beard or anything. But he was quite a long way away, you know. I couldn't even promise to recognise him if I saw him again."

"Still, it's a possible lead for Daniyaal to follow up. The delivery company will have records. Thank you so much, both of you. Please let me know if anything else comes back to you. I'm so very grateful to you for looking after Chloe for me. I don't know how I would have managed without you two."

"We love to have her here, you know that. It does your mother good to have her to look after. She actually copes better with her aches and pains when Chloe is here. So you are really doing us a favour when you ask us to help."

I knew Dad was worrying about Mum too. His voice sounded more emotional than usual and he gripped my hand hard. I smiled gratefully at him.

"I'll see you again soon. Thanks for lunch."

Chloe was delighted to see Vitaly again and immediately said something which sounded very much like the beginning of the word 'train'. She was managing more and more recognisable words each day now and trains were some of her favourite toys. He ran off to fetch some of his set from upstairs and I knew they would play happily together for a while.

Beth, on the other hand, was evidently extremely nervous. She could not sit still, but was up and down, alternately peering out of the front window and wandering out into the hall. To give her something to do, I asked for a cup of tea.

"Of course, of course. That's no problem. But I was going to make tea when they arrive. But we don't know when that will be. So of course we can have tea now. If you really want some."

I could see that the panic was really building.

"Look, you make tea and I'll ring Stephen and see how he got on. He might have some idea who will come and when. It could even be tomorrow."

Beth's scared eyes flicked between me, the children, and the kitchen, and then she rushed out.

It was a relief to hear Stephen's calm friendly voice on the other end of the phone.

"I'm so sorry, Sam, I intended to ring at lunchtime to let you and Beth know what had happened, but I had an unexpected bereavement visit and couldn't put it off. But I did have some success. My contact actually has quite a senior position in children's services and said immediately that she would come and see Beth this afternoon. I think around three, although she may be delayed by other visits. But you have no need to worry. She's really nice and very supportive."

"I'm so grateful to you for arranging this, Stephen. It has to be done and the sooner the better, I think. I'll just go and let Beth know."

"Will you ring me this evening and tell me how you got on? I would like to support Beth in this, as far as I possibly can."

"Of course. I'll ring as soon as Chloe is in bed. Thanks again."

Beth began to calm down a little once she had a clear appointment time and knew that it would be a woman who came. She was much more comfortable in female company and often found men intimidating. I did not know why, whether it was just instinct, or if she had suffered a bad experience in the past, but that was partly why I had been so happy for us to be able to share a joint interview with Daniyaal.

Just before three o'clock the doorbell rang, sending Beth into a spin. Reassuring her with a glance, I sent her off to answer the door. She came back in accompanied by a confident and obviously very capable black woman, perhaps in her early forties, whose ready smile and warm friendly voice soon relaxed us all.

"Hello everyone. Nice to meet you. My name is Elizabeth Buchanan and I'm a social worker here in the area. Now, I know a lot of people find the idea of a social worker coming to their home scary, but I promise you that I am not here to criticise or cause trouble, just to check that everything is going well and help you to take the next steps you need to in these difficult circumstances."

You could almost see the tension leaving Beth's body and she breathed out slowly, closing her eyes for a moment in sheer relief. She offered her visitor a drink, but Elizabeth said she had just had a cup of tea and was fine.

"If I accepted tea and biscuits in every house I go to, I would spend all my time in the loo and weigh even more than I do already! But thank you, it is a kind offer."

It was a very mild joke, but we laughed, all the same, as

much because of the lightening of the atmosphere as out of amusement.

"Stephen told me some of what has happened to put you in this position. I am so very sorry, both for your loss and for the situation you find yourself in. He said your name was Beth, is that right? Are you an Elizabeth, like me?"

"No, my name is Bethan, Bethan Denning."

"Right, well then, Beth, I'll explain why I am here and what I need to do."

Kindly and very clearly - she was obviously used to dealing with people who were upset, frightened, or not confident in English - she told us that, if Beth was looking after Vitaly, it would come under the private fostering arrangements. This meant that she, representing local social services, needed to see that he was safe and well, and that his environment was suitable. It also meant that she would need to run some background checks on Beth.

"Nothing to be afraid of, just checking you don't have a criminal record or anything else like that, which might make fostering unsuitable. Nowadays we can do most of it online, if you are able to use a computer?"

"Of course, no problem."

"If you have a passport or other photo ID available and a bank statement or bill and birth certificate, I will be able to confirm your identity while I'm here and the rest can be done online."

Elizabeth reassured us that if, as expected, everything went through with no red flags, there would be no problem with Beth fostering Vitaly immediately, on a temporary basis.

"You don't have to make a long-term commitment at this stage, you know, Beth. Give yourself and Vitaly time to settle. But if you wish to, later on, you could apply for a special guardianship order or even adopt him."

Beth brightened.

"I haven't dared to hope for that. I would really like to adopt him, but I understand that it might not be possible. But that's what I want."

She had evidently been thinking seriously about it.

Elizabeth explained that there were several benefits she could claim to help with looking after Vitaly, and that there would be support, should she need it, from local fostering services, including finding an interpreter if necessary. The council had some experience of housing lone refugee children, and knew where to find the appropriate resources. Then she turned and called the little boy over.

He went to stand by Beth, holding her hand tightly, as he spoke to this new stranger.

"How are you, Vitaly?"

"I am well," he stated proudly, looking up at Beth for confirmation and praise.

"Do you want to stay here with Beth?"

"Yes, Miss. I love Beth. Please, I stay here with her."

"Of course, if that is what you want. You speak very good English. Will you show me your bedroom?"

Vitaly's eyes glowed at the compliment and he hopped from one leg to the other with excitement.

"Come. I show you. Very good bedroom. Come!"

He led her out and Beth followed. Chloe, left alone again, came back over to me and I gave her a big cuddle. Seeing Beth and Vitaly made me realise how very fortunate I was. And also that I needed to sort out guardianship arrangements in case anything happened to me. It was not likely to occur, but after my own recent experiences, as well as what had happened to Daria, I should know that you could not rule it out. I definitely needed to be certain that Chloe would be safe and cared for, come what may.

Beth had retrieved her documents while Vitaly was showing Elizabeth around the house, so things progressed quickly once they returned to the living room.

"Well, Beth, I can certainly see that you have everything very well-organised for Vitaly and that he feels safe and secure with you. He even had the confidence to show me his pull-ups! You should know that he may have further reactions to the immense amount of personal trauma he has been through and the fostering service will be happy to support and guide you through any issues that arise. Counselling can be arranged if need be. For now, though, I am amazed at how settled he seems, given the sudden loss of both his mother and father. You have done a brilliant job. Just don't be surprised if he struggles with things unexpectedly and is very sad or even angry some of the time."

Beth nodded seriously.

"I know. He can go from being super happy to desperately sad in a moment. And I understand, because I feel much the same. We'll grieve for his mother and father together and be sad when we need to, but enjoy life when we can."

I looked at Beth in astonishment. I had never heard her speak in such a mature way about her own emotions. This situation had really changed her.

"I'm extremely impressed, Beth, with both the practical and the emotional side of your care for Vitaly. Please carry on, with the full support of the council. Take my card, and don't hesitate to contact me if you need some kind of help, whatever it is."

"Honestly, Elizabeth, I can't thank you enough. You've given me so much confidence, going forward, that I can actually do this. I'm very grateful."

After the social worker left, Beth came over and gave me a hug.

"Thank you for being there, Sam. I know I managed pretty well in the end, but your presence and support made all the difference, especially at the start."

"She was lovely, wasn't she? She's really changed my view of social workers. She was so supportive and positive. And she's right. You have done a fantastic job with and for Vitaly. You are the one he needs right now. I'm so proud of you."

"Do you know what, Sam? I'm actually starting to feel like a mother. It's not easy, but the positives definitely outweigh the bad parts."

I smiled at her.

"That is exactly what I think most mothers would say. Are you taking Vitaly to nursery tomorrow?"

"Yep. I think it's best if we both get back to routine as soon as possible. Caroline is so good - she says he can come whenever I want him to, and even on days when I don't work there. That'll mean I can still help at the Food Bank, too."

Chloe was reluctant to leave her hero, Vitaly, but it was time for us to go. It felt as if we had a new family somehow. I had always wanted Chloe not to be an only child, and her growing relationship with Vitaly seemed to be developing as if he were an older sibling or a cousin.

But it was so painfully sad that he no longer had his own mother. Every so often that tragic fact, and the image of Daria lying dead in a ditch, forced itself into my mind. Who could have done such a terrible thing? I desperately hoped that the culprit was not someone I knew.

CHAPTER 22

Fortissimo

I slept a little better that night, partly from exhaustion, but also because I felt more secure about Vitaly's situation. It was a comfort to know that he could have a family again. Not his birth family, but so much better than nothing.

But the nightmarish vision of Daria's dead body would not go away. I did not want to let it go yet, either, just allow it to drift away with time. Somehow, we had to find the murderer. If it was a stranger, it would be difficult and distressing, but if it was someone who knew her, or someone I knew, that would be even worse. Something was nagging at the back of my mind and my subconscious kept trying to bring it back into my dreams.

I did not know what it was that did not fit. That logical, puzzle-solving mentality was not my way of thinking. But, viscerally and emotionally, I knew that something somewhere was wrong. I sensed it, but could not bring it to the surface.

I took Chloe to nursery for her regular session that morning and hoped that a walk would clear my head and enable me to think things through properly. She was doing her first full day that Tuesday and I knew I had plenty of time until three o'clock when she finished.

As I came away from the long, low building next to the school,

I suddenly remembered that I had not passed on my parents' observations from the street party to Daniyaal. I quickly messaged him to suggest a phone call, but he replied that he would prefer to see me if possible, since he was in the area anyway. We arranged to meet at my house in fifteen minutes.

He looked dreadful. His hair had none of its usual shine and bounce, his eyes looked dull and bloodshot and his lips were tight with tension.

I did not comment on it, but invited him in and provided him with coffee and sandwiches, without even asking him. He sat and ate ravenously, but obviously hardly aware of what he was putting in his mouth. I did not speak until he had finished.

"OK, Daniyaal, if that is what you call looking after yourself, I would hate to see you neglect your health! You desperately need a few hours of rest. And probably a proper meal. You can't survive on snacks and doughnuts."

He managed a faint smile.

"I don't actually like doughnuts. It's a bit of a television stereotype. But it's true that we do tend to fill up on sugar and carbs to get us through the fatigue."

"But you can't possibly do a good job in this state. Your brain won't function properly. You could even miss some vital clue or ignore a crucial witness. You know that really. I'm sure the inspector would say the same."

"Touché. She actually ordered me to get some rest but I felt I needed to keep going, to lead the team. You're right though. My brain feels like mush and I have started to become irritable with colleagues. I promise I will go and rest for a few hours when we have finished here."

I was relieved. I had seen him tired before, but never at this point of utter physical and mental exhaustion.

"OK, that's good, Daniyaal. I'm sorry, I forgot to contact you yesterday about a couple of things my parents noticed at the street party, which might help the investigation."

I told him first about Adam. I knew it was not an alibi as such, but it should help to explain where he was for the rest of that afternoon.

"I suppose it makes him a less likely suspect, Sam, but it's hardly conclusive. He could have gone to find her at the end of the party or slipped away without your mother noticing. However, it gives me something more to question him about. I'm intending to speak to him again tomorrow. In some ways, he seems the most likely killer, with the most obvious motive, but the lack of a car would make disposing of the body difficult. But not impossible. He might even have 'borrowed' his mother's car."

"I honestly don't think he has it in him, Daniyaal. I know that's only my instinct, but I think he really cared for her."

"If you knew how many murders came from twisted love, you wouldn't see that as an exonerating factor! Was there anything else your family saw? Your mother seems to be unusually observant."

I told him about the delivery driver. He made me repeat it for recording and seemed happier with this revelation.

"That certainly gives us something to go on. Even if the driver is completely innocent, he may have seen something which we can use. Please thank your mother for me. It's very helpful, and no one else has mentioned it so far. Obviously we're interviewing as many people as we can who were at the street party, but most of them seem to have been totally absorbed in enjoying themselves with friends or family. Sophy has given us a list of names from the ticketing website, although we don't know who actually attended."

I had not thought of that. What a good idea.

"Is that everything?"

I hesitated. Should I tell him what my father said about Stephen? To be honest, I did not want to, but in the end, I decided that it was essential. After all, it was only a short absence and I knew, beyond a shadow of a doubt, that he was innocent. It was even possible he might have noticed something useful on his way there and back, without being aware of it.

But Daniyaal did not see it like that.

"That's very interesting. We haven't interviewed him or Celia yet. And I have not heard about that absence from anyone else. Was this meeting a secret? I will have to look into who he was supposed to be seeing, but even half an hour could be enough. We know the body was not moved until some time after she was killed, so it is a possibility. He could even have arranged to meet her in the church, and killed her there."

I was flabbergasted and appalled.

"But you know Stephen! You know he wouldn't do a thing like that. He's - he's a truly lovely man and so very gentle. He spent a lot of time explaining our church practices to Daria and praying with her for Bogdan, when she was alive. And he's been so helpful in looking for her, and supporting Beth and Vitaly. You can't treat him like a suspect, just because he had to go and meet someone."

Daniyaal's tired face hardened and he spoke harshly.

"You are blinded by your feelings, Sam! Of course I have to take it seriously. He's unmarried, unattached, and may be hiding all kinds of twisted, unhealthy desires. You say he spent time with her, at times alone. So you cannot possibly know how their relationship developed. She probably looked up to him as a priest. And we have all heard about how they sometimes abuse their power and influence. I definitely know how he looks at you! And how he seems to react to me if I am with you."

"What on earth are you talking about? How he looks at me? He's a friend, a very close, dear friend, someone I can trust and rely on. I have a good deal of affection for him. He helped to save my life. But you - you sound as if you were jealous of him!"

As soon as the words were out of my mouth, I regretted them. What possible reason would Daniyaal have to be jealous?

I was about to apologise and take it back, when he spoke, much more calmly now, in a hard, cold voice.

"Perhaps you are right. It is obvious to me that you have very strong feelings for the vicar. That makes you an unreliable witness, where he is concerned. But I promise you that I will not allow my personal sentiments to influence my conduct of the investigation. I will question him as I would any other witness or suspect. Nothing more, nothing less. I must go now. Please ensure that you let me know if you hear anything further about the case."

He stood up stiffly, not looking directly at me, and stalked out of the house without another word. And I did not know what to say to him. I was in a state of shock. He had never spoken to me like that before, and I was confused by what it revealed of his and my own emotional state.

CHAPTER 23

Subito

What on earth had got into Daniyaal? I felt quite upset by the unexpected confrontation. I was so used to him being a comfortable friend and supportive professional. Yet those powerful emotions seemed to have sprung out of nowhere. My knees were wobbly as I stood up to pace and think, so I sat back down immediately. I even felt slightly queasy and unsettled.

Suddenly, I realised that I would need to tell Stephen that a police officer might shortly be coming to interview him about Friday afternoon. Perhaps with a hostile approach. Feeling intensely guilty about having mentioned it to the police at all, and especially to Daniyaal, I messaged him immediately, asking if I could go round. He responded at once, inviting me to lunch. In looking after Daniyaal, I had forgotten all about eating myself. Again.

I was glad to find that Celia was there too when I arrived. After what had been said, I was unaccountably uneasy about being alone with him. We sat together eating a light meal of salad and bread. After a few mouthfuls, I felt somewhat better and able to broach the subject.

"I'm terribly sorry, Stephen, but Daniyaal knows that you left the street party after speaking to my parents. For about half an hour, wasn't it? I think he will want to speak to you about it very soon."

To my relief, Stephen looked completely unconcerned.

"That's no problem, Sam. After all, it is a fact. I had to meet unexpectedly with a member of the congregation, who rang me in the throes of a spiritual crisis. Of course, it is completely confidential, but I only went to the church for a short talk and prayer and then was able to return, knowing we would meet up again on the following day."

"Will you be able to give Daniyaal their name?"

Stephen looked doubtful.

"Only with their permission, which they may well not give. It's a very private matter, and I think it is unlikely that they will be willing to speak to the police, even about meeting me, let alone what we discussed."

Oh dear. Stephen might be comfortable with that, but it would reinforce Daniyaal's opinion that he could have committed the crime, and possibly his unfounded prejudices against the unmarried vicar.

Celia must have seen something of my concerns in my face, because she began to be angry.

"If it comes down to you being arrested, that person will just have to come forward, Stephen. You are too generous with your time in any case, especially with these kinds of intense last-minute demands. And you, Sam, were you the one who told Daniyaal that Stephen left the party? I would not have believed it of you. I thought you were his friend."

Shame brought the colour to my cheeks. I did feel that I had let Stephen down.

Before I could answer, he intervened.

"It doesn't matter if she did, Celia. It is the truth, and I would have told the sergeant myself, if I had thought it was relevant. I don't believe that the police will arrest me for something I haven't done and for which there can't be any evidence. Not having an alibi is not enough."

Celia looked doubtful, but tried to smile.

"I suppose you're probably right. I hope so anyway. But I can't help remembering how awful it was last time you were a suspect. Not only for you. All the gossip in town. People can be so horrible, so spiteful."

"I know, it's not an experience I want to repeat either, but that time was different. I had been at the scene, and actually spoken to Charlotte just before she died. This time, I didn't see Daria, and I have no real connection to the murder. It'll be fine. You'll see."

I felt that Stephen was talking to me as well as to Celia. I reached out and touched his hand fleetingly.

"Thank you and I'm so sorry you are involved at all."

"I suppose we are all involved, really, especially those of us who were close to Daria. I do hope there will be some kind of breakthrough in the case before long. The uncertainty, and an atmosphere of mutual suspicion, are very unhealthy within the community. It could undo all the good which is coming from our lovely Jubilee celebrations."

"I know. I expect the media will turn up shortly, as well. The finding of the body was mentioned on the news last night. And that's the kind of invasion I particularly hate, as you know."

Celia's eyes flashed.

"Just let them try to talk to me about it! Those vultures always arrive when something bad has happened. I can't stand them."

I nodded in agreement.

"I can't help feeling that I know something which would help with the case. Something I've heard or seen. I've been racking my brains, but I just can't think of it."

Stephen looked at me gravely.

"You are very perceptive, Sam, and it would not surprise me if you had subconsciously noted an inconsistency somewhere. But racking your brains is unlikely to help. These things normally don't come back until you stop trying to access the memory."

"You're right, Stephen. I'll go for a walk and see if it pops into my mind. But I have a feeling it may have something to do with something you mentioned to me, Celia, at some point recently. Can you remember what we talked about at the street party?"

Celia shook her head at first, then closed her eyes in an effort to remember.

"We talked about Daria's bad news to start with, I think, and then I told you about the child who wasn't going to be able to play in the concert. And Jessica's teacher accompanying her. That's all I can remember."

Again something jangled in the back of my mind, but I could not place it.

"Oh well, either it will come back to me, or I'll have to accept that it was never anything important. Thank you so much for lunch, Celia, and thank you for being so forgiving, Stephen. I really appreciate it. I'll go for my wander now before I have to pick up Chloe."

"Let me walk you out," said Stephen, warmly.

As we said our goodbyes, he clasped my hand in his and told me not to worry. My initial discomfort had eased, and I was able to give him a brief hug. Such a lovely man. How could Daniyaal not see that?

I decided to walk along the road Daria had taken, in case anything jogged my memory. I let my mind float free and enjoyed the physical sensation of walking, the brush of the breeze on my face, and the sparkling birdsong. I was lucky to live in a town with plenty of green space and wildlife.

Suddenly, it came back to me, in a shocking moment of clarity, which brought me to an abrupt stop in the middle of the pavement. I remembered that Celia had been looking for John Deering and had not been able to find him. He said he was carrying out more 'discreet' tasks, because he was upset by his encounter with Daria. But where? I had not seen him and neither had my observant mother. Was he actually there?

I had never liked the man, although his behaviour since Daria's death had been less patronising to me and more tolerable in general. Was I just prejudiced against him, as Daniyaal seemed to be against Stephen? Or was there a possibility that he had somehow been involved in the murder?

I was only a few hundred yards beyond his large house. It stood out from the rest of the ordinary suburban buildings on the street, because of its size, age, and architecture. I had walked past it without noticing, but perhaps it had somehow triggered my memory. I turned round and began to make my way back towards it.

All at once, I remembered something I had read, possibly in a Lord Peter Wimsey novel. Something to the effect that characters in novels who ended up in deadly danger had generally not taken any sensible precautions. I was about to go and speak to John Deering. That much I had already decided. But if he actually was the murderer, that could be a very dangerous step to take. No one even knew where I was. I had not told anyone about my suspicion.

Pulling my phone out, I messaged Stephen.

Where was John Deering? Am going to speak to him.

Not accusing him, but putting the question and saying where I would be. After a long hesitation, I also forwarded the message to Daniyaal. No additional tick from either of them to show that they had seen it yet. Daniyaal would almost certainly be working and Stephen probably with a parishioner or even praying. But at least I had partially covered my back.

Not that I actually thought I was going to beard a murderer in his den. Much more likely that I would endure more patronising smugness from an older man I really did not like, who invariably brought to the surface my incipient inferiority complex.

Taking a deep breath, I walked briskly up the winding path to the front door and rang the old-fashioned doorbell. As I waited, half hoping he would not be in, I took in the beauty of his period house, partly covered in green Virginia creeper, with deep set sash windows laid out with Georgian balance and elegance. It was impressive, and almost as subtly intimidating as I sometimes found its owner.

Just as I was about to leave, the door opened and he was there. I looked afresh at him, trying to spot any tell-tale signs of murderous intent. But there were none. As I had mentioned to Daria, he seemed to cultivate an older appearance than his age warranted. His hair was already close to white and he wore thick round horn-rimmed glasses, which hid his eyes somewhat and made their expression difficult to determine.

Although he looked avuncular, harmless and elderly, there were very few lines on his face and I put his age at mid-fifties. It was his mouth which I had always found irrationally repugnant. Full lips but mostly turned inwards, as if he were running his tongue along the inside of them.

I jumped as he addressed me, with apparently polite sarcasm.

"To what do I owe the pleasure of your visit, Samantha?"

He knew I disliked being called by my full name but insisted on doing it.

"Please call me Sam, Mr Deering. Or may I call you John, now that we know each other a little better?"

He inclined his head in acceptance.

"Sorry, I was distracted by your beautiful house. I had never really looked at it before. You are very fortunate to live in such a gorgeous place."

"'Beautiful', yes, I can accept that description, but I'm afraid that 'gorgeous' is a most inappropriate adjective. However, your use of language is not the issue at hand. I was asking what you required of me."

"Sorry, I thought I had said. I was hoping to ask you a few questions about what Daria told you about her Ukrainian friends and contacts."

"Ah, yes, you like to try to assist the police, don't you? Given their evident lack of progress, even your input may be useful. I suppose I can spare you a few minutes. Do come in."

He led the way into a large study situated in the front of the house, with tall windows overlooking the front garden. It was furnished in a typically 'gentlemen's club' style and should have seemed trite, but it was well-used and matched the house and its owner perfectly. The hide-bound books on the shelves were evidently read regularly and the leather armchair near the desk was worn pale in places.

He indicated a smaller chair for me to sit in and arranged himself like a professor in his own, hands folded, with an air of patience and longsuffering, waiting for me to speak.

"I'm so sorry to intrude on you like this, but you are such a crucial witness and so observant," I apologised, rather sycophantically. No point in annoying him right at the start.

"I just wondered if you might have remembered any more about Daria's Ukrainian friends, the ones you mentioned to the police.

Unfortunately her phone was damaged, so the police haven't been able to extract any information at all from it, as yet."

Was it my imagination, or did a tinge of relief flit across his sober face?

"That is extremely unfortunate. So you have no idea with whom she was in contact? I will carefully examine my memory."

There was a long pause. I did not dare to break it.

"I am almost certain that she mentioned the name Tomas, because I remember her explaining that in Ukrainian it did not have an 'h'. But I cannot be sure that this was in connection with a personal contact from her mobile telephone."

"Nevertheless, that could be extremely useful, Mr - John. Thank you. Were there any other names she brought up?"

"Perhaps Maria. We were discussing nativity traditions in both countries, and I believe it arose, but whether she had a friend or acquaintance of that name, I do not know, Samantha."

"I really wish you would call me Sam, John. Samantha doesn't sound at all like me. It sounds like an elegant lady in a long floaty white dress, delicately arranging flowers!"

John smiled for the first time.

"You do not consider yourself to be a young lady? This is one of the major ills of our modern society, I believe. The feminine side of the female gender seems to have been lost. Young women now desire to be treated like men, to have the same rights and duties, and have lost the ability to shape themselves into ladies, or into wives and mothers as they used to. Much has been lost in the process."

I was taken aback.

"I'll have you know that - " I began impetuously, before deliberately calming my voice.

"Sorry, that was rude. I was a wife, and am now a mother, but that does not mean I should not have the same opportunities and career choices. My relationship with my husband was a partnership of equals."

He smiled pityingly at me.

"I'm sure you would like to think so. But it is part of our human, our biological nature that someone must take charge, and I am sure your former husband would have wanted to do that, to protect and cherish you, as in the marriage service. I am quite certain that you will disagree with me, but I would wish to follow the old ways, where a wife should promise to obey her spouse. Submission is, after all, the highest form of love."

"I really can't agree with that. True love wants what is best for the loved one. It has nothing to do with submission."

He was really enjoying his topic now, glad to have someone to whom he could propound his regressive theories.

"Even the act of sexual intercourse should be an exercise in absolute submission by the female. This is how it was designed, how we often see it in the natural world."

I felt deeply embarrassed to be discussing sex, even in these vague terms, with this man.

"I can see that you are uncomfortable at the thought, Samantha. But the reduction in male fertility, women having their children late or not at all, the growth of homosexuality, all of these stem from the modern reluctance of the female to embrace submission as part of her femininity."

I goggled at him.

"You really can't be serious."

"Look at me. I have much to offer a young wife, money, security, a wonderful, protected, and luxurious life. Yet I remain single, involuntarily celibate, unable to pass my unique genes on to a successor."

His words disturbed me deeply. I was sure that I had heard that expression, 'involuntarily celibate' somewhere and not in a pleasant context. Somehow related to violence against women.

"I'm sorry, John, I just can't continue this conversation. It is making me very uncomfortable. Did you talk to Daria like this?"

"Not quite in this depth, Samantha, since her linguistic skills would not have permitted it. But she was a much more confidently feminine and attractive woman than you and seemed to have a much better instinctive understanding of her role in society."

Thanks, I thought. I don't find you attractive either.

I had always known that he disliked me as much as I disliked him. I needed to escape from his oppressive company as soon as possible.

"Just one more question, if I may. When you returned to the street party after meeting Daria, you said you sought out more 'discreet' tasks. I didn't see you, and Celia couldn't find you. So I was hoping that you might have noticed, from the more retired position where you were working, someone leaving the party early, and not returning or behaving oddly."

"That, at least, is a sensible question. But I'm afraid I was so absorbed in what I was doing, using it to distract me from concern about Daria, that I did not notice anything or anyone. Now, if that is all, perhaps I can show you out?"

"Of course," I agreed humbly, just anxious to escape.

In the cool, spacious hallway, I once again could not help but admire the gracious elegance of his house. I caught sight of the end of a piano in a room on the other side of the house.

"Oh! You have enough room for a grand piano! Daria told me you had a wonderful music room, but I did not realise that you had such a beautiful piano. May I see it?"

I really do not know why I asked that, why I did not just make good my escape. Something just put it into my head and it blurted straight out.

With some reluctance, he allowed me to look inside.

"Is this where you had your lessons? What a lovely room."

It was beautifully proportioned, with a high ceiling, French doors to the back garden and plenty of space for a magnificent shiny grand piano, as well as a comfortable sofa and low table. There was also a classical fireplace with a very expensive rug in front of it.

"Oh no! You've damaged your rug."

I could smell that he had used bleach on it and it had whitened quite a large section.

"One of my piano pupils had a nosebleed the other day. Probably due to picking it excessively, knowing schoolboys. I tried to remove the stain this morning, but have only succeeded in ruining my precious rug."

I laughed.

"As a former teacher, you can't tell me anything about the revolting habits of schoolboys that I would not believe!"

But suddenly it struck me. This could be where Daria died. If I could get the police in, they would surely be able to detect human blood, even if it had been thoroughly cleaned.

Unfortunately, I am no poker player, and John could immediately see a change in my expression. He turned towards me and his face darkened ominously. I tried to smile, to pretend that I had not put two and two together, but it was no use.

"Well, thank you so much for showing me your music room, John, and for answering my questions so patiently. I must be going now. My friends are waiting for me."

For one hopeful moment, I thought it might work. He stood back from the door, as if to allow me to pass, but as I reached the threshold, I felt a tremendous blow on the back of my head and everything abruptly turned black.

CHAPTER 24

Attacca: Libera me

The first thing I became aware of was a stabbing pain in the back of my head, where it seemed to be pressing on a very hard floor. I tried to move to ease it, but could not lift it, not even a little. Other discomforts intruded gradually, and I realised that my wrists were tightly bound together with something sticky and immovable, like duct tape. As I tried to roll a bit, to change a position which was becoming increasingly painful, I discovered that my legs too were tied at the ankles. My feet seemed to be completely numb already, so the bonds were tight.

Even before opening my eyes, I knew where I was. The smell of bleach was much stronger than before and almost made me retch. That rug.

"Do not pretend to be unconscious."

The familiar voice made me shudder. I forced my eyes open.

"Why did you really come here? Whom did you inform of your visit? Which friends are expecting you?"

My brain felt like porridge, useless and mushy. Should I tell him about messaging Stephen or Daniyaal? Would it make me safer if he knew they were coming, or just encourage him to be rid of me more quickly?

Since he could not afford to release me after knocking me out and tying me up like this, I thought the latter would be the more likely outcome. Keep it quiet. He could not see my message on the phone as I had a security pin installed.

I moistened my lips and tried to speak. After an initial croak, my voice seemed to work after all, although it appeared to come from far away.

"Wondered where you were at the party. Didn't tell anyone because I wasn't sure. No one would believe me. Nearly everyone likes you. The ones you bother to be kind to, anyway. They think you're just a nice old man."

He laughed unpleasantly and moved around to where I could easily see his face from my prone position.

"Sweet old John Deering? Yes, I like that persona. It's very effective. I don't waste it on everyone, because it takes a great deal of effort. With people like you and Celia - well, it just is not worth it. You are not worth it. But it worked very well with the lovely Daria, I must say."

The image of that beautiful, kind girl, dumped in a ditch like trash, convulsed my stomach suddenly, out of the blue, and I began to vomit, trying, in spite of the shooting pain and flashes of light, to turn my head to the side, so that I would not choke. He came over to where I was lying, quickly grabbed my hair and wrists and turned me roughly onto my left side. The acute pain eased a little, but the retching continued even more violently, even bringing my knees up close to my stomach with its intensity.

"I need to be certain that no one else knows you are here before you die, you unutterably stupid and annoying woman. Now you've completely ruined my rug."

As the nausea and convulsions eased off, I made myself open my eyes and look over at him. He had decided to sit comfortably at his ease on the sofa, so that I could not help but see his face from where I was lying. Vaguely, I reminded myself that I had left two messages, with reliable people, which might bring help. But I would need to keep him talking, to play for time. I cleared my throat and spat a little, to try to get rid of the foul residue out of my mouth, then forced myself to speak to him.

"I just don't understand you. Why would you want to kill Daria? She really liked you."

I knew he loved the sound of his own voice and that, somewhere deep inside, he would be desperate to tell his story, to boast to someone of his cleverness, or explain his real motivation.

"Well, I suppose I have plenty of time to talk. I can't take you down to the quarry until after dark. Yes, that's what I'm going to do with you, Samantha. Drop you into the deep, cold lake in the old quarry and take pleasure in watching you sink. Not too fast. Slowly enough that you can suffer the full experience of knowing that you are going to die, but are totally helpless to prevent it. Unable even to call out in your desperate flounderings, since I will gag you tightly. Your inane chatter silent at last and forever. With any luck, no one will ever even find your corpse."

He was searching my face for a reaction and I made an effort to look terrified. With some success, because I was genuinely frightened of him now. I had known that he had a nasty side, but this was real sadism. Seeking pleasure in another's pain.

"I can see that scares you, my dear. So it should. It will not be long now. But I will keep you entertained until then, don't you worry."

He was enjoying himself. Relishing the sense of power over me. Using the ironic endearment like a sharp knife to prod a further response from me.

"I did not intend to kill Daria, you know. I have never been the violent type. At least, not since boarding school. It was, in fact, more or less an unfortunate accident."

I closed my eyes for a moment. To hear him justifying himself, describing the killing, this was not something I wanted to do. But it was essential to keep him talking. I tried to shut the words out, but it was impossible. And part of me also needed to know exactly what had happened to poor Daria.

"I met her, much as I told the detective, just outside the garden gate, and she was genuinely in a dreadful emotional state after her difficult encounter with that fool, Adam. Almost hysterical, out of control. She managed to tell me, between tearful outbursts, about Bogdan's death."

There was only a slight trace of sympathy in that cold voice.

"I listened to her sympathetically, of course, calmed her down and invited her in, as I said. But, in actual fact, she did agree to accompany me inside for a few minutes. She knew that she needed to regain control of herself before walking any further, and she was at ease in and familiar with my home. I made tea for her, and sat with her on this very sofa, patiently listening to her sorrows, her poignant sadness at the untimely death of her young husband. I soothed her, put my arm around her, stroking her fine, silky blonde hair. Her head was resting on my shoulder. Such a perfect moment for me."

His voice was more remote now, almost dreamy. It was sickening.

"I felt such a sudden surge of desire for her, was so mentally and physically aroused, that I simply had to put both my arms around her, to hold her properly. At first, she did not struggle against me, she saw it as mere comfort. It was very pleasant, almost satisfying, but I wanted more."

I was revolted, but could not help but continue to listen.

"I put my finger firmly under her chin and raised her head to look up at me, then kissed her on the mouth, relishing the quiver of her sweet lips beneath mine. Truly wonderful, for a fleeting second. But I could sense the very instant when she suddenly realised that this was not an embrace of consolation, but rather one of eager, hungry passion. Her body jerked away from me so suddenly, she pushed me back forcefully with her hands and rose abruptly to her feet."

His face changed. Anger and frustration were clear in the tension in his neck.

"I stood up as well and tried to take her back into my arms, to recapture the moment of pleasure, but she shouted at me roughly to leave her alone. I held onto her shoulders, told her that I only wanted to look after her, to protect her, to care for her, that I would happily marry her, make her my wife, give her the security she and Vitaly needed now that Bogdan was gone."

I could almost hear a pleading note in his voice.

"But she would not listen. There was absolute revulsion in her face. She called me a horrible old man. She even said that I was worse than Adam. That he would never have touched her like that. That was the final straw. My hands slid up from her shoulders, moved around her neck to throttle her, to stop her saying those unpleasant things. I squeezed harder and harder, my eyes tightly shut against the revolted expression on her face, just so relieved that she had stopped shouting at me."

I was shaking. It was too much, listening to this perverted man talking about killing my friend. But although I could not help making a small noise of disgust, he continued as if I was not there.

"Suddenly, I found that she had gone limp in my hands. I opened my eyes, let go of her throat and she half staggered to her feet, then fell sharply backwards, and hit her head on the marble fireplace. I knew at once that she was dead. It's unmistakable. Her beautiful wide open eyes staring up at me. Such a waste. She could have been my wife. She would have filled the role so well. She had the potential for so much elegance and grace."

He sounded faintly regretful, as you might feel if you had broken your favourite vase, or dropped an ice cream you were half way through eating. Then he actually shook himself, before he looked down at me directly, smiling mercilessly at the distress in my face.

"So what was I to do? It was an accident, I did not mean to kill her, but no one would have believed that. So I had to rid myself of the inconvenient corpse. But I needed darkness to do that safely and that was hours away. I therefore wrapped her, with some considerable difficulty, in a large towel and managed to manhandle her body into the boot of my car. I thought about using the rug, but I knew I would be able to wash the towel more thoroughly. It was hard work moving her, but I have a side door which leads directly into the garage."

I shuddered. I had always hated the idea of being shut in a car boot. It was a common trope in thrillers and had haunted my nightmares as a teenager.

"Yes, Samantha, you have it correct. That is what I will do with you. Only it will be a little harder, as you will not be dead. I might need to render you unconscious again. But I will make sure that you wake up while still enclosed in the boot. Just a gentle tap on the head, to keep you pliable while I move you. I will probably leave you shut up in there for a few hours this evening before I leave. I do not want the car to be noticed when I go, so I will wait until it is quite late to finally dispose of you, I think."

With every word, a vice seemed to tighten around my heart. I did not want to beg, did not want to give him the pleasure of my surrender. But it was impossible not to ask.

"Please don't do that, John, Mr Deering. I - I would rather you killed me here."

My voice was small, craven, pathetic, and I was ashamed of myself. I should hold on, try to live as long as possible, for my darling Chloe's sake. There might still be a chance of rescue. But I was so terribly afraid. I was trembling inside, quivering with fear like a small trapped animal.

"I'm sorry, my dear," he said, with a false sympathy which turned my stomach. "I cannot do that. I already have to dispose of the rug which you have now soiled again, after I worked so hard to clean the blood off. I must not risk any more traces being left in my house. No, my plan is the best. But they do say drowning is quite painless, don't they? So I am being generous enough to show you undeserved mercy at that point."

Suddenly, clanging loudly, the doorbell rang. Hope surged within me and I took a deep breath, ready to scream. But he had seen it in my eyes, moved unexpectedly swiftly, and clamped my mouth shut, holding my nose closed as well, until I began to lose consciousness again, my chest heaving desperately as I tried in vain to breathe. His hands moved away then, and I came back to the surface just as he stuck more tape over my mouth, laughing at the utter terror in my eyes.

It was another of my fears. Did I really have so many weaknesses? I hated the thought of being gagged. What if my nose became blocked? I would suffocate. He could see the pleading in my eyes, heard me manage to produce a quiet moan in my throat, as I tried to appeal to him, but he just patted the side of my head contemptuously, and went out of the room, closing the door carefully behind him.

I could not think of anything except breathing. Controlling my breath. I must not cry. That could block my nose. I struggled to lift my heavy arms up towards my face, to try to rub the tape off my mouth with the back of my hands, but to no avail.

In and out, in and out. Slowly and steadily. I could do this. Eyes closed, I prayed in desperation, but as calmly as possible, for rescue, for the person at the door to realise I was here.

My eyes flew open as I heard the door handle move. Hope faded as I saw him enter, alone, and quite relaxed.

"Nothing to worry about, Samantha."

He enjoyed pronouncing distinctly all the three syllables of my full name. A minor cruelty, but it obviously pleased him.

"It was just my neighbour asking if there was any news about poor Daria. He knew I was terribly upset by her death, and wondered if I had heard how the police investigation was going. He actually paid his condolences and brought me a sympathy card! The irony was so rich, I could barely hide my mirth."

Indeed, he now laughed heartily, raising his head in loud gusty guffaws.

"There is no need to worry about anyone hearing my amusement, Samantha. The walls here are so thick, barely a sound passes through without the door open."

That was another scintilla of hope gone.

"Now, where were we? Oh yes, I had Daria in the boot of the car. Poor thing, she looked sadly squashed. You are somewhat taller and less deliciously slender than she was, aren't you? It will be an uncomfortable squeeze, I'm afraid. You will be very cramped in that dark, airless space."

The deliberate taunting, continually poking at an open wound, actually had a positive effect. Anger overwhelmed my fear and I was back in control of myself. He looked disappointed that I was not in tears. Yet.

"I had to change my clothes, of course, but I was soon able to stroll up to the street party quite steadily, and, surprisingly, with no physical tremors or mental anguish at all. I had thought that killing a human being, especially someone special like Daria, would have a greater impact on me than it did. In actual fact, I was full of a sort of clarity and calm I did not expect. I enjoyed playing my role of concerned well-wisher. And I did it well, didn't I?"

I stared at him with contempt and disgust. I made sure that I projected not a single gleam of the admiration he so obviously craved.

"I know I did. I convinced you, at any rate. Not that that is much of a triumph. You're not the - what is it they say nowadays? Not the sharpest pencil in the pot."

I agreed. I was a failure. I should have been able to see through his hypocritical mask to the foul, rotten soul at his core.

"For just a moment, when I first had you tied up, I wondered whether to make full use of your body. You're no Daria, but it would have been so easy, and forcing your submission, after all you said, might just have been mildly satisfying. But you really are not my physical type at all, you do not attract me in any way, and I just could not bring myself to feel the slightest twinge of sexual desire for you, even helpless and completely available as you were, as you remain now."

The disdain in his voice was designed to hurt me, to make me feel inadequate and remind me of my absolute vulnerability. Not even attractive enough for this evil old man to want me. But I was not hurt. I did not allow myself to feel ashamed or worthless. I was profoundly glad not to appeal to his perverted tastes.

He saw the renewed resistance in my eyes and decided, vengefully, to rip the duct tape violently off my mouth. It was a searing wave of pain, but the relief for me was indescribable. I sucked in several deep breaths of vomit- and bleach-tainted air.

"If you behave yourself, I can make this relatively easy for you, even at this point, Samantha. Otherwise, I can choose to make your death very difficult, protracted and painful. You are completely at my mercy. So do not even think of lying to me or tricking me. I ask you once more: does anyone know that you are here?"

I tried staring him out, but then thought better of it and decided to appear to cave. I denied it quietly, meekly, with feigned despondency.

"I have taken your phone and switched it off. As you have a security pin, I couldn't check your messages, but I have even removed the battery and I will shortly destroy the sim card. I do not want it traced. No one must know that you were ever here. Will you disclose to me your pin now? Checking your messages would help me to know what you have said. If there is nothing incriminating, I could make things much easier for you."

I shook my head in a confused way.

"Do I have a pin? I don't remember it. I'm sorry."

Would he believe my pretence at memory loss? He moved closer and looked deep into my eyes. I forced myself not to look away, to meet his stare but vaguely, as if unsure of what was happening.

"You do look confused. I suppose the concussion could have that effect. But I promise you, if I find out that you are lying to me, I will make you, and those you care for, suffer."

I knew that my eyes were not working properly, that there were flashes at the edge of my vision, that I would look, and actually was, concussed. So the important thing was to make him believe that I was not deceiving him.

"I'm sorry. I really don't remember. Please believe me."

I made myself sound despairing, lost. I was desperate to make him believe me. I actually could not have remembered my pin if I had wanted to. I might possibly have been able to type it in from instinct, but intellectually, it was gone for now.

He sighed with disappointment.

"I really don't think you do. Not much of a brain, is it? Oh, well,

I suppose you can only work with the talent you are given."

His contemptuous tone was reassuring, in a way. He believed me.

"How - how did you send the messages from Daria's phone?" I ventured to ask.

"Her phone was not secured, so I could use it as I intended. I was concerned that you and the others would have the whole town out searching for her, if you did not hear from her. That would have made it very difficult to dispose of the body. So after I came back home from the street party, I turned her mobile phone back on for a very short time, and composed a brief message for Bethan. Something to make you all think she was safe. But I actually walked along and sent it from the bus stop outside town, just in case anyone could or would trace or track the phone. Then I switched it off again immediately."

His cold calculation was frightening.

"I sent the second message from the place where I left the body. I thought it would lend verisimilitude to the idea that she might have met a Ukrainian friend, who had killed her for some reason. But, just in case, I disinfected the phone before taking it apart and destroying it. No prints, no DNA. I had brought a bleach-soaked cloth just for the purpose."

He certainly seemed to like his strong cleaning products. But even bleach could not clean the rotten filth from his soul.

"I'll probably drop yours into the quarry with your body. It should remain undiscovered and if it is found, it will contain no useful evidence, after I have taken and destroyed the sim. I am quite looking forward to volunteering for the search party, once you are known to be missing. It should be an agreeable source of amusement. I will be such a keen volunteer. Perhaps I can even misdirect their well-meaning efforts. It will be an exquisite continuing pleasure."

He sounded very pleased with himself.

"The police will find evidence, fibres and other clues which will lead back to you," I insisted, trying to persuade myself. "Your boot will be full of evidence."

"But they do not have sufficient evidence for a search warrant, Samantha. Nothing points to me at the moment. I am just that nice old John Deering. Such a kind gentleman. So distressed by Daria's death and the absence of my poor friend, Sam Elsdon."

He plastered a fake expression of sadness onto that innocent-looking face, which was becoming increasingly repellent to me. To shut it out, I closed my eyes, pictured Stephen and Daniyaal, and prayed that one of them might finally read my message and come to find me. In spite of his recent anger against me, I knew, in my heart, that Daniyaal would still come, if he knew that I needed him. But it might be too late.

"Well, Samantha, we are coming to the crucial moments for you. I need to begin to move you into the car. I do not want to leave it until the last minute, when I might feel rushed and make an involuntary error. I will fetch a sheet to wrap you in, but I think it will be very challenging to proceed whilst you remain fully conscious. Even if you agree not to struggle, I will not be able to trust you fully, and you may not even be able to help yourself, your body might react instinctively to the danger. So I think another little tap on the head will be best. You are already seriously concussed, I can see that in your eyes. One more blow should put you under for long enough."

I had been about to promise to be compliant, but he could see the lurking anger and continuing resistance in my eyes. He came to his feet and picked up the roll of duct tape.

"I will gag you once more while I go upstairs. I don't think anyone would hear you, even if you screamed, but I am not willing to take the risk."

"Please, please don't. I promise that I will not scream."

I whispered the plea, not exactly begging, but hoping I could persuade him not to put the tape on again. The fear was churning in my bowels once more. Not again. Not that suffocating terror of being unable to breathe.

"But you have nothing to lose now. Nothing to bargain with. Nothing I can take away if you break your promise, other than the promise of a quick death rather than a slow painful one. Unless - well, I suppose there is still your daughter."

My heart jumped in horror. Fear for myself was bad enough. I could not endure it for Chloe as well. Now the tears did come, because I was afraid that I had somehow given him the evil idea. When I was gone, who would be able to protect her?

"I promise that I will be quiet, I will do as you say."

I spoke in a rush, too fast, too obviously terrified by his threat, almost choked by the tears I could not hide.

"On your daughter's life, then."

I tried to nod my head, but it was too painful to move.

"On my daughter's life."

It was a dreadful thing to say. I could hardly breathe with the tension of it. Swearing on Chloe's life. The worst thing I could ever imagine.

Looking down at me, calculating my ability to resist, he seemed to accept that I was finally cowed enough to be no threat, and walked calmly past me and out of the room.

Left alone, I fell prey to utter despair for the first time. No one was coming to save me. My precious Chloe was now at risk. I bit my lips hard to try to hold back the sobs, but they burst out anyway. I closed my eyes and prayed. I did not know what to say, but my heart poured out, to the God I did not know, but had to believe was there, all my misery and hopelessness, my shame and fear. Pleading for him to help me. From somewhere, perhaps from a film I had seen, words came to me.

Out of the depths I cry to you.

Gradually a strange, supernatural calm came over me. An acceptance of where I was. A letting go of the pain and torturing anxiety. A sense of no longer being alone.

I opened my eyes, slowly, to see that foul murderous man returning, with a dark sheet in his hands, an anticipatory gleam in his cold and ruthless eyes, which I could discern even behind his thick old-fashioned glasses. The second time around, with a victim he genuinely despised, he was looking forward to this.

But the calm did not leave me. I felt held, surrounded by love, unafraid. He could hurt my body, but my soul, my essence, was beyond his reach now.

He looked down at me, puzzled.

"You do realise what I am going to do to you, don't you, Samantha? You do understand that you cannot prevent it? That you are totally in my power?"

I still could not move my aching head, but my voice was steady now.

"I understand. Get on with it, old man."

"It must be the concussion, I suppose. No more pleas, no begging for your life? How disappointing."

He sounded genuinely let down, as if I had deprived him of an anticipated pleasure. I watched him passively, motionlessly, as he approached, the heavy paperweight, which he had obviously used to knock me out last time, held threateningly in his right hand.

CHAPTER 25

Da capo al fine

Suddenly, the room was filled with sound and movement. The French windows burst open, some of the rectangular panes of glass smashing, with a sudden tinkling and a crystalline rushing sound. There was a correspondingly loud banging noise from the hall, followed by men's voices shouting aggressively from both directions. I could not help wincing. It was overwhelming.

A body flung itself to the ground next to me, leaning over me to protect my head from any debris, or violent movement from my captor. But I could still see part of what was going on and hear every small noise. While they shouted at him to get down, John was manhandled to the ground well away from me, hands cuffed behind his back, and then hauled roughly to his feet again.

He had changed persona again and was attempting to look baffled and innocent. The paperweight had been dropped in the scuffle and his hair was tousled, his glasses askew. Looking plaintively around, he spoke more shakily than usual, sounding like a worried, rather confused old man.

"Officers! What is this? I'm not the one you need to be taking into custody. This woman, Samantha Elsdon, seems to have got it into her little head that I had something to do with Daria's sad demise. She apparently came to interrogate me, but became quite violent when I denied it, and actually tried to attack me with a paperweight. I was forced to restrain her. I was about to call the authorities, when you forced your way into my house in this aggressive manner. You will need to pay for the damage you caused, I'm afraid."

You had to admire his quick thinking and acting abilities. The force of his personality was so great and his tone so very convincing that, for a moment, I feared he would be believed.

But the burly policeman in front of him simply laughed in his face.

"We've been watching you from outside for the last few minutes. You can't pull a fast one now. We even have a quiet little audio recording from our bugs. You're going down, mate. Come outside and I'll read you your rights, while the others secure the scene."

It was a sergeant I did not recognise. He pulled John Deering out of the patio doors into the garden and the atmosphere changed immediately.

I closed my eyes in relief and sent up a little prayer of thanks, short but heartfelt.

"Sam! Are you OK? Look at me."

A familiar voice caused me to open my eyes. It was Daniyaal, of course. He was the one whose body had been trying to shelter me. His voice was rough with worry and emotion, and his hand just gently brushed my sore cheek where the duct tape had been. I could not help wincing away from the hot sharp pain. He turned his head and spoke much more loudly.

"Constable Parker! When is that ambulance due to arrive? It looks as if she is seriously injured."

"Should be about another hour, they said, Sergeant. Constable Wells has done some recent First Aid training, so I can get her in to look at the victim in a minute, if you like."

Daniyaal nodded, his face unusually grim. He turned back to me, his mouth trying to smile, but eyes anxious and lips tight.

"I'll apologise to you properly when we're alone. For now, I just have to say, I'm so sorry for what I said. Can you forgive me?" he whispered into my ear.

I wanted to nod, but knew by now that it would not be possible.

"Yes," I breathed. "You came."

He looked searchingly at me, then moved carefully away from my vulnerable body and stood up, projecting his voice to speak clearly to all the officers in the room.

"It's fairly obvious that this particular perpetrator has no intention of pleading guilty, so we need to process this scene carefully. It's too late for all of us to wear overalls now, but please put your gloves on and anyone new in the room must gown up. We need photographs of everything, exactly where it is."

He looked down at me where I was lying, so helpless and passive, unable to move.

"I'm afraid that means I can't release you just yet, Sam, and you'll have to put up with us taking rather intrusive pictures of you, but I can't risk this one getting away. It looks as if he could afford a good lawyer, so let's try to do this by the book."

I cleared my throat and tried to raise my shaky voice a little, not very successfully.

"He killed Daria in this room, too. He told me how it happened. He strangled her, let her go and she fell and hit her head on the fireplace. There - there should be traces. Probably underneath me."

I could not help shuddering at the thought. Daniyaal saw, and bent to touch my arm reassuringly.

"Thank you, Sam. That is really helpful to know. This is now a murder scene, not just a crime scene. We'll try to get this done as quickly as possible and then take off that tape. But I'm not sure about moving you. Your head injury looks quite nasty."

I tried to smile, but it wobbled a lot.

"It certainly hurts more than you might think."

Daniyaal stood up once more and asked PC Parker to send for the specialist scene of crime team, now that they knew what else had happened here. A murder needed additional care. Then he went out into the garden, avoiding looking at me again. I felt bereft, left alone again in such an exposed, vulnerable position.

The police photographer apologised quietly for the flash in my eyes, and then took multiple photographs of me where I was lying, from every possible angle. My sore face and head, the embarrassing pool of vomit, my wrists and ankles. It was somehow humiliating. I felt like a lump of useless flesh. Almost like a dead body. But I understood that it had to be done. It was part of catching that horrible man.

Then Daniyaal was back, bringing a PPE-clad Stephen with him, much to my astonishment.

"I have to get on with things now, Sam, but since we don't want to move you yet, I thought having some company might help. Your friend, the vicar, is here, and I hope he can bring you some comfort, and talk to you while you wait. The First Aider will be in shortly and I'll be back to remove that tape in just a few minutes."

A single tear rolled from the outer corner of my left eye into my hair, which was smeared on the floor and full of my own congealing vomit.

"Thank you," I murmured.

"You - you've been very brave, Sam. Not much longer now, I hope."

He turned away abruptly, hiding the pity and concern in his face.

With his permission, Stephen sat carefully on the floor next to and partly behind me, not on the rug, which was so full of evidence, but on the woven wool carpet underneath. It took a minute for his tall, gangly frame to fold itself sufficiently, but then he was close to me and I could look at him by slowly moving my chin up a little. Painful but worth it.

I could see that he was shaking slightly. He put out a hand and stroked the matted hair away from my forehead.

"Oh, Sam, I wish you hadn't come here on your own. I didn't see your message at all until Beth called me. I was so bound up with work, I just didn't look. I'm so sorry."

I managed to smile comfortingly at him.

"Not your fault. I know I should have waited or called. Such a foolish thing to do, going in on my own. Good thing Daniyaal looked at his messages."

Stephen shook his head.

"I don't think he did, or if he did, he didn't take it seriously. It was Beth who raised the alarm. She knew at once something was wrong, when you didn't pick Chloe up, after her first full day in nursery. And you weren't answering your phone or even looking at messages. It reminded her too much of what happened to Daria, so she rang 999 straight away. I don't think they were all that interested in looking for someone who was only a few minutes late in picking up a child, but they did give her the direct number for the local station. She called me first, concerned about what to do, and I finally saw your message."

There were still traces of that hideous gnawing anxiety in his voice.

"I told her to ring the local police and she did, and insisted on speaking directly to Daniyaal. She would not be fobbed off, not even with being told to make a missing person report. As soon as he spoke to her in person, he made the connection with your earlier message and took it on board as an emergency situation. He rang me and asked what it was about, since you had just forwarded the message to him from mine. He sounded very strained, genuinely anxious about you."

"That was so brave of Beth. She doesn't like confronting people. It will have been hard for her to push back like that."

"She took Chloe home with her and Vitaly, and called your parents to come and collect her, before ringing me back. Celia decided she should go over to help her with the two children, but not before she remembered that she had also spoken to you, at the street party, about not being able to find John Deering. That made more sense of your message and I began to get really worried. I was coming over here to try to find you, when Daniyaal rang again."

I could hear the edge of that worry still in his voice.

"I was here before the police, actually, but he had made me promise not to go in, so I hung around outside, trying to look inconspicuous. I saw a neighbour go to the door and speak to him, so I realised that if John was still there, you probably were too. But if it had taken any longer for the police to get here, I think I would have had to come in on my own. The waiting was simply hideous."

He bit his lip until it bled again and tried to calm his breathing. I wanted to comfort him, but was completely unable to move at all. Even speaking was a challenge.

"I thought they would storm the building immediately, but Daniyaal said they needed to find out what was going on first. Otherwise we might put you at greater risk. Some officers waited with a ram to force open the front door and the rest of us climbed over the wall into the garden. We crept up to the French windows. It was awful. We could see John's back, knew he was sitting on the sofa, but there was no sign of you. They had some listening equipment, but the walls are so thick, they had to risk putting it on the bottom pane of the window, and even then, they could hardly hear what was going on."

"I wish I had known you were there. It would have helped. I was so very frightened."

He looked down at me tenderly and touched my forehead softly with his hand.

"I was praying so hard for you. We were so worried that you might already be dead. Then he stood up and left the room, and we could see you, part of your body anyway, lying, so completely still, on the floor. One of the officers was sure that you must be already dead, but Daniyaal told him - swore at him and told him to be quiet. I wanted to go in straight away, but they waited until he returned and picked up the paperweight. I - part of me wanted to hurt him, to punish him, even to kill him. I'm ashamed of that instinct, but it was really powerful at that moment. I'm glad it wasn't me who had to go in and arrest him."

Stephen's voice had deepened remembering the overwhelming emotional reaction.

"I think - it's understandable, Stephen. Murder is a terrible crime, against all of us, the whole of society. We feel such revulsion towards someone who has deliberately taken a life, especially someone - someone as innocent and vulnerable as Daria."

It took a great deal of effort to get it all out, but he needed to hear it.

He smiled suddenly.

"You are so wise, Sam. But it's not an acceptable reaction for a vicar, for a Christian, and I will have to work hard to put away such instincts, to learn to leave vengeance to the Lord, whatever that man has done. And I'm afraid my feelings were as much about protecting you as for poor Daria. I felt so guilty that I had not seen your message sooner, that I hadn't been there when you needed me."

I was about to tell him about the strange sense of calm I had experienced, when Daniyaal came back with a female officer, both of them now in full protective equipment. He had a sharp knife in his hand, and very carefully cut through the middle joining sections of the tape, so that I could at last move arms and legs. Or at least I would have been able to, if they had not been numb, heavy, and uncontrollable.

"What do you think, Susie? Shall I remove the tape now or is it better to wait?"

She squatted down beside me, again avoiding touching the rug. I was embarrassed by the vomit next to me and in my hair and could not help reddening, turning my face away as far as I could. She gently pulled at the end of the tape on my right wrist, which was uppermost as I lay on my side, where Deering had rolled me.

"It's pretty firmly fixed, Dani. I wouldn't. I think they'll be able to get it off more gently at the hospital, and she can have analgesia there. I don't think she's in a fit state for more pain just now."

Very gently, she moved my head around a little, so that she could see and touch the wound on the back of it.

"This looks like quite a serious head injury. Definitely concussion. There is a chance of a fractured skull, especially given the fact that she has vomited. I think her neck is OK, so we could try to move her, but I would prefer to wait for the paramedics. Sorry, ma'am. I'm being as careful as I can."

I had been unable to suppress a physical jerk at the surge of pain when she probed the wound.

"It's OK. Sorry about the vomit. It was - it was remembering Daria, lying in that ditch, that set it off."

She touched my shoulder reassuringly.

"It's not uncommon after a head injury. That emotion may have set it off, but it most likely stems from your wound. I would like to get you to hospital as soon as possible, but the ambulances are very busy just now. Can you bear to stay there on that floor a little longer? I can find something soft to go under your head and bring some water to clean up your face a little."

Her matter-of-fact kindness was overwhelming. My throat tightened and the tears almost came.

"I can cope. He put me on my side when I threw up, so at least it's better than having the bump pressing into the floor."

She stood up and spoke quietly to Daniyaal, then went to fetch a soft towel for my head and a cloth and some lukewarm water to bathe my face and clean off the horrible dried-on sick and some of the tape residue. Stephen held my hand while she worked, gently massaging it to bring it back to life.

It was a strange sensation, feeling so helpless and being cared for so kindly. The wave of peace I had experienced earlier crept back into my heart and I closed my eyes, breathing softly and evenly. Trust them to look after you. Chloe is safe. Do not fight it. Let go.

Remarkably, I drifted into a doze. I was vaguely aware of things happening around me, sounds, touches and movements, but I floated somewhere on a softly rocking sea, secure and relaxed.

I slowly came back to the surface and became aware of Stephen rhythmically stroking my right shoulder. I could hear him faintly muttering prayers. I forced my reluctant eyes open.

"Hush, don't move, you're doing fine," he murmured. "The ambulance has just arrived and the paramedics will be with you in a second. It's nearly over."

Taking him at his word, I closed my eyes again and tried to recapture the floating mood, but it would not return. When the paramedics touched me and spoke to me, I was tense and anxious and found it hard to respond to them at all.

Being moved onto a stretcher was a difficult and at times sharply painful experience, however careful the paramedics tried to be. They insisted on using a neck brace just in case and moved me very slowly and cautiously. They talked me through everything they did, repeatedly calling me Samantha, until Stephen asked them to use Sam instead and I smiled gratefully. Once it was over, in the rocking ambulance, I drifted away again, not sure whether I was falling asleep or losing consciousness, but glad to escape the hurt for a while.

CHAPTER 26

Cadences

Although they had assured me, after the X-ray, that there was no actual skull fracture, my head injury must have been quite serious, because I did not surface properly until Thursday morning. Before that I had slipped in and out of sleep and consciousness, hardly aware of my surroundings and unable to bring myself to wake up fully. I was vaguely aware of visitors, be they nurses, or family and friends, and occasionally felt the light touch of a kiss or a hand, the prick of a needle, or water being held to my lips without being fully aware of where I was, or even who I was.

But on Thursday I woke up suddenly to harsh bright light streaming in through the window, making me blink. I was aware of a dull headache in the background, but nothing like the pain of Tuesday and I found that I could once again tentatively lift my bandaged head and look around the room. I had been given a side ward and was very grateful for the peace and quiet. Even small noises aggravated the headache with jagged twinges.

My mouth felt very dry and claggy and there was a cold drink close to my bed. I reached clumsily for it, but felt better for the movement as well as the hydration. My body felt so very stiff. Lying still would not help - I needed to move, but slowly and carefully.

Instinctively, I looked around for my phone, but, of course, John Deering had taken it. I supposed it was evidence for now. So I had no way of contacting anyone or finding out what was happening. It was a strange feeling to be cut off from the mobile, cut off from the outside world. Not knowing what was going on was intensely frustrating, even in my weakened state.

After being checked over thoroughly by the nurse and managing to force down some not very palatable breakfast, which helped me to feel stronger, I was ready for visitors. The nurse had said I might be able to go home soon, but would have to wait to see the doctor and they were very busy with emergencies that day. Waiting around, without even a phone for company, was an exercise in enforced patience, not one of the qualities I was best known for.

So I could not help feeling excited when the door opened slowly, and even happier when Chloe toddled in, holding my father's hand.

"Chloe!" I croaked.

"Mama!" she responded, holding her arms up to me for a cuddle. Dad lifted her onto the bed, and I hugged her as if I had been away for weeks. Mum was there too, looking searchingly at me, to see if I was really recovering.

"You look a bit better, Sam. You were so white yesterday, apart from the raw patches on your cheeks where that horrible tape was pulled off."

"I'm sorry to have worried you so much. I'm feeling mostly fine, or at least much better today. They say I might even be able to go home later, as long as I have someone to keep an eye on me."

"I'm not going to lecture you, just now, on the terrible risk you took going into that house, Sam," said my father, rather severely. "You will know already how we must feel about that. I do have to tell you, however, that you have caused your mother very acute anxiety, and that I cannot tolerate. It must not happen again. But we are both so glad that you are safe now. When you are released, you will come home with us for a few days until you are fully recovered."

It was a statement, not a suggestion. I agreed humbly. I had done enough to make them worry. I knew that they would want to make certain of my recovery and help out with taking care of Chloe. Guilt was, however, a hard burden for me to bear.

"It's so good to see you all again. I thought - for a time, I thought I might never …"

My lip trembled and eyes filled with tears.

"Don't worry about all that now," said Mum, briskly. "It's all over and that dreadful man is behind bars, where he can't hurt anyone else."

I found that I could now nod, as long as I did it very slowly and carefully.

I was surprised at how very tired I felt after they had left. All my energy seemed to go with them. But I was pleased to receive another visit, this time from Deb.

She seemed strangely subdued. After a few questions about how I was, she fell silent, and I asked her what was wrong.

"I feel so bad. I've known John Deering for years, and I suppose I always took him at face value. A pleasant, cultured old man. I don't understand how I could have been so wrong about him."

"Mmmmm," I responded, noncommittally.

"I knew he could be quite rude to people sometimes, like you or Celia, unintentionally I thought, but I put that down to the abrupt way the upper classes talk sometimes. He was obviously rather intellectually arrogant and dismissive of anyone who disagreed with him. But you - you never liked him. I suppose you sensed that there was something underneath, something nasty. It's really knocked my confidence in my ability to judge people, to choose who to trust."

I tried to reassure her.

"You weren't alone in thinking he was a pleasant person. Most people did. I thought there must be something wrong with me for not liking him. He - he told me, that afternoon, that he didn't bother putting on his 'nice' persona for everyone. Celia and I, well, we weren't worth the effort. So I think he tried a great deal harder to hide his true nature with people like you, people he either respected or thought could be of use to him."

"That's interesting. I suppose I did always find it odd that he was so dismissive of Celia, in particular. It didn't fit with the personality I thought I knew. But that was actually his real character."

I gulped.

"I'm afraid his real personality was much worse than he ever allowed us to see. He had a nasty sadistic streak and - and seemed to enjoy hurting and frightening me. I don't know if that was always there, waiting to come out, or whether it was killing Daria that released it or created it."

Deb looked at me with real concern.

"You've had a really bad time of it. Again. Let's not waste any more thoughts on that foul man. He's not worth the effort."

I nodded carefully.

"I'd much rather give my attention to his victims, Daria and Vitaly, and even Beth. Oh, Deb, I wish I could get the vision of her lying in that ditch out of my head. It keeps flashing back and it's hard to remember her as she was, full of life and love for her son."

"I can imagine. It must be horrible. We'll have to see what we can do about that. Perhaps the doctor will have some suggestions."

That was more like Deb, always looking for solutions. I felt I had to ask her a question which had been on my mind all that day.

"Deb, will you - would you be willing to help to look after Chloe, if something - if anything happens to me? I know my parents would care for her, but they are getting older and - "

Deb looked horrified.

"Sam, darling, don't. Of course. I promise you that I will do whatever you want. But nothing like this is going to happen again."

I reached out for her hand.

"I know, but - it could even be a car crash, illness or just some stupid accident. When - when I saw Beth dealing with Vitaly, who had lost both his parents - I just knew I needed to put something in place to protect Chloe."

Deb brushed a tear away.

"I - I'm honoured you would think of me. We can set up something official if you will feel better about it."

I nodded, relieved to have that settled.

"One good thing is that the media only have the bare minimum of the story, and nothing about you at all. The police seem very anxious to keep the details private so that the court case is not prejudiced. We're all glad to have the journalists out of our hair."

She did not stay much longer, clearly aware that I was tiring very easily and still in a pretty fragile state. In the end, they kept me in hospital for one more night as my blood pressure was fluctuating wildly and my vision was still disturbed by flashes if I moved too much.

The next day, Dad drove me to their house, where I was able to relax and recover in peace and safety. It took some time. But after a few days, still feeling vulnerable, but physically almost back to normal, I knew it was time to go back home with Chloe.

I wanted to catch up with my friends and hoped that Daniyaal, who had kept away so far, might call or visit. We had unfinished business.

My phone had finally been returned to me, seemingly intact and undamaged, by a female constable, so I was able to message my groups to say that I was back and I soon had some meetings and play dates planned. Chloe was going back to nursery too, so life seemed to be about to take on a more familiar routine.

But before I had the chance to see any of my friends, I received a very formal text from Daniyaal, asking me to go to the station to give my full statement about what had happened to me. I agreed, somewhat reluctantly, to go in on the first nursery morning.

I was nervous about seeing him again, but also anxious about going through the whole traumatic event once more. Mum and Dad had ignored it as far as possible, and I had tried to forget what had happened. It worked well enough during the day, when I was distracted, but at night I was often unable to sleep and, if I did drop off, was troubled by vivid and disturbing dreams. Perhaps telling someone exactly what had happened would help, but I was rather concerned that it might instead make things worse, by bringing half-buried and deeply frightening memories up to the surface again.

I reported in at the front desk and Daniyaal came to meet me. He still looked tired and there was deep anxiety lurking in his normally bright eyes. For once, he did not smile, but greeted me more formally.

"Good morning. I hope you are feeling better now. Thank you for making the effort to come in, Sam. It is better if we do this properly, by the book. John Deering is still protesting his innocence, so we must make sure that everything is as clear as possible for the CPS, so that the prosecution goes ahead without excessive delay."

"I understand."

"When it is over, I would like to take you out for a coffee so that we can talk properly. I - I know there are some personal things which need to be said. But let's get the business side out of the way first."

I agreed and tried to put those puzzling and uncomfortable emotional reactions out of my mind.

When we entered the interview room, I saw that the inspector was there waiting for us. I was relieved, in a way, that the other officer present was someone I knew already. It made it a little easier that she took the lead with the questions, addressing me throughout as Mrs Elsdon, and taking me through from my lunch with Stephen and Celia to the arrival of the police.

My voice was unsteady at times, but the events were still very vivid in my mind. The inspector asked me to use Deering's words as far as possible and I found it difficult to say those awful things aloud. I tried to keep it matter-of-fact, but it was not always possible and I needed several breaks to regain my composure.

At last it was done. The recording was switched off and I sat back, drained and exhausted.

"Well done, Sam," the inspector praised me. "That wasn't easy, but you held it together very well. You have a very clear memory, especially given your head injury."

"I don't think I'll ever be able to forget it, unfortunately," I responded. "But I do feel slightly better for sharing it with you. Once you put it into words, the disturbing images seem to fade a little."

"I hope so, but you will still have to work through the emotional side of it, as you know. It isn't just events, it's your feelings, the incredible stresses you went through."

"I'm sorry to have made such a mess of the whole thing," I

apologised. "I know I should not have gone there on my own. It was stupid and dangerous."

"It was certainly dangerous, but I am not sure that it was stupid. He felt confident that he could deal with you, so he was off his guard. If we had gone in to speak to him, as the police, he would have reacted very differently, and we might not have found enough evidence to search the place, let alone charge him with Daria's murder."

I nodded. He could be very convincing when he made the effort.

"And now we have other charges to make, of grievous bodily harm and false imprisonment in relation to his treatment of you. It's very unlikely that we would have got through to the truth as quickly without your intervention. There is some pretty telling forensic evidence, but he is exceptionally quick-witted and is able to find apparently reasonable explanations for everything to do with Daria's murder. If he hadn't attacked you, we would still have had a difficult job proving his guilt beyond all doubt."

"I can imagine that he would make a very credible witness. Is he still insisting that I attacked him?"

"He's now saying he might have misinterpreted what you were doing! He couldn't really continue with his former line in the face of so much contrary evidence. Why would he have taken your phone and removed the battery and sim? Why would he have tied you up with duct tape? And kept you imprisoned for so long? It just doesn't make sense. But I have no doubt that he will change his story, or alter the emphasis at least, several times before he comes to trial."

"I suppose he hasn't admitted to killing Daria."

"Not yet, but the evidence is building and it is pretty damning, from her stomach contents - the tea he mentioned to you - to the towel fibres and trace evidence of bodily fluids in his boot. We'll get him, don't worry. He has been remanded in custody for now, and refused bail so far, so you don't need to be anxious about seeing him in town."

I had not thought of that. What an awful situation that would have been! I shuddered at the thought of seeing that long white face, the repellent mouth and camouflaging glasses again.

"Anyway, we are, once again, grateful to you for providing a quick solution to a very nasty case."

"All I ever seem to do is get myself into difficulties and need rescue! I'm not exactly an effective sleuth."

Daniyaal intervened at this point.

"You don't think like a detective, that is true. You are not particularly proficient at weighing up evidence or eliminating alibis or suspects, I have to admit - that is difficult to do without police resources. But what you do have is a kind of emotional intelligence, which seems to be able to sense how people really are, under their public mask. Your brain must be picking up tiny signals that others miss. Adam was an obvious suspect to me and my team, for example, but you never really felt that he could be guilty. The rest of us took John Deering at face value, a nice old man. Only you, and perhaps Celia, saw through him. You disliked him from the start, without knowing why."

I was embarrassed, but also flattered that he had taken the time to figure things out like this.

"You also have a special way of drawing people out. They talk to you, reveal things to you. That is an enormous advantage in this kind of case."

I remembered with a rush of discomfort that John Deering had spoken slightingly about silencing my 'inane chatter'. Strength or weakness? At least the police seemed to value it.

"That's true," confirmed the inspector. "In all three cases, you have found out a great deal more, just by having conversations with people, than we have been able to, using traditional police methods. I hope you will never have to be involved in a case like this again, but if you ever are, we will certainly listen to your observations with even greater attention than before."

I knew my face was flushed, but I was genuinely touched by what they had both said. It made me feel that I had done something more important than just discovering things by accident, that I had perhaps even made a valuable contribution.

Daniyaal led me out, and insisted on paying for coffee and cake at the nearby café.

"I told the inspector that I owed you an apology, that I had treated you very badly, and she has allowed me to take this time with you. As you will have realised by now, I hope, she has enormous respect for you."

I lowered my eyes, focusing on taking a small mouthful of my lovely piece of carrot cake. What was coming next?

"Look at me, Sam, please. I feel absolutely terrible. There is simply no excuse at all for the way I treated you. Yes, I was exhausted and under enormous stress, but you are my friend and you did not deserve that."

His anxious eyes were fixed on mine, his voice pleading for forgiveness.

"Of course I forgive you, Daniyaal. But I still don't understand why you said what you said."

Now it was his turn to lower his gaze and I was surprised to see his dark skin flushing.

"This is hard to admit, Sam, and I do not understand it properly myself. I was not thinking straight at all. But I seized on the idea of your vicar friend as a suspect, when it should have been obvious, even to me, that he was not likely to be the culprit. As you said, I know him. I know he is not a pervert, that he is nothing like the rabid religious maniacs you often see portrayed in fiction."

He stopped, gulped down some coffee and went on, more hesitantly, tapping his index finger on the table and watching it intently.

"But - you were right, I suppose. I am jealous of him. I don't have any reason or right to be, but it's there, deep down. I - I really do value and enjoy your friendship, Sam. It's something I would find it very difficult to do without. And you are so close to Stephen, you talk to him so much, about such intimate, personal things, that I feel - well, I feel envious of your relationship, jealous of his closeness to you. I'm sorry. I'm not normally a possessive person, but for some reason I find it hard to share you, at least with him."

There was silence. I did not know what to say, how to respond. There was something else here, something deeper, which neither of us was daring to mention, or even to think. I was profoundly unsure of my own feelings and it seemed to me that Daniyaal was just as uncertain.

So let it be friendship again. It was down to me to repair it.

"Daniyaal, I really appreciate and want your friendship too. I miss you when you are busy and we don't meet for weeks. I like to talk to you. You have a really different perspective from the other people I know, and I value that. So let's be friends again, and maybe arrange to spend a little more time together, so that you don't need to feel envious of my other close friends like Stephen and Deb. But you will have to share me. I can't lose them either."

I had added Deb into the mix to reduce the obvious tension related to Stephen. Was it sexual tension? I did not know and, for the moment, did not want to know.

"Thank you, Sam. You are being unbelievably generous. I would appreciate that. And I will try very hard not to be possessive. I hate that kind of behaviour. I don't know where it has come from. But I won't let it take over again."

The warmth in his voice told me that it was probably going to be OK. We just needed to navigate our way back out of these deep emotional waters and back to our normal companionable relationship. I laughed.

"I'll never refuse a piece of cake and a strong coffee, Daniyaal, you should know that! Let's do this again next week, shall we? I would like to hear more about the case from your angle anyway, but not today, not straight after making my statement. That took a lot out of me."

He grasped my hand for a moment and smiled, still speaking less formally than usual.

"You're on. What about Tuesday when Chloe goes to nursery?"

"Great idea. I'll message you nearer the time."

And, just like that, the storm seemed to have passed. For now. But it had made me very aware that there were dangerous rocks lurking under the apparently calm waters of our relationship.

Once I was settled in, back at home, my first visitors were Beth and Vitaly. I was very much touched when the little boy came straight over to me and gave me a hug, before being pulled off by Chloe to play with her toys.

"I told him you had been ill and he was worried about you. He's such a caring child. He seems to have a lot of his mother's sensitivity."

I felt the prick of tears in my eyes at the thought of Daria and changed the subject hastily.

"Beth, I just want to – to say thank you. You - you saved my life by contacting the police and Stephen so quickly. I had sent a message to him and Daniyaal, but neither of them had seen it until you rang them. Honestly, I hate to think what might have happened if you hadn't reacted so quickly."

I put my hand over hers and squeezed it. Her naturally pale face was deeply flushed with red.

"You don't have to thank me, Sam. It was all I could think of to do. Caroline, at the nursery, was sure that I was overreacting and thought I should wait at least half an hour, but - it seemed so horribly familiar. Just like what happened with Daria. I knew, I was absolutely certain, that you would not be late picking up Chloe. Not on her first full day. And you know we insist on everyone having their phone on and available, in case of accidents, but you did not answer my call."

She gulped.

"So I couldn't, really couldn't let it go, not when I might lose you, too. I don't like making a fuss, and I find it especially difficult, when it's a man telling me I'm rushing into things, or being hysterical, but - well, this time I knew I just had to. And Stephen pushed me to do it as well. I'm starting to understand why you like him so much. He really is good in a crisis."

"You're so right, Beth. You can always rely on him. But you were so brave. I honestly am deeply grateful."

"The most important thing is that they got there in time. But I'm so sorry that you had to suffer so much. That wicked old man. Did he - did he tell you why he killed Daria?"

She spoke hesitantly and looked nervously at me. I did not really want to go into John Deering's twisted motivations again, not so soon, but she deserved an answer. She had been so close to Daria, lived through the trauma of her going missing, faced the tragedy of her murder, and she was now caring for Vitaly. One day, she might have to explain all this to him.

Looking down and focusing my gaze on my left foot, I tried to explain as best I could.

"From what he told me, John Deering had developed some kind of feelings for Daria during their lessons together, and it quickly became a fixation. But, from what he said, he might have always been obsessed with the idea of having a Ukrainian wife or girlfriend. Do you remember, he said at our first meeting that he had tried to take in a refugee himself?"

Beth sounded shocked.

"You're right, he did. Do you mean he might have planned something like this all along?"

"Not killing someone, no, but I think he was looking for the kind of relationship that he had failed to find previously, in this country. He - he told me he wanted a young wife, someone pliable, submissive and feminine, that he could dominate and mould into the person he wanted."

"How horrible! He was never very kind to me, always a bit patronising, but I thought he was basically a nice man. He seemed so knowledgeable, so educated and superior, I thought it was quite natural for him to look down on someone as ordinary and unintelligent as I am. And he was relatively sympathetic when my parents died."

"He wore that persona as a mask, I think. His feelings underneath were - seemed to be full of frustration and anger at the way society had changed and left him without the type of family he expected and wanted."

"But I still don't understand why he would murder Daria."

I looked over to the children, playing happily together and lowered my voice a little. I knew they would probably not understand, but it was instinctive to try to protect them from it.

"He met her, after she had that confrontation with Adam, right outside his own house. She was very upset. He comforted her, invited her in. She trusted him and felt safe in his company, in his home. And then he tried, well, he tried to go further, to express his feelings towards her, to be passionate with her. But, of course, she didn't want that at all. Can you imagine, just after you have found out that you have lost your husband, someone says they want to look after you, to be with you, to marry you? He had no idea what he was asking."

Beth covered her mouth with her hand.

"You mean he asked her to marry him, right then?"

"Worse, he kissed her, with – with passion, held her in his arms, until she broke free. She was furious, understandably. Told him he was worse than Adam. And he couldn't take that. He - he strangled her until she fainted, then let her go and she fell and hit her head on the fireplace. She died straight away. She didn't suffer. At least that is a comfort. One day - one day you can tell Vitaly that. And that she truly loved her husband."

Beth was crying now, huge tears pouring down her face.

"What a terrible thing to do. I know it was hard for you to tell me, Sam, but I'm so glad you did. I needed to know. And you're right, one day I will tell Vitaly."

The little boy heard his name and raised his head from the game to look at us. We both smiled lovingly at him and he waved, before going back to playing with trains with Chloe.

"How are things going with him, Beth? I'm so sorry I haven't been able to help out for the last few days."

She was calmer now, fundamentally reconciled to the situation, in spite of all its challenges.

"It's not easy, as you will understand, but we're getting there. Deb has helped me with the forms I needed to fill out, and I've paid Annette to do some babysitting at the weekend, so that I can go shopping, and everyone else has been so helpful."

"You know we're all here to help you, Beth. You'll never ever be on your own with this."

"I know. It makes such a difference to have help on offer from every side. People have been so generous."

"How is Vitaly getting on?"

"His English is improving every day, and he's such a little sweetie. We support each other. Nadiya has translated for me on the phone a few times when we've got stuck. And I've learnt to use Google to look up single words when I need them. I've agreed with her that she will take him to Ukrainian church for me once a month. I want him to stay in touch with his culture and heritage, as well as his language, and the church was so essential for Daria. I need it to remain as a strong feature in his life. In fact -"

She paused and looked at me rather apologetically.

"In fact, I'm hoping you will take him to Stephen's church sometimes for me too. He liked it there and I don't feel ready for it at the moment. Maybe one day, but not yet."

"I'll try, Beth. I'm not sure where exactly I am with the church and God and everything. But I will try to go more regularly, and certainly don't mind taking Vitaly with me. You might have to look after Chloe for me though. I don't think she's quite old enough to behave yet."

Beth seemed relieved. But then she took a deep preparatory breath and looked rather anxiously at me.

"I've got something else to share with you, Sam. I think it is good news, and I hope you will too."

I stared at her in surprise. More changes? Not like Beth at all.

"I think I told you I had made some good friends among the clients from the Food Bank? Well, my best friend there, Laura, is really struggling at the moment. She's on her own after a relationship break-up and, although she is holding down a minimum wage job in a local warehouse, she just can't make ends meet. Her rent has gone up again and the energy costs are just impossible. The future bills look even worse."

I nodded understandingly. Inflation and energy prices were crippling for so many people at the time.

"Anyway, I've offered her the chance to come and live with me for a while. She's keen to help me with Vitaly, and even if it doesn't work out, she'll be able to save for a deposit on a better place to live. But I think we'll get on really well. We'll be like a new little family for Vitaly. And I think it will help me a lot to have someone to talk to when things are tough. And someone to babysit when I need to go out."

That really was a surprise. I knew Beth had the space, but she had always been a rather private person, in spite of her readiness to entertain and be hospitable. I wondered if there was something more than friendship there, but it did not look as if Beth was thinking in that way, for the time being, anyway. And taking in Daria and Vitaly had prepared the ground for accepting a new lodger and sharing her home again.

"I'm really happy for you, Beth, and I hope it does work out for you both. Parenting on your own is tough. I can only manage because I have my parents nearby, as well as friends to help out. Having someone to live with you is a brilliant idea."

Beth looked so relieved.

"I wasn't sure how people would react, Sam. But it seems like an ideal solution for me, as well as for Laura. We really do get on and I trust her implicitly. It's so tough coming to a Food Bank, you know, admitting that you need help. The shame and embarrassment can mean that you see people at their worst, as well as their best. But she's such a kind person and so caring. Even generous, although she has so little to give, in material terms. She's met Vitaly twice now and they seem to get on well. Deb suggested we have a proper tenancy agreement, a very simple one, just in case of problems, so we're going to get that organised first, but she should be moved in by the beginning of August at the latest."

I gave her a hug.

"It sounds as if you have really thought it all through. I'm sure it will be fine. More than fine! It could be exactly what you and Vitaly need."

So nice, after all the misery and trauma of the last weeks, to hear something positive.

I could not help being a bit nervous, after my meeting with Daniyaal, about seeing Stephen again. I was very uncertain about my feelings, and was concerned that our friendship might be knocked off its even keel. So it was good to meet him, entirely by chance, in the park, while I was taking Chloe to feed the ducks.

He looked quite normal to me, and I could not see that he was looking at me in a strange, intense, or passionate way. Perhaps it was all in Daniyaal's jealous imagination. He certainly smiled when he spotted me, but behaved just as usual, stopping to chat to me, but not demanding my attention in any personal way. My internal tension began to relax, as he spoke to me, in a completely ordinary, casual way.

"Hi Sam and Chloe! How nice to see you. I've just escaped from my study to come down here. I find the sermon flows better if I walk, especially in a green area like this."

"Hello, Stephen. Your sermons are very good, I think. They always have a personal message and make me reflect on things I had not considered. So maybe the ducks are helping!"

He laughed.

"They never give me the right words though! Just quack, quack, quack. I need a bit more inspiration than that. Have you brought some food for them? I would love to help Chloe, if you'll let me."

"Of course."

I watched them throwing the food out. Well, Stephen was throwing and Chloe was dropping. Their faces bright with enjoyment and unselfconscious fun. A lovely moment of shared pleasure between the two of them, nothing to do with me.

When they came back, we went to the cafe to buy ice creams, and Chloe had a milk ice lolly.

"How are you, Sam?" asked Stephen, in a more serious tone.

"I think I'm going to be OK, thank you. It's been a tough time and I still have flashbacks and nightmares, but that's only to be expected. I'm rather dreading the court case, but I've been told that it won't come up for some months, so I have time to prepare myself."

"That's good. I hope we may be able to hold Daria's funeral quite soon and that will give the whole town a chance to mourn collectively and pay its respects. She had become quite well-known and was extremely popular with everyone she met."

"I know. We all miss her so much. Is the Ukrainian priest still going to help with the funeral?"

"Yes, Father Mikhail will lead much of the service, but we want some parts in English, so that we can include the local people too."

"That's so thoughtful. It will be an emotional experience, but we all need some closure. And I really trust you, after the brilliant job you did of my memorial service for Thomas last year, to make it work for everyone."

He flushed.

"That's very kind of you, Sam. That was easy to do, he was so much loved. But so was Daria. We intend to also make it a memorial for Bogdan. I know she would have wanted that."

"You're right. One of the last things she expressed to me was her sadness that he would only get a military funeral. Those things mattered so much to her."

We walked back into the centre of town together. I suddenly felt that I needed to mention the sense of calm, of clarity and being surrounded with love I had experienced. It was a difficult subject to broach but I managed to get a few incoherent words out.

He turned to me in surprise, with joy on his face. Not happiness, joy.

"Oh Sam, I am so pleased for you. Not many people have such a clear memory or experience of the Spirit's presence like that. Your prayers took you to a very special place. Treasure that moment, as awful as the time surrounding it was."

I was amazed that he would classify it so clearly as a spiritual experience, but now, when I looked back, it did seem as if my terrified prayers had been answered with a special kind of peace.

"I - I don't feel as if I know who God really is, Stephen, or as if I have any kind of relationship with him, not yet. But if that was him, well it was truly extraordinary, and I do want to know more."

It was strange to walk along a familiar street and have such an intimate but alien type of conversation. It reminded me of some of my discussions with Daria.

He reached for my hand and pressed it.

"I'm here for you when you need me, Sam. You only have to ask."

Somehow our relationship had changed again, but I still felt safe within it. He was not pushing me. Just waiting for me to be ready to explore the rather scary unknown.

Feeling much stronger in myself, I decided to invite Annette and Simon over to lunch. I was eager to see how she had been getting on, and to follow up on my plan of giving her more support, without offering money. I therefore decided to prepare a proper cooked lunch for us all, with a filling pudding as well. Chloe and I normally had our main meal in the evening, but it would do us no harm to eat at lunchtime instead.

I could see immediately that she looked better. The frown lines had gone from her forehead and her eyes looked brighter and less sunken. She had brought me some fresh flowers from her garden.

"Sam, it's so lovely to see you. Have you properly recovered from your ordeal? I couldn't believe you were in such danger again."

I popped the flowers straight into water.

"I think I must be becoming a crime magnet! It would be nice to have a more normal life, I must admit. Hopefully the next few months will be free of murder cases."

Annette laughed.

"You'll have to keep away from your policeman friend, then. Although, to be fair, this one didn't start with him, did it?"

"No, you're right. And - and I couldn't avoid being involved. Not when it was Daria."

My unruly feelings were out of control again. Annette saw that I was struggling and gave me a hug.

"It's OK, Sam. I understand. Don't think about it any more."

Over lunch, much enjoyed by both of the children, we talked about other, less stressful things. The trials of working for Mrs Donnington-Browne, who insisted on windows being cleaned with vinegar and newspaper. The progress of the cat-sitting business, which was already looking like a roaring, or rather a purring success.

"Oh, and I forgot to tell you. Mrs D-B is going to use John as a handyman too. He can fit it round his shifts, but she is delighted to have someone to call on for all those fiddly little jobs. And he actually likes doing maintenance work, so it's a win-win."

"That sounds perfect. Is all this extra work helping financially?"

Annette smiled.

"It definitely is. Things are far from easy and I'm still frightened of the energy price hikes they're predicting in the autumn, but we feel more secure than we have for months. Thanks to all of you. I'm so lucky to have such wonderful friends."

"I feel the same, Annette. I'm so fortunate to have all of you to support me. I don't know how I would manage without you."

We had such a good time together and Chloe and Simon played so nicely that we arranged to do the same thing the following week. The summer promised to be a time of fun and friendship. What a contrast with what had gone before.

CHAPTER 27

Coda: In pace

On the following morning, I was surprised to receive a visit from Daniyaal. It was unusual for him to come round without calling or messaging first. Chloe was in nursery that day and I was catching up on much needed cleaning and tidying around the house.

"Do come in, Daniyaal. Would you like a coffee? I was just about to stop for a short break."

There was a pause, as he thought about it, and then he accepted willingly enough. Why the hesitation? I was not sure. It made me a little anxious.

I left him in the sitting room, while I made coffee and opened a packet of biscuits. I wondered whether this was an official visit or a private one. He had not said. I began to feel even more nervous.

He looked up from his phone, with a serious expression on his face, as I entered the room with the tea on a tray.

"Thank you, Sam. I am sorry to intrude on you like this. It's official business today, I'm afraid."

"More questions?"

He shook his head, rather solemnly.

"No, I have some surprising news for you, and I am not sure how it will affect you. That is why I didn't want to deliver it over the phone. Come and sit down next to me."

I started to tremble. News from the police never seemed to be good. I sat down abruptly and he took my shaking hands in his, while he spoke gently and seriously to me.

"I have to inform you of the fact that John Deering is dead. He was killed in prison last night."

I looked at his serious face in total astonishment. Did he really think that this would be bad news for me?

"It seems he offended some important gangland prisoner with his patronising air and contemptuous manner, and someone killed him for it, on the following day, with a homemade knife."

I was waiting for more. He seemed to mistake my silence for distress.

"I know that many victims feel cheated out of their day in court when the criminal takes their own life, or is killed in jail this way. I want you to know that we understand how you may be feeling, and that victim support can help you to deal with the frustration."

I grinned at him. So that was what had been worrying him.

"Honestly, Daniyaal, you had me really worried there! I thought there was some dreadfully bad news coming. I don't care at all about having my day in court. I was worrying about it already, having to face up to him, and go through the whole awful experience all over again. I know I'm not supposed to be happy when someone dies, but I truly am."

He let go of my hands and sat back, his face showing relief, but also surprise.

"Never to have to see that man again, for me, that's the best possible result. Not to have to hear again about what happened to poor Daria. Not to listen to him lying, trying to pretend he was innocent. Not to suffer him trying to put me down, to make me feel and look bad under the guise of giving evidence. I'm so very relieved, genuinely glad about it!"

It was true. There was a strange growing bubble of happiness inside me.

He started to smile too.

"I see what you mean. You're right that he would have milked every moment in court, and tried to use it to his advantage, to portray you as an unreliable witness. And you would not have had your own lawyer to protect you. I thought you might want to see him taken down, punished, but I can understand what you are saying. The process would have been very traumatic and painful."

"Yes. Awful. It makes me shudder to think of it, of his revoltingly smug, contemptuous face. I'm sorry if I ought to pretend to be sorry that he's dead, but I can't. It's not as if I had anything to do with his death. It sounds as if he brought it on himself. So I am just deeply pleased that he is gone from this world. I'm free of him forever."

Daniyaal laughed, the worry gone from his dark eyes.

"I have to say, that is essentially how we reacted to the news down at the station. He has been extremely difficult to interview, and this case was looking like a tough one for us."

"I can imagine. I guess this means we can have Daria's funeral as soon as we want to now?"

Daniyaal confirmed it, and we sat together companionably enough, enjoying our coffee together. The day seemed brighter and sunnier. A shadow had lifted from my future.

The whole town seemed to come together to pay for, plan, and prepare Daria's funeral and Bogdan's memorial service. Everyone wanted to participate, to be involved. We had more donations than we needed, so the additional money was put away for Vitaly's future needs. On the day of the service, we had to set up speakers outside so that the crowd, which could not fit into the church, could hear what was happening. The streets were lined with people as the hearse pulled into town. Many of them were wearing Ukrainian colours or holding flags.

The Ukrainian parts of the service were impressive and solemn, but obviously most of us could not understand them. A contingent from Father Mikhail's church had accompanied the priest and they intoned the appropriate responses in the right places, with real gravitas.

Vitaly had been allowed to attend, despite some misgivings amongst the rest of us. Nadiya had insisted that he would need, later on, to know that he had been there for his parents. He stood between Beth and Nadiya, who both guided and supported him through the service, a small erect figure, dressed in formal black. I could not look at his back without the tears coming into my eyes.

Full honour was paid to Daria and Bogdan's lives, their achievements, their personalities. It was moving to hear what was said. But the formality of most of the service enabled me to keep my emotions under control.

The service ended with Jessica singing the Eva Cassidy version of *Somewhere over the Rainbow*. It was heartrendingly beautiful, felt unbelievably appropriate, and moved us all to tears. As my eyes drifted towards little Vitaly, I had to hold back the convulsive sobs which threatened to burst out.

I also found the burial itself difficult to cope with. Somehow lowering a coffin into the ground was much more graphic than a discreet cremation, much more final. But when Stephen spoke the words: *'in sure and certain hope of the resurrection to eternal life,'* I felt more at peace. I knew that Daria had maintained a very strong faith throughout her trials and that I could, somehow, entrust her to the God she had served so well.

As the committal came to an end, a low male voice began to sing the Ukrainian national anthem and gradually others joined in, some with words, the rest of us simply humming the tune. It was a very powerful moment of unity and respect.

As I walked slowly away, I encountered Adam and his mother, who had been standing at the back of the crowd surrounding the grave. Claire had her arm around her son's shoulders, trying to soothe the poor boy, whose thin body was racked with sobs he was desperately trying to keep silent. I stopped.

"I - I'm so sorry for your loss, Adam," I said quietly. "I know that Daria meant a great deal to you, as she did to me. We will miss her very much. But I think she is at peace now."

Claire smiled gratefully at me and Adam raised his head a little, revealing part of a face ravaged by grief and shame.

"I - I - I so wish - "

I could not help myself. I gently touched his arm.

"Don't, Adam. It doesn't help to dwell on your regrets. We all have them. I - I should have gone with her. But I didn't. I can't change that now. I know, from bitter experience, that I can't hold onto those thoughts. It eats away at you."

I gulped a little, shook myself, and carried on, not sure if I was saying the right things or not.

"You spoke to Daria that day out of love and only wanted to apologise. I believe she will know that now. She understood you better than you think. She knew how hard it is to be young and feel alone."

The tears fell as I remembered what she had said.

"Let's - let's try to remember her as she was, a beautiful, special person. If you ever want to talk about her, later on, you can contact me and we can meet up."

He could not speak, but he thrust his hair off his face, looked into my eyes with unutterable sadness, and then nodded.

"Thank you so much, Sam," his mother said, her own voice trembling a little. "We're not coming to the wake, it would just be too much, but I think Adam might like to talk to you one day soon."

The church hall and its grounds had been taken over for a real community celebration of Daria's life. It was unlike any wake I had previously attended. So many people helping out, talking about her, looking at the pictures of her that Beth and Sophy had put up around the place.

The Ukrainian group had brought a great deal of food to share and Sophy had tried some more recipes, with mixed success. We also had scones with strawberries and cream, Daria's favourite, and sausage rolls and pork pie, which Vitaly loved.

I was sitting in a corner, near Beth, Laura, and Vitaly, and was impressed by the number of people, some of whom I had never even met, who came over to talk to them and offer practical help and support, not just for now, but for the long term.

A number of them spoke to me, too, about what had happened, and how glad they were that the case was all over. No one was sad that John Deering had died and been buried, without ceremony, far from the town. He was not mentioned. Expunged from our memories, as far as possible.

Towards the end of the afternoon, Sophy stood up, asked for quiet and addressed the crowd.

"Thank you all for coming to remember and celebrate the life of our dear friend Daria and her husband Bogdan. We may never have known him, but we honour his life and his service to his country in its hour of need. It is simply wonderful to see the community coming together in this way to do our best to do them justice, and to support Vitaly and Beth as they move forward together."

Everyone clapped and smiled their approbation.

"As you know, we asked for donations to the Ukraine appeal fund instead of flowers, and I can already tell you that we will have raised over a thousand pounds just from today's events. Thank you so much to everyone who was able to contribute, especially at what is such a difficult time, financially, for so many of us."

More applause and some waving of Ukrainian flags.

"After the devastation caused by the brutal acts of what I have to call evil people, we commit ourselves to be there for our lovely Vitaly throughout his life here. There is a famous African proverb, which states that it takes a village to raise a child. Well, Beth and Vitaly, we are pledging ourselves to be that village for you. You need never feel alone with a problem or a challenge. I promise you, we are all here to help."

Thunderous applause.

Beth, tearful but happy, had her arm around Vitaly, who had understood perhaps one word in ten, but whose eyes were glowing with the uncomplicated happiness of childhood.

I hugged Chloe and my parents, who had brought her down for the wake, full to the brim with admiration for this warm welcoming community, which was so determined to ensure that love and friendship would triumph in the end.

THE END

ABOUT THE AUTHOR

Rosie Neale

A former languages teacher, Rosie has always wanted to write and is relishing the opportunity to continue the Sam Elsdon series. She is a keen reader of murder mysteries herself and likes to give full rein to her imagination, while rooting her stories in contemporary life and national events.